KING OF BLOOD

BOOKS BY KATHRYN ANN KINGSLEY

The Masks of Under series
King of Flames
King of Shadows
Queen of Dreams
King of None
Queen of All

The Iron Crystal series
To Charm a Dark Prince
To Bind a Dark Heart
To Break a Dark Cage
To Love a Dark Lord

For a full list, visit www.kathrynkingsley.com

KATHRYN ANN KINGSLEY

KING OF BLOOD

SECOND SKY

Published by Second Sky in 2024

An imprint of Storyfire Ltd.
Carmelite House
50 Victoria Embankment
London EC4Y 0DZ
United Kingdom

www.secondskybooks.com

Storyfire Ltd's authorised representative in the EEA is Hachette Ireland
8 Castlecourt Centre
Castleknock Road
Castleknock
Dublin 15 D15 YF6A
Ireland

First published by Limitless Publishing in 2019.

ISBN: 978-1-83618-350-1
eBook ISBN: 978-1-83618-349-5

ONE

"My apologies. I am Rxa, the King of Blood. And I believe I have arrived just in time." The angel—Rxa—straightened from his bow and folded his opalescent, nearly translucent wings back behind him.

She had been about to die in another fight between Edu and Aon, when, all of a sudden, *this guy* had shown up. Or rather, *this angel*. Lydia was still trying to recover from the whiplash from everything that had just unfolded. One minute—certain death. Next minute? Literal angel.

"Oh," was the best she could muster for a brilliant response. He was another king, that much was clear from his full porcelain face mask. And judging by the fact that he was covered in white ink, he was from Lyon's House.

She knew the other kings and queens were sleeping because the world had been doomed. She had such little time to think about what had happened to her, it never occurred to her they might wake up now that it *wasn't* about to get sucked into the no-longer-encroaching void.

Damnit all.

Things were about to get more complicated, not less, weren't they?

Her life just seemed destined to keep going from bad to worse—from simple to more and more complex. The angel was watching her with his perfect, angular, emotionless white mask. It, like all the others, had black eyes for holes, showing nothing of what was underneath.

With a blink, she realized she was being rude. "Oh! Sorry. Really. It's an honor to meet you." She took a step back and wished she could retreat further. "Things have been—a bit much. I'm a little overwhelmed."

"And injured, I see." Rxa looked at Edu briefly, tutting at the big man. "I can only imagine what you have suffered. I, too, feel rather as though I am missing significant pieces of recent history." The angel placed a thin-fingered hand against his chest and bowed his head to her slightly. His voice was soft, but she had no problem hearing him. "I do not know who you are, and for that I apologize. I do not know how this has all come to pass."

"It's a hell of a story, bird-man, and you just showed up in the middle of season two without watching the recap."

Rxa looked up at Q, where her winged snake was still curled around and over her protectively, like a mother tiger protecting a cub. "I... see." It was clear he didn't.

"Master Edu demands that you take your leave of this situation, Rxa. You are not necessary here," Ylena interjected. For a moment, Lydia had almost forgotten about Edu and Aon.

"I am offended you do not seem happy to see me. Regardless of your objection, I still beg to differ your point." Rxa shook his head as he turned to face Edu. "For I find you ready to pitch our world back into chaos. It has known salvation for... two weeks, by my measure? And you wish to destroy it again? For what reason, brother?"

"Aon is the cause for her rise. She is corrupted and serves his desires," Ylena insisted.

Q snickered, taking Ylena's comment to mean something dirty.

Lydia elbowed the snake in the side. Luckily, the three men seemed preoccupied with each other and didn't notice.

"Then tell me, how has this come to pass? How has Aon gifted the girl with the marks she wears on her face? I do find it odd that she wears no mask, but... as I noted, I have been absent and feel I am lacking in a great many details." Rxa glanced back to Lydia briefly. "Do you know how Aon is the cause for her rise, Edu? What methods he used?"

"No. Master Edu does not feel the need for the specifics. The truth is plain to see." The leather of Edu's gauntlet creaked as he tightened his grip on his sword.

"Is it?" Rxa turned now fully toward Lydia and took a step in her direction. Q hissed down at him and flicked his tail dangerously like an angry cat. Rxa raised his hands in a show of surrender. "I mean you no harm, my lady. I swear it."

Lydia swallowed thickly. She nodded, and Q relaxed.

"Watch yourself, bud. No sudden movements."

"Duly noted." Rxa stepped nearer, closing the distance between them down to a few feet. He reached out, and she hesitated before accepting his hand. His touch was warm like a sunbeam. He bowed, placing a kiss, shrouded by a mask as it was, on the back of her hand. "What is your name, my lady?" he asked as he straightened. Her face warmed; she was blushing.

"Lydia."

"Tell me, my lady Lydia... how is it you have come to be this way?"

Lydia chuckled, a sound that was weak and sad and ended in a sigh. "That's a long story. Probably for another time when these two aren't ready to kill each other. Or me. Or all of the above."

"Quite fair, but I insist. I must know at least the summary. Tell me... what are your dealings with the warlock? What is the nature of your knowing each other?"

Lydia flinched and looked away. "Fine. I'll try to give you the short version. I went into the Pool of the Ancients and came out as a mortal. Edu was convinced I was some kind of threat to the natural order of the world, so he vowed to kill me. Aon saved my life and took me into his home. He never once hurt me. Not once. I helped him in his library, and we... I don't know. He never asked me to do anything that had anything to do with any of this bullshit. Edu wasn't convinced and hunted me down and killed me. I died. Aon buried me in the pool, and... I came out like this."

"Hum." Rxa tilted his head back slightly as he watched her. He was silent for a long time, scrutinizing her, and Lydia tried not to blush again under the gaze. "Fascinating... very fascinating. You poor creature... you have spent all this time afraid, haven't you?"

"Yeah. I have."

"And now, just when you think you have come to establish your rightful place in this world, Edu comes to kill you a second time? All for a crime of conspiracy with the warlock who shared with you his home?"

"Winner, winner, chicken dinner."

Rxa glanced up at the snake but didn't seem to understand or register Q's comment. He looked back down at Lydia. "What else did the warlock share with you, my young sister?" His voice was soft, a warm and tender whisper. It was a question meant only for her and not for the two angry kings some twenty feet away.

Lydia's eyes shot wide.

"Aon has never stood his ground like this for the safety of another... not in five thousand years. But there, just there... in your eyes, I see the truth. I see in your soul what must have transpired." Rxa made to touch her cheek but paused as he heard a deep snarl. It didn't come from Q.

"Do not dare touch her, Rxa." Aon, speaking up for the first time since Rxa arrived.

"And so, he confirms my theory." Rxa let out a warm chuckle and lowered his hand. He leaned his head down toward her to whisper once more. "He loves you. And you, him. And Edu is too set in his hatred of the warlock to see it, even though it shines in the sky as brightly as your Earthen sun. My dear sister, I am so sorry." Rxa straightened and took a step back.

"No," Rxa said louder, for Edu and Aon's benefit. "I do not believe you are right, Edu. She is not corrupted. Not by anything other than the work of the Ancients."

Lydia was dumbstruck. Whatever the train named Rxa was that had just hit her, she hadn't seen it coming. She felt like she had been opened like a book and laid out on the table. How'd he figure it out that easily?

But looking at him, at those wings... knowing what Under was, it all made sense. Thousands of years of human history made sense in a snap. Lydia couldn't contain her curiosity. "So... which one of the myths are you?"

"Excuse me?" Rxa asked, sounding deeply amused.

"Whose myth did you start? Michael or Lucifer? Or Sammael, I guess, depending on who you're asking." Folding her arms across her chest, she tried not to feel defensive. Tried was the keyword.

Rxa laughed. It was a clean, soft, pleasant sound. It was sincere. There was no malice within it. "That is a long story. Probably better for another day." He echoed her previous sentiment, then paused for a brief moment. "I am overjoyed it was by the actions of the Ancients our world is restored. I am relieved to see Aon's experiments never came to fruition."

"*You knew?*" Ylena howled in rage. Edu went to storm toward Rxa and Lydia. The angel whirled, and with a gesture of his arm, golden chains burst up from the ground and wrapped around Edu, dragging him to the dirt. Tangling around his arms and legs, forcing him to his knees. Edu struggled but couldn't do anything. Still, Ylena shouted. "You knew of his mad attempts? *Traitor!*"

"Of course, I knew." Rxa shook his head and left Lydia to approach Edu. He unfurled his wings, and she watched in fascination as the light glinted off everything around him. "Aon was seeking to save our world. How could I not agree with his goal? I do not wish to see our world perish. Edu, my brother... you are wrong. You must stand down."

"Never!"

"You are now utterly outmatched," Rxa warned, his soft voice turning dangerous for the first time. "Need I remind you with whom you now stand opposed?"

Then, all at once, Rxa changed.

Everything in Under had a dark side. Everything in this world was not exactly as it seemed. Even an otherworldly, dazzling, perfect depiction of an angel had something looming underneath.

And in this case, it was his shadow.

Out from Rxa stretched the darkness cast by the light of his wings, and there were too many shadows for one man. Too many twisting figures that seemed as though a dozen people were standing in one spot—each doing something different. Each varying slightly from the previous one. Each moving just a little bit off from the other.

When Rxa raised his hand, the shadows moved out of sync with him as if either hurrying or reluctant to catch up. Rxa took a step toward Edu—and to the side, and back, and to the other side—all at the same time.

The man split into four versions of himself. Then eight and then a hundred, each a translucent reflection of the main. It looked like a kaleidoscope or a magic eye, fractured and impossible versions of himself projecting out from the center. She had never seen anything like it before.

Each version of Rxa had wings of a slightly different color. Each like a tone of ink was removed from the man and split off into another. No, not ink—*light*. Each version of Rxa was a piece of a spectrum of light that was separating from his main body, changing the original man's coloring as it did.

Lydia staggered backward and half fell, half sat on Q's tail. It was too much for her to take in all at once. Her snake curled a coil near her protectively.

Within an instant, all the versions of Rxa had seemed to separate out. They were nearly countless now, blurred and blending on top of each other. The man who approached Edu in front of her wore wings of jet black. They were hard to see and only seemed to barely reflect the light of the moons overhead.

Even as the versions of Rxa split apart, they phased back together, meshing into the whole as he stepped forward once more. As they came together, he returned to his original glowing white tone. The moment had only lasted a second or two. His shadow seemed to calm down, as whatever the angel had just done faded.

It was a show of power. A threat to Edu, as much as it was for her benefit, she suspected.

Rxa glanced over his shoulder at her. "Whose name did I create, my lady Lydia, you ask? Michael or Lucifer? Sammael or Azrael? Raphael or Mammon? I fear it is not so simple. I am not one name. *I am them all.*"

* * *

Edu was forced into the dirt on his knees like a prisoner of war. He watched Rxa's display of his true nature and knew the show was not meant for him. It was the easiest and most succinct way of displaying who he really was to Lydia.

And like all of them, Rxa had a flair for the dramatic that would not be denied.

Judging by the wide-eyed look of shock on her face, it had worked. Edu was not so impressed. He had fought the King of Blood on the field of battle many, many times. The dragon and the archangel were no strangers to hurting each other and the various tricks they could employ to do so.

Now, it seemed they may have reason to come to blows once more. That was, if Rxa had enough honor to release him from the chains that kept him trapped. The angel held the magic that kept the Ancients chained at the bottom of their lake of blood. If he wished Edu never to stand again, it would be a simple task.

The chains were unbreakable.

"Release me, Rxa," Ylena demanded for him.

"No, brother. Not until you have calmed down. Not until you see the fallacy in your reasoning." Rxa came to stop in front of him. "I understand your hatred for Aon. I know your desire to see him pay for his crimes. But the man has committed enough sins for which to be paid recompense without engineering more from where there are none."

"Are you so certain so soon? You have just awoken from where you lay in your crypt, having surrendered control of our dying world to the madman who doomed it." Edu's emotions were still raging, and he felt sympathy for Ylena, who would be laid out from the exertion when all was said and done. She might sleep for days after this.

"Aon. Your experiments—did you ever succeed in transmuting the ink we wear to other colors?" Rxa asked without even glancing over his shoulder at the warlock in question.

"I do not see why it matters." Aon looked away. His words were curt and stiff.

"Humor me, brother," Rxa urged gently.

Aon sighed heavily and folded his arms across his chest. "No. I failed at every turn. I have learned to rearrange the marks at my will, but I cannot change their hue. Not even between two Houses who still live." Aon sounded none-too-pleased to admit this. "Not even between blue and purple, whose natures are so similar. Let alone resurrect a House that was... extinct."

"You did not, at any point, find the means to create ink of turquoise?"

Aon was silent for a very long moment, the warlock looking off toward the jungle at the edges of the ruins that Edu both recognized and yet, with the influence of the new dreamer, had become foreign to him. "I did not even come *close*, Rxa. My work was doomed from the start."

"Yet why did you continue?" the angel asked.

"I wished to save this world." The warlock held a moment in the air before he finished. Edu watched as his shoulders sank just slightly. "After all this time, I still did not wish to die."

Rxa turned back toward him. "Tell me then, King of Flames, how Aon was responsible then for her rise if he could not gift her with the ink she wears? Do you think he is lying to us of his failure?"

No. Edu did not. Aon was never one to admit defeat, even in the interest of maintaining a greater falsehood. His ego would not allow it. And if he could wield ink of turquoise, he would have given Lydia more than just the ones she wore on her face, certainly.

"Then do you think he controls the Ancients now?" Rxa tilted his head to one side, his blond hair falling along the angles of his perfect white mask. His soft voice was as pervasive as Edu remembered it. The man did not need to speak loudly to be heard. "Do you think he sways their minds?"

Edu clenched his hands into fists in the dirt where he was forced to keep them pressed. He shook his head once more.

Controlling their primordial creators was a power far beyond the abilities of even Aon.

"There is no shame in admitting when one is wrong."

"Master Edu has never thought such a thing. He has always had the honor to admit when he is beaten." Ylena was regaining control of herself, and Edu of his own rage.

Hanging his head, Edu let out a long, ragged sigh.

This war would not be won today.

"Very well. Aon may not be responsible for her wearing the marks of a queen. But answer him this, Rxa. How can you be so certain he does not control her? She has spent much time in his care. You have been asleep and blind to the goings-on of this world. He has had more than enough time to bend her to his will."

Rxa let out a thoughtful hum, and he turned to look at Lydia. "I believe you have answered your own concern, brother."

"How so?" Ylena asked for him.

"I do not see a woman 'bent to the will' of the warlock." Rxa gestured a hand, palm up, at the Queen of Dreams, who was still standing beneath the protective wingspan of her bizarre and freakish snake companion. The woman looked exhausted, terrified, and most of all—angry. "Do you see her cowering behind the warlock now? Do you see her kissing his hand? I do not. Aon's proclivities are no secret to us all, Edu. If he wished to have a pet dreamer upon a leash, do you think she would roam free? Do you think he would be able to resist the temptation?"

"It is an illusion. To keep us from seeking war."

"Then he failed miserably, didn't he?" Rxa tilted his head slightly. "For here you are, seeking just that. Seeing through what you claim to be a falsehood. A lousy plan for a man known to be so brilliant, if it was so easy to predict."

Edu growled low in his throat. Damn the angel. Damn him to the pits.

Rxa continued, seeing his line of reasoning gaining purchase. "Have you ever known Aon to have such restraint? He covets all that he owns. If he wished to possess the girl, she would be his slave. He would not care for war or for what we think. Five of us could barely threaten him during the Great War. If he had the Queen of Dreams for his slave, do you think the two of us would pose much of a threat against them?"

Edu felt his jaw twitch.

No. No, they would not.

"If he wished it, she would wear his chains with pleasure. Yet, she is here, in her home. And judging by the expression she wears, she wishes nothing to do with any of us. I believe—correct me if I am mistaken, my youngest sister, for I do not wish to speak for you—but you merely desire to be left alone."

"I have stronger words for it." The blonde girl snorted with laughter. "But yeah. That sums it up nicely."

"Including Aon?"

Lydia shot a withering glare at the warlock, who was watching the scene unfold with continued uncharacteristic silence. "He can go fuck his ass with his metal claw. *Sideways.*"

"I. Well..." Rxa paused, as if trying to picture how that might work, before clearing his throat and glancing down at Edu. "Case in point. Tell me again how she serves him mindlessly?"

"It is a clever ploy, nothing else," Ylena argued, but the conviction was gone as the pegs were being knocked out of his stick-house argument one at a time. Finally, it collapsed. Besides, there was another way to find the proof of her corruption one way or another. "But you are right, brother. I cannot chase the man for his potential crimes, when there is plenty enough before me to condemn him over. Tomorrow, he stands trial regardless."

Come the dawn, Edu would see if the girl truly served the warlock, and then he would judge her with proof laid before him.

"Oh?" The King of Blood was ignorant of Aon's recent crime, after all.

"Master Edu wishes to stand, King Rxa," Ylena insisted. "He does not enjoy speaking to you from the dirt."

"You do not seek to take her life?" Aon finally interjected.

"No. At least, not for the moment." The chains around him released and disappeared through the swirling, small gold circles from which they originated. As the gold chains disappeared through them, they vanished. Edu stood with a low breath and didn't bother to brush himself off. "Edu concedes that murdering the girl on suspicions alone may be... imprudent."

"Imprudent? That's what you want to call it! That's adorable! What'd you call it last time, asshole?" Lydia shouted at him. He found himself rather quite glad that the Queen of Dreams was without her full power.

"Master Edu had a prophecy last time. And this time, a neutral party has interceded on your behalf, Queen of Dreams." Ylena's tone was now devoid of emotion. "He would be unwise to ignore Rxa's counsel. He will no longer seek your death until the point he has proof that Aon has perverted you and by what means."

"Sure. You had a prophecy the *second* time. What about the *first* time you wanted me dead? Where was the proof then? This is number three, after all." Lydia snapped at him. The little Valkyrie of a queen was likely to stay furious for some time. He understood and did not hold it against her.

"Noted," Ylena replied for him. "And you are correct. He had none. Merely theories. This time, perhaps, he has learned not to act on paranoia alone."

Lydia huffed. "Right. And I'm Albert *fucking* Einstein."

He did not know who that was, but he got the point of the statement.

"Tell me of this crime, brother." Rxa resumed the previous conversation. "Speak to me of why Aon faces trial."

"Aon murdered a shifter in cold blood." Edu motioned for Ylena to join him at his side. They would be leaving soon. His business here was concluded, and it was clear the new queen was not keen on his presence for very obvious reasons.

"Aon. You know the cost of such an act." Rxa looked over at the warlock with a disappointed shake of his head. "Why have you done this?"

"You will learn tomorrow, it seems, when I stand trial for the crime." The warlock was unusually standoffish and quiet. It never did bode well when the warlock held his tongue.

Rxa tilted his head curiously at the warlock. "Are you not reigning king at the moment?"

"I abdicated in light of my crime. I had hoped doing so would convince this idiot to scatter the armies he currently amasses to fight me." He gestured aimlessly with the claw that Lydia had so colorfully suggested he put into his anatomy in a physically impossible manner.

Rxa groaned and looked back to Edu. "You gather for war?"

"Aon held the dreamer as his prisoner until recent history." Edu grunted. Ylena continued to speak at his behest, if now reluctantly. "In light of the trial tomorrow, Master Edu will not march upon Aon or Lydia. He will order his forces disbanded."

"Thank you, brother." Rxa bowed his head.

"Do I have to go to this trial?" Lydia chimed in.

"Yes," replied Ylena, Rxa, and Aon, all at once.

Lydia groaned loudly, much like a child.

Rxa was the only one who chuckled, though Edu found himself smiling somewhat, though she would never know.

"All royals must stand to judge the accused," Rxa explained, taking pity on the girl's clear ignorance of her situation.

"Great! So can you all seriously fuck off already?" Lydia said wearily from where she was now sitting on her ghastly snake's tail. "I need to get drunk and to go to bed." She threw her hands up in frustration. "Apparently, I have somewhere to be tomorrow."

"After you, Edu." Aon gestured at him, demanding he leave first. Ever protective of the girl. The question still beggared Edu like a biting insect beneath his armor. It was clear that the warlock would fight to the death to shelter her...

But why?

TWO

Lydia watched as Edu and Ylena disappeared in a rush of flame. Aon looked to her, and she shot daggers at him, willing him to go away.

She was still not ready to talk to him after what he had done to Nick.

The memory of her friend's death was still raw in her mind. The sound of his rasping final breaths.

It was as though her glare had carried real blades, for how his shoulders winced at her expression. He took a step back, folded his gauntleted hand before him, and took a deep bow in her direction. "Tomorrow, my darling, you may cut the pound of flesh you so clearly desire from me."

And with that, the warlock was gone in a swirl of black smoke.

Lydia sighed and walked over to a stone at the edge of the reflecting pool and leaned against it. She needed something firmer than Q's tail to lean on as she put her hand over her eyes.

She wanted to scream, or cry, or both.

She was exhausted and completely at her wits' end. She had been through a grueling fight with Edu where he kicked the living hell out of her and then had to witness a two-way argument about her life turn into a three-way one.

Everything just kept getting more and more complicated.

Now, she was told that Aon's trial was tomorrow. It's not that she was honestly surprised. All the things that had happened to her since she arrived was one unexpected and unwelcome heap of crap on top of the other. But one thing remained consistent—all of it happened too fast. Screw everything in her life right now.

All of it.

"The notion of this trial brings you great duress. I think, if I may be so bold, it transcends your attachment to the man accused. Who was it whom he killed?"

Rxa. She really hoped he would just take his cue to leave, but unfortunately, he had stayed. She looked up at the angel. He stood a respectful distance away from her, watching her, still wary of Q. His pose, hands clasped behind him, accentuated his athletic frame. He was muscular but thin, built like a soccer player—not a spare ounce of anything on him. He was still too beautiful to be real, and it gave him an almost eerie and unsettling quality. She understood exactly why humans must have fallen at his feet for centuries.

"The shifter he killed was my best friend. From Earth. He killed him right in front of me. Made me... watch him die."

Rxa exhaled as if the wind had been punched from him. "My lady... I am so very sorry. What inspired him to do such a deed? Jealousy?"

She let out a sharp laugh. Aon? Jealous? "No. Although if it came down to that, I'm sure he would have." She had no doubt that Aon would kill anyone who came near her. She had no misgivings about the man and his personality. Involving herself with someone like him came with a very sharp double-edged sword.

"What, then?"

"A prophecy Ziza gave him. She said that a king would rise to destroy me, and a friend would be my undoing. He killed Nick to prevent it from coming true. He did it to try and prevent Edu or anybody else using him against me."

"He did it to... protect you." He looked off thoughtfully. "What an abject tragedy. It is so obvious that he loves you. And with the pain I see upon you, it is ever more apparent that the feeling is mutual. If you did not, you would not burden yourself with such angst. You would choose to hate the man instead. You are angry with him—furious, even—but you do not *hate* him."

The glare she shot him might have withered plants.

But Rxa held fast. Something told her he'd had far worse stares from far scarier people than her in his thousands of years of life. "Tell me I am wrong, and I will relent."

Shutting her eyes, she dropped her head, and her argument. "Please, you can't tell anyone."

"I fear it will be a secret not long worth keeping, but I will do so."

"What do you mean?"

"It is plain for anyone to see."

"Edu doesn't."

"Edu is simply too blinded by his loathing for Aon. When he calms down long enough to observe you, he will know." Rxa chuckled. "That is another reason we hide our faces. Perhaps you should consider doing the same."

"The masks are stupid and mine was ugly."

"Qta's would not suit you, you are right. Make your own."

Lydia didn't realize she could. She blinked and then shook her head. "No. They're still stupid."

"As you wish. It is refreshing, I must say, to be able to see the expressions of a fellow royal. To see your eyes and know how it is you feel. And you are not subtle in your projections. It will not be long before the world knows that you love the warlock."

Lydia cringed. "I don't know if I do."

"Then let me confirm it for you. It is scrolled across you, stronger than the ink you now wear."

Maybe he had a point. Because right now, hiding was extremely tempting. Not from Rxa, per se—but from everything. "I don't know how to forgive him."

"It is not the same, anger and love. Both may be true at once." Rxa let out a small hum of realization and shook his head. "And now, I must beg for your forgiveness. I have spent so many thousands of years providing counsel, I forget it is not always welcome. Nor am I, here in your home. I am an intruder all the same. I was entrapped by my curiosity over you, but it is no excuse."

Lydia smiled. "I see where Lyon gets his manners."

"Oh, you have met my regent?" Rxa sounded pleased, almost excited. "I fear I have not been home to see him. I was too eager to see what—or who—had saved our world."

"He's not your regent anymore, but yeah." Lydia felt weird being on the giving end of any kind of information for once. "He married Kamira and gave up his mask."

He placed a hand over his masked face and groaned. "Of course, he did. Well, he will regain his proper status immediately."

"I thought elders couldn't be married?"

"The letter of the law states that heads of House cannot be wed. He is no longer the head of a House now that I have returned. Therefore, he may regain his rightful place as my High Priest." For the first time, he had the tone of a man who was used to commanding law. "Who reigned in his stead? Do you know?"

"Otoi." The disgust was impossible to keep out of her voice.

Rxa let out a sudden laugh. "Oh, how this world has suffered!"

She couldn't help but smile at the man's somewhat operatic sense of humor. The man acted like he was on stage, and his gestures matched. She supposed he was accustomed to being the center of attention.

But still, he was creepy. He was glowing and beautiful, but she felt wary around him. It wasn't until then that she realized what it was exactly that kept giving her the willies around the man. His shadow was still wrong. It always was. Just slightly offset from the man's movements as though it were two people trying to keep sync but missing the mark.

It was dumb, but she had to ask. "Rxa? What's up with your shadow? What is it that lets you split apart like you did before?"

He took a step to the side, and in that motion, a piece of him seemed to separate away from him. Another duplicate of himself stood nearby, like a refraction of light. This time, the angel wore blue wings. And with his absence from the whole, the blue shades out of Rxa's wings disappeared. When he talked, they both did, slightly out of phase with each other. It felt like looking into an infinity mirror. The two men weren't copies; they were reflections. "I am many, even though I am merely one. A thousand minds live inside my own." And with that, the reflection stepped back into the main and was gone.

Oh, that made sense why he seemed to be the only one so far who could tolerate Aon. They were both nuts. "So 'you are Legion?'"

"Indeed!" Rxa seemed incredibly pleased and impressed she knew the name. "Do you know the myths?" He sounded both hopeful and flattered all at once. It was oddly endearing.

"I do," she said with a smile at his eagerness. From horror movies, sure, but she knew enough about angels and demons to get the references.

"I am sorry if I frightened you earlier. It is just much easier to demonstrate my nature than to use words."

"It's fine, I just wasn't expecting it. Slowly but surely, I'm starting to get used to all your melodrama around here."

"If you are accustomed to the warlock, trust me, all the rest of us will fall flat in comparison." Rxa took a step back. "I should leave you to your rest. Tomorrow will not be an easy day for you. I have imposed upon you ruthlessly enough. But, when the trial is said and done, will you call on me at the cathedral? I wish to know you better, sister."

I bet he means it in the biblical sense. Bow-chick-a-wow-wow.

Q had kept the commentary inside her head, and she appreciated that much. That way, she didn't have to shout at the snake for making stupid insinuations. "I'd like that, thank you, Rxa."

Ooooooh...

Shut up, Q.

"Then may you sleep well," he said with a bow. "And I will see you on the morrow."

"You"—Rxa vanished in a flash of light that left her wincing and covering her face with her hands—"too."

Damn it, Lydia really did need sleep. And a drink. Maybe not in that order. She started to walk back toward her home. As she did, Q shrunk down and curled up on her shoulder, finally dropping his defensive stance of her since everyone else was gone.

Wanna tap that angel ass?

"No, Q. I don't."

Sure, you do. Who wouldn't? I'm sure it's... heavenly.

Lydia groaned at his awful pun and bonked him in the head with her palm.

Ow! How about divine?

Lydia bonked him again.

Quit it. I'm funny and you know it.

"You deserved that."

No, I didn't! I still think it's funny.

Making her way to her bedroom, she shooed a strange little lizard off one of the pillows. It skittered under her bed. There were little critters just about everywhere now. She supposed that made sense. It was a jungle, after all.

Deciding she was too tired to drink, she flopped down onto the pillows. As she did, she heard something crinkle. Looking up, she saw a piece of paper sitting on one of the cushions that were piled up and served as her mattress.

Next to it sat a rose. But this rose wasn't normal. It was made of glass—black glass. She picked it up, and she knew instantly who had left it. It wasn't subtle. The message of why this rose wasn't real also wasn't lost on her. A normal rose would wilt and fade in time. This one would last forever.

In case she never let him give her another one.

In case he wasn't around to give her another one.

She realized she didn't know what the possible outcomes of the trial tomorrow could be. Death? Imprisonment? Torture? What kind of awful things could Under really do to a person?

The rose was beautiful. It was a piece of art, and she couldn't bring herself to chuck it against the wall and shatter it. Instead, she held out her hand and summoned a small stone cup to her palm. Doing those kinds of stunts still made her snicker like an idiot. She wondered when it would stop being endlessly entertaining.

She put the cup on her nightstand and put the rose in it.

You still love him.

Yeah.

She did.

She didn't even bother arguing with Q. She knew the truth. But one question still burned in her as she flopped back down and looked at the note Aon had left her. She loved him.

But could she forgive him?

Lydia finally opened the note. It wasn't very long. It wasn't an apology or a lengthy explanation. It was only one sentence, and it stung her heart harder than any lofty scripture could have done. It made her shove the note under a nearby pillow and roll over onto her stomach, willing sleep to come for her and push away the turmoil she felt.

Do what you must. –A

* * *

Lyon had felt the return of his king and master the moment Rxa rose from his crypt. He had wondered how much time it would take for the other royals to wake from their slumber. The answer was not long at all, it seemed.

He could only pray it meant peace, not chaos.

But he was not so certain. This was Under, after all.

And with the rise of Lydia, it seemed all was thrown into disarray.

It was his nature to worry, though—and he would have to try to set that aside and greet this new world with a level head and easy heart.

He was not surprised it was his own king who woke first— for Rxa was the last to give in to the seemingly unavoidable end to their world. Rxa was the one who, unsurprisingly, maintained the highest faith that all would be well.

When Rxa did not come to the Cathedral of the Ancients, he knew without a doubt where the vampiric angel had gone.

To see the new dreamer.

It would be clear to each of the royals as they rose from their crypts as to why it was that they had awoken. There was only one event that would stir them from their fugue states— the return of the dead House. It was Lyon's experience that the royals could sense the presence of the others. They were joined in some intrinsic way, as were the Ancients. It was from their creators' power they drew their own, after all. They would feel Lydia's existence as any might the warmth of a nearby candle.

Lyon did not blame Rxa for going to investigate. Lydia was a topic of no small curiosity. The world was abuzz with rumors and news of the new queen. The void was continuing to shrink away, and their world was ever healing to the size and majesty it had once known. Whole cities and countryside ranges that were lost to the emptiness of the void were returned.

New beasts roamed the forests and the cities—creatures unlike any that Lyon had ever witnessed. They were warped, cartoonish and terrifying at the same time. These were creatures that were born of the depths of Lydia's mind. Qta's creations had not been nearly so fantastical and twisted as the modern child's dreamings.

This morning, Lyon had come across a being that could replicate any household object. He had discovered it in a rather unfortunate moment with his afternoon tea when it had been masquerading as his kettle. Luckily, the bite marks in his hand had healed in short order—though its venom had burned for some time.

The return of a dreamer made Under once more unpredictable—once more unknown, even to those elder creatures such as he. Kamira had complained to him for an hour about some massive, robotic chicken-creature who belched green flame and had rampaged through her woods and destroyed several groves of trees her pack called home.

Lyon had successfully not laughed at the mental image, though he had been sorely tempted.

Although now, frenzied newborn monsters were to be the least of Kamira's troubles.

His mind traced back to the worry of the other royals. What would they do? How would they react?

Dtu, her king, would follow quickly behind the King of Blood, he suspected. Kamira would dread Dtu's return.

That was not to say that Kamira didn't adore Dtu. She was devoted to him more than perhaps any other elder that served their king. Therefore, in turn, it came to pass that no elder was so profoundly wounded by the loss of their royal. Save for one, perhaps.

Maverick had fallen to Under long after Queen Vjo had turned to slumber in lieu of facing the end. Vidor, Maverick's predecessor, was never the same after her departure.

Each of the kings and queens of Under had retreated to their crypts to greet the void in silence for their own reasons. Yes, the press of oblivion upon them was the cause. But for each one, the precise emotion that inspired it had differed slightly.

For Ini, it was utter grief at the death of the world she loved so much, and she went first. The Queen of Fate had the most straightforward, least nuanced motivation.

For Vjo, the Queen of Words, it was that their world no longer held her interest. For what could not grow and learn held no value.

For Dtu, the King of Moons, it was the admission of defeat that sent the werewolf king to his tomb. Surrender amongst the shifters was a greater sin than any other.

And lastly went Rxa, the King of Blood, and for him it had been an acceptance of the fate the Ancients had created for them. The angel believed that the influence of the Ancients was at work in all things. Therefore, this must be how their world would end. His had been the tragedy of faith.

But oh, how Kamira had been furious at Dtu when he crawled into his crypt. He, as Kamira had issued vehemently at the time, "tucked his tail between his rotted legs and shrank away like a whipped dog." She would be in a rage when he returned. Dtu would pay for his abandonment in blood.

Lyon's relationship with King Rxa could not be more different.

Shifters were defined by passion—by emotion. Whatever they felt, they did. Reason and rationality weighed little on their minds. He was grateful for their impulses, for it was the lack of a logical temperament that had spared his life the night Kamira decided to take Lyon as her lover and not a trophy.

He remembered that night fondly. He always would.

No, his order was not one of passion or impulse. His was a House of careful thought—of reasoning and words. Of lengthy veiled expositions upon intentions where a simple fist or an embrace may do the same. Perhaps Lyon had spent too long amongst the beasts of Kamira's House. Perhaps his disdain for the coldness of the priests of the House of Blood had grown too large over the years.

Not to be mistaken, Lyon was happy for the return of Rxa. He was kind, even in his esoteric darkness. Lyon found great peace in the presence of the vampiric angel who was the most devoted servant of the Ancients. Even though it was his power that kept the Ancients prisoners in their depths, there was none who loved their primordial creators quite like him.

It was with a warm heart that Lyon lit the candles upon the altar in the cathedral's main sanctuary. The one over which he had kept watch these past four hundred and some-odd years for his king. The carved depictions of their creators were dramatically lit in the flickering candlelight.

Their world was saved and yet would surely be sent into upheaval once more. Tomorrow, Aon would sit trial for murder. He may be condemned to an eternity of imprisonment for the crime or be stripped of his title and disfigured and maimed, if not more. There were many options for how the future may unfold.

His heart wept for Lydia, forced to stand in judgement. Forced to decree what may become of the man she loved. Lyon lit a candle for the soul of Nicholas and prayed to his Ancients that he may find peace.

Lyon felt Rxa's presence a moment before he appeared. Lyon turned and dropped to one knee as white light flooded the room from the angel's presence.

"Oh, rise, foolish man." Rxa's bare feet touched the stone floor of the cathedral. His rebuke had been a warm one. "Come now, dear friend."

Lyon stood and smiled at the angel before him. With only a few strides, Rxa crossed the stone floor and embraced him before Lyon could even speak. Lyon returned the gesture and felt great relief well in him. His king had returned.

"The new queen said the truth." Rxa took a step back from Lyon and tapped his finger on Lyon's cheek over his soulmarks. "My regent has abandoned his post for love."

Lyon flinched and sighed, embarrassed. Yes, his mask was gone. Rxa could see the markings that ran down his face from temple to jaw. While Lyon and Kamira had been together during Rxa's reign, it was only the past three hundred and fifty years that they had been wed. Not until after the white angel had gone to his tomb and Lyon had surrendered his mask in exchange to call Kamira his wife. "Yes... my king."

"Do not be so doleful, Lyon!" Rxa laughed. "Do you think I am surprised? You, the ever-honorable one? I could not be happier for you, dear friend. I am merely sorry that I was not there to officiate the ceremony!" Rxa clasped Lyon by the shoulders and squeezed reassuringly. "But you left Otoi in charge. Really?"

"He was the next successor."

"Whatever did this world do to deserve your revenge?"

Lyon chuckled despite himself.

"Well." Rxa released Lyon and walked past him to look up at the carved depiction of the Ancient that held reign over their own House of Blood. "He is removed from his rank immediately. You are my High Priest, my regent, and none other. You are hereby restored to your post. You may replace your mask." Rxa placed his hand to his chest in his symbol of prayer to the creature that gave him his power.

"I accept my title. But I..." Lyon paused. "I think I would prefer to remain unmasked, with your humble permission, my king."

"Wherefore?" Rxa turned to look at him, his tone curious.

Perhaps it was inspired by Lydia's defiance of the old rules. Maybe he had just become accustomed to not wearing the piece of porcelain that had hidden half his face for so very long. "I find others seem more apt to trust and listen to me. I have made more allies and acquaintances since I have gone without. I think, truthfully, I prefer it this way. It shows honesty and trust, if nothing else."

"You have always been an odd one, Lyon. But, if that is your wish, then of course. Remain as exposed as you see fit. It seems that this is now all the fashion," Rxa teased him with the last few words.

"I see you have met the new dreamer."

Rxa laughed and folded his wings at his back. "I have indeed. She is quite a marvel. I see in her such strength."

Lyon nodded. "I have had the pleasure to know her since she arrived. Ms. Lydia is a curious thing. I thank the Ancients for having chosen this path for her. I do not know if I have met another who is better suited to wear the turquoise in lieu of Qta. I hope that we may all find a respite for her coming."

"Indeed. It seems she has brought a miracle to many, in more ways than one." Rxa paused, his words a quiet insinuation that left little room for Lyon to wonder. "I interrupted what appeared to be Aon protecting the girl from Edu's wrath. I have never known the warlock to defend another. Never once. What do you think of their friendship?"

"I do not know." Lyon tried to keep expression from his

face—but his king was a talented reader of emotions. It was part of his gift. His reticence to speak of what he knew was confirmation enough for the angel.

"You are a horrid liar. You always have been. And you are painfully loyal to your old friend, even now and after all he has done. I respect that. I take it, then, you know of her mutual accord with the warlock?" Rxa waved a hand at him, as if to assuage some fear. "It was so very plain to see upon them both, I am even surprised Edu did not see it for what it was."

Lyon nodded reluctantly. "After Edu murdered Lydia, I was there when Aon chose to bury her lifeless body in the pool. I knew then that he loved her. As for Ms. Lydia—I know she still debates the value of her affection, but it is plain to see upon her when she is near him."

"What do you think of our mutual friend finding a companion after all this time?" Rxa cast his gaze back up to the statue of the Ancient that loomed up high over them. The Ancient of Blood. In the wings of the cathedral, each with their own alcoves, were the other six. An Ancient for each of the Houses that ruled.

While Rxa did not know the precise reason as to why Aon murdered Qta, he knew of Aon's plague of loneliness. He was perhaps the only other soul upon this wretched world that believed Aon may have a heart that could feel love for another. Lyon remained the only one who had heard Aon's true motives from the warlock himself, although he was certain Rxa suspected.

All Rxa knew for certain was that Aon had taken Qta for his own ends. It was at that point that all five remaining kings and queens had rallied against Aon. They had all failed. Aon was unstoppable when he was prepared, and only by benefit of his surrender were they not all destroyed by his wrath. Aon had given up his fight, unprompted and unexpectedly, when he was poised to wipe them all from the face of Under. Once he had killed Qta, it seemed Aon had no reason to continue with his war.

"I hope she brings him peace," Lyon said after his thoughtful pause. "I hope they are allowed to be happy together." Rxa was accustomed to his long silences and did not press him to speak before he had chosen his words. For that, Lyon was immensely grateful. "I believe he has paid his penance and deserves to know contentment. I believe Aon deserves to know love."

"Hm. I agree. I think the Ancients have chosen to grant Aon a companion after all this time. I find it no coincidence that the one they chose to replace Qta was already enamored of the warlock before the deed. Perhaps it will be a boon to us all."

The subtext was clear—that if Aon knew a kind of tranquility in his existence, mayhap they all might share in the calm that may bring. He could only pray to the Ancients that it was true.

"I am troubled that she seems to be split from the bulk of her power," Rxa observed. "Her companion seems to be her shelter from the storm."

"I do not blame her. No one has ever been gifted the power of a royal in such a fashion. As she died a mortal, devoid of any link to the Ancients, it would have likely driven her mad."

"It is still an unnatural state for her to be trapped in such limbo." Rxa looked up at the statue of the Ancient looming over them. "She still does not accept her place in this world."

"She will adjust. I have faith in her."

"I hope you are right. I do not know the young thing. I will have to take time to do so. Now," Rxa turned to face him and gestured for them to exit the sanctuary of the cathedral and retreat to somewhere more private, "tell me everything that I have missed. Every detail."

THREE

How exactly was she supposed to prepare for the trial of her lover—who murdered her best friend—when she was a newborn queen in an underworld of monsters?

No frickin' clue.

The only thing Lydia knew for certain was that this sucked.

And that she really didn't know who she could trust and who she couldn't.

When she had woken up that morning, she felt like death warmed over. She hadn't slept well. She had tossed and turned the whole night, unable to shut her mind up from the raging debate that was crashing over her and pulling her under like a riptide.

Aon killed Nick. *To protect me.* He loved her. *But he killed Nick in front of me.* He was a monster and a sadist. *And I love him.* Once more she was arguing with herself about the warlock. She wished she could forgive him. She wished she could hate him. She wished she could make up her goddamn mind. But there was one thing she couldn't deny any more... she loved him. She really did.

Why won't you tell him how you feel? Q asked her from where he was perched on her chest. He was curled up like a cat. She scratched his head accordingly. He leaned into the touch, flicking his tail happily.

"It's betraying Nick if I do." Her tone was as morose as she felt.

Is it? Well, then, I guess you'll have to pick, huh? The man you love or your dead friend. But maybe Aon'll get some cement slippers and be dropped into the bottom of the ocean—now that we have one again—and it won't matter! You'll never see him again.

The creature was trying to cheer her up, but holy hell it wasn't working. Shooing him off her, she sat up. It was time to get going, anyway. The black glass rose was still sitting on her table where she had left it. Ruffling through her pillows, she found the note that had been left with it. As if expecting the writing to be different, she re-read the note. She wouldn't have been surprised—especially with the Warlock involved. But to her odd disappointment, they hadn't.

Do what you must. –A

In his own weird and egotistical way, he was giving her permission to do what she felt was right. Dread and heartache hit her both at once. She realized suddenly that she wanted to scream and shout at him—to throw things at him.

But she wanted to talk to him.

She *missed* him.

No small part of her was eager to try and sort this all out. To either decide she hated him or to forgive him. One way or another, she couldn't stay in this purgatory of feeling both and neither all at once.

With a beleaguered sigh, she went to try to clear her head

the best way she knew how. Wandering through her new house —which was slowly becoming more and more Boston and less an Aztec ruin although the influence was still very clearly there —to find the bathroom.

It had a shower. A real shower. Sure, it was carved out of rock and the water poured out of a hole in the wall and down a stone slab like a water feature in a garden. It was hardly modern. But it was amazing. It was relaxing. The water was hot, and she miraculously had soap, and that's all she cared about right now.

Picking up a little stray lizard that had crawled inside the shower, she put it down on the bathroom counter. It looked like a chameleon had mated with a lobster, and she thought it might be able to breathe fire, judging by the red glow in its throat through the skin.

It was still so bizarre to think that she had "poofed" it into existence. That it was a monster born out of her mind. It was adorable in its own weird way, and she wanted to stop and name the little thing, but the hot water was calling her.

Stepping into the stone shower, she let the wonderfully hot liquid pour over her head. The steam rushed over her, and she shut her eyes with a long sigh. It gave Lydia time to think, if nothing else.

Loving Aon didn't cure what he had done. The unavoidable truth of how she felt didn't change the memory of watching him burn Nick's face away in a blaze of black fire. It didn't do anything to dull the fact that Aon was capable of the worst kinds of acts, even if he felt righteous in the deed.

But Aon had submitted himself to this trial. He said he stepped down from the throne willingly to face recompense. He could have fought it or come up with some lame excuse as to why he had to do it. Especially with Edu having been preparing for war. Aon could have pulled all sorts of loopholes that she was sure she had no idea even existed. But Aon had abdicated the throne to Edu and was allowing this all to take place.

Why?

It was clear he didn't care about anyone's opinion of him. Aon didn't give a crap what the elders or Edu, or likely even Rxa, thought of his morality or honor. He had no issue with taking a life, especially not when he felt it was justified. So why let this trial take place?

Then it dawned on her all at once.

It wasn't for their benefit... it was for *hers.*

He was surrendering to a conviction from *her.*

This was her one chance to either get her revenge on him for what he had done or let it go and move past it. This was Aon, forcing her hand in a very public fashion. Either make him pay for his deeds or forgive him. He wouldn't let it drag on in ambiguity.

"Son of a bitch!" Lydia slammed her palm into the stone wall of the shower.

Just figured it out? You're cute, but not terribly quick, Q teased from where he had perched atop the waterfall.

She didn't bother fussing about him seeing her naked. They were the same person, after all. He was bathing like a bird, dipping in the water and fluffing his feathers and shaking off, sending droplets flying in all directions.

"Shut up." Leaning her head against the wall for a moment, she appreciated that it was cool against the hot air, and let herself focus on that instead of her anger. "I don't know what I expected. He's always playing a game." This was a chess move by Aon, that's all any of this was. And she was going to be outplayed. There was no question of it.

Yup. That's why the others don't trust Aon. For some reason, you trust him because of the games.

"In spite of," she corrected him.

Because of, Q argued. **You think that because Aon's a step ahead, he's already got it all figured out. There's comfort in that.**

"Whatever," she said, dismissing the comment and yanked on the rope that controlled the stone slab that shut off the water. Stepping out, she wrapped a towel around herself and went about getting ready. She dressed fancy—as fancy as she could, anyway—without taking Q's suggestion of wearing feathers. There was no way in hell that was going to happen. Silk turquoise blouse, black pants, boots, and a dark turquoise coat and scarf that was at least printed to look like peacock feathers.

Q warned her where Edu lived was cold and that they were, for the first time in well over a thousand years, experiencing winter.

But she should probably dress nice for Aon's trial.

Of Nick's murder.

Damn it all.

Every time she remembered why she was nervous, it just made it worse.

Gold jewelry, turquoise makeup, and she was ready to go. Well, physically, anyway. She gripped the counter with both hands and leaned over, stretching her back and her legs, trying to get the tension out of her muscles. "Q, I don't know if I can do this."

Tears stung her eyes and threatened to ruin her makeup. She bit them back angrily.

You kinda gotta.

"I don't know what to do. They're going to ask me to condemn Aon, and I don't know if I can. I don't know if I can't. And if Edu catches wind that he and I are... whatever we are, he'll kill me. Again." She cringed. "And I don't know if I can trust Rxa."

I know, Cupcake. You'll be okay, though. Just do what feels right.

Straightening up, she let out a weak laugh. Patting her

shoulder, she invited the snake over. When Q flitted over from the counter to the spot on her shoulder, she scratched him on the head. "I just wish it wasn't so soon."

I think that's on purpose. He knows that forcing the matter when the issue is still fresh, you're more likely to not let turn into a bitter scar. If he does this while it's still raw, he thinks he has better odds of stitching you two back together.

Q was probably right again. Aon would want to intervene on her feelings to push her one way or the other before it grew into resentment. Before she learned to hate him like the others had. The asshole knew what he was doing. "Yeah." There was some comfort in knowing at least there was somebody behind the wheel of this crazy train.

See? You trust him *because* of the games.

"Shut up." She hated arguing with herself. It felt stupid and she always lost no matter who won. "Let's just go get this over with."

A swirl of feathers and a blast of cold air met her face. Going from a hot and humid jungle into a walk-in-freezer made her head reel with the abrupt change.

It was snowing. More accurately, it was blizzarding. "Holy shit—" Ducking her head against the wind, she raised her arm to cover herself from the biting cold. "You weren't kidding!"

She was standing on the steps to Edu's keep. She recognized it from the night she tried to escape, although now it was painted with a thick coat of white. Lydia had to squint to see through the driving snow. Walking up to the door, she could hear her boots crunch into the inches of the cold fluff that had already fallen.

Well, at least she hadn't dressed like she usually did for her jungle.

Pounding on the wooden door, it swung open a moment

later. Lydia nearly fell inside, blown in with the force of the wind at her back. Someone was laughing. Under his breath, maybe, but laughing all the same.

"Fucking *hell*—" She shook off her arms. Looking up, she blinked in surprise and recognition. That was a face she hadn't seen in what felt like forever. It had only been weeks. "Tim?"

"Hey there, toots." He grinned at her after shutting the door behind her, having to put his shoulder into it to slam it shut. The howling wind and pounding snow stopped the moment the massive wood door was closed, and what was left was the kind of warmth that could only be from burning fires.

Tim looked precisely the same as he had the first night she met him, in the Cathedral of the Ancients. Or the night he helped corner her so Edu could kill her. The memory of precisely the last time she saw Tim made her shove him with both hands, sending him staggering back into the door. She'd caught him off guard and nearly threw the man toppling to the ground.

Or, maybe she was stronger than she used to be.

Fifty-fifty shot.

"The hell was that for, you crazy—" Tim paused and blinked, seemingly coming to the same realization as to why she was angry at him. He straightened up and brushed himself off. "Oh, right, that. Yeah, I'm sorry. I didn't want to have anything to do with it, but when your king tells you to do something, you do it."

The poor greaser had nothing to do with her death. Not really. With a half-hearted shrug, she decided small grudges weren't worth it considering what she had to deal with. "It's fine. Consider that shove my revenge." She combed her hands through her hair. "So. How're you?"

Tim looked deeply surprised at her having forgiven him so fast. But clearly, he wasn't someone to look a gift horse in the mouth. He flashed a bright grin. "I got off easy!" he joked. "I'm good, Lyd. I'm good. How're you? You look... great." He looked down at her, pointedly staring at her chest again, before giving her another cheeky smirk.

Laughing, she shook her head. Tim was a simple man, and she appreciated that right about now. "I'm holding up as well as can be expected. And thanks, I guess. It's good to see you."

"How about a hello kiss instead of a shove next time?"

"Go to hell, Tim."

The greaser laughed. "Well, can't fault a man for trying. Everybody's gathered in the main hall. Still waiting for Maverick, but other than that, we're ready to go. Maverick is *always* late."

"Bunny? Oh hell, Bunny!"

Someone shrieked from behind her, and before she could even turn around, they had nearly tackled her to the ground. Thin arms were around her, and she was almost flattened by a small, very excited wild animal.

"I am so happy to see you! He said you'd be here, I'm so happy!"

"Evie!" She exclaimed as she finally managed to whirl around in the girl's arms to see her. Lydia hugged her tightly, and almost cried out of joy. "You're okay!"

"I am! And you're—ooh..." Evie trailed off in wonder as she suddenly took Lydia's face in both of her hands, clearly caught up by the sight of the ink on her face. "It's true. It's really true. Edu told me, but I didn't really buy what he was sellin', but bunny! Look at you."

Lydia felt her face go warm in a blush. She hated the scrutiny and the attention.

"Are you two gonna kiss?" Tim interjected from where he was still by a wall. "Please tell me you're gonna kiss."

"Shut up," Lydia shot back.

The greaser made an exaggerated and disappointed finger snap in response.

Rolling her eyes, she turned back to Evie and pushed away from the girl long enough to look down at her and see that her friend had all her limbs. "Are you okay, Evie?"

"Of course, I am! Why wouldn't I be?" Evie looked a lot better as Edu's prisoner than she did as Aon's. The last she had seen the girl, she was strapped to a table and being tortured. Now, she was dressed in furs and leather, which suited her long curly red hair and freckles perfectly. There was somehow even more shine in her yellow eyes than there had been before.

"What're you doing here?" Lydia wondered out loud at her.

"Oh, well." Evie grinned and leaned into her to whisper. "It seems like we've both bagged us a king." At Lydia's shocked and confused expression, she cackled in laughter and hugged her tighter. "Edu came to find me when you made Aon let me go. He took me here, and I've been with him ever since. Oh, bunny, I never got to say thank you. You saved me!"

Lydia smiled at the girl. "It was the least I could do. You saved me first, after all. I couldn't leave you there like that. But you're here... with Edu? Are you okay? Is he hurting you?"

Evie laughed again and grabbed Lydia's arm to pull her off away to somewhere a little more private and away from Tim's harmless leering. "You're worried about me? You're the one with the warlock! I couldn't be better. Edu's a sweetheart; he really is. Just a big soft cowboy down underneath all that armor. I know you two haven't gotten on, but he's good to me. I promise. He's a good man."

Relieved that her friend was okay and seemed none the worse for wear, she still couldn't help but give Evie a half-hearted smirk at her comment. "Saying that we haven't 'gotten on' is probably the biggest understatement of the year."

"I know, I know. I was so angry when he told me what he did. I was so upset, bunny. I broke a lot of his house the night he came back from—from—" Evie couldn't bring herself to say the words and choked off, unable to say that Edu had killed her.

"But he thought he had no other choice, y'know?" Evie nudged her arm.

Lydia did know. She did understand. She was angrier at Edu for not believing she wasn't some hypnotized slave of Aon's, than over him killing her, to be honest.

Something told her that the drama that was ahead of her *now* was a lot worse than what she had to deal with when she was a human. Somehow.

Nodding, she sighed. "I get why he did it. I need him to stop trying to re-kill me, and then maybe I can actually try and have a conversation with the man." Lydia blinked. "Well. Mostly. Through that lady, anyway."

Evie giggled. "You'll be fine. He's stubborn, but he'll get there. The straight six is just so worried and afraid about what that warlock might do, he doesn't want to give him an inch." Evie leaned into her again in a hug and squeezed as hard as she could. "I'm just so happy to see you!"

"Right back at you." And she really was thrilled to see Evie. They hadn't spent much time together, all things considered. But she thought of Evie as one of her closest friends. She may have lost Nick, but at least there were still people in this world she was happy to see.

Tim was chanting, *"kiss, kiss, kiss,"* at them under his breath.

"Tim!" she shouted at the man, who cackled in laughter but obediently went quiet.

Evie was grinning at Tim's antics, which she was sure only encouraged the greaser, before turning her attention back to Lydia. "Hey, maybe I can convince Big Red to come bring me to your place later? I'd love to see it!"

Big Red. Cute. The way she said it was with such affection, it was clear to see the two were together in more than just a physical way.

She hoped the feelings were mutual, for Evie's sake. But the little spitfire seemed so impervious to the world and its troubles, she'd probably brush it off and keep going like nothing had happened. It was a skill and personality trait that Lydia was keenly jealous of. It was one she was sorely lacking.

"I'd love that." The smile on her face hadn't faltered since Evie had shown up.

"Well." Evie nudged her arm again. "I'm holdin' you up. You should get this mess over with."

"Yeah… I don't want to. But I should."

"I'll see you later, bunny." Evie rocked up onto her toes to kiss Lydia on the cheek and then walked off with a chipper, "Bye, now!" and a wave. It was so over-the-top it made her smile and shake her head.

"Next time, kiss her goodbye on the lips, goddamn it!" Tim shouted after her.

"Oh, put a cork in it, Zippers," Evie shot back to him. Tim laughed loudly, and Lydia couldn't help but smile at the exchange. He walked off with a broad smirk, and she could read his enjoyment clearly across his features. They could be friends, if fate let it happen.

Now, she was alone with only one option left as to what to do. It was time to face the music.

As she walked toward where she assumed the great hall was, she could take the time to look around at Edu's home. Last time, she had been too busy trying to escape it to really pay attention. It was beautiful in a rustic, hand-carved, medieval Viking kind of way. Now that she knew he was supposed to live in the frozen north, his decor and clothing choices made a lot more sense. Last time she had been here, it had been the ambient lack of weather that the whole world had been stuck with. They hadn't had anything resembling seasons or changes in temperature until she became a dreamer, and the Ancients saw fit to save the world they created.

It was another reminder why she had to be this way. It was yet another thing on the list.

Lydia rubbed her hand on the back of her neck, trying not to feel overwhelmed again. One thing at a time. Just a murder trial to help oversee. No big deal.

No big deal *at all*.

FOUR

Damn me and my stupid life.

Walking through the open doors to the main hall, she wasn't sure what to expect. What she got was something fitting out of a *Lord of the Rings* movie set. A giant pit of fire burned in the center of the room, lighting the carved wooden beams that soared up two stories in stark highlights and shadows. Every surface of the wood structure was carved with twisting knots that resembled warped and morbid Celtic designs or figures and monsters. Dragons seemed to be the repeated motif here.

To one side of the room at the end was placed a large table upon a stone landing, a few steps up from the rest of the room. It was rectangular and just as rustic as the rest of the motif of the room. It looked as though it had been hewn out of entire trees. It was placed at a perpendicular angle to the rest of the chamber, and at it sat familiar figures, all on the far side like a panel of judges. At the center sat Edu, dwarfing the others, even in his non-armor attire. He was wearing his typical pile of leather and furs that made him look like the Viking that he apparently was. Yet again, she wondered which came first—Under or Earth.

Kamira and Ziza she knew on sight. And it was hard to miss the glowing angel, standing behind a chair, his wings unfurled behind him. The white, opalescent feathers casting an eerie glow on everything around him. Upon seeing her, Rxa bowed his head in greeting. Otoi had already apparently been removed from his duty, as the obnoxious little man was nowhere around. She was glad for it.

Lydia just smiled back faintly at Rxa, feeling a little too much on stage for her liking, with everyone present turning to look at her.

There was another man at the table, dark-skinned and dressed entirely in black that she didn't recognize. He wore a black metal mask over half of his face. On second thought, he might be vaguely familiar, but she didn't think they had ever been introduced. It was clear, judging by the color he was wearing and by the metal mask, that he was from Aon's House.

Maverick, as Tim had said, was late. But where was Aon? It took her a second to find him as he wasn't sitting with the others, in the glare of the fire like a shadow within a shadow.

There, in a chair sitting opposite the table, closer to the center of the room and at the base of the stairs on which everyone was seated. The warlock was in the armchair, leaning back, ankle on his knee and head propped up on his hand, looking utterly bored.

Walking toward the table, she tried to at least look like she belonged there, even if she felt like an idiot. Trying to pretend, even if it was bullshit, that she wasn't nervous, confused, and had little to no idea what was happening. There was a time not so long ago that she would have run from this room in horror. That seeing those people seated at the table, staring at her, would have sent her into a fit and running for cover.

She was one of them now, one way or another. Slowly but surely, that fact was getting through her thick skull.

The chairs at the table were painted and color-coded. One for each House, decorated in roughly hewn wood carvings. Hers was a twisting array of winged snakes and placed next to the man in the black mask and suit.

Doing her best to move with any kind of conviction, she sat in the chair, smiling back at Kamira who had greeted her silently. You knew it was cold when Kamira was wearing a fur cape.

It's a tit nipply out, huh?

Man, she was glad her snake was invisible, and nobody heard that. *Shut up, Q.*

Lyon was looming in the shadows of the room, and he shot her a gentle, piteous smile. He likely understood and empathized with what she was going through. She was glad he was here, even if he wasn't welcome to sit at the table with the others and therefore wouldn't be able to help her directly.

Looking over at the brooding, angry-looking man in black next to her, Lydia reached out her hand to him with the friendliest expression she could muster. "Lydia. Nice to meet you. I don't think we've met."

The man looked at her, visible eye wide and wary, before glancing to Aon where he sat.

"Oh, for the *love of*—" Aon sighed dramatically. "Yes. You may speak to her now, Navaa. Things have changed, in case that had wholly escaped your notice."

Well, Aon was irritable today. She guessed he probably had a decent reason, all things considered.

After being rebuked, Navaa took her offered hand and shook it. "A pleasure, Ms. Lydia. It is nice to finally meet you." The man had a deep voice, strained as it was in the moment of being snapped at by his boss. But there was a sharpness and a danger to him that was obvious. She could tell he fit in perfectly in Aon's House. "I am Aon's elder and regent when he sleeps, Navaa."

Aon's second in command? Huh. Lydia had never really thought about it. She hadn't cared or paid much attention to the politics in Under before. She was too busy trying to stay alive. "He wasn't letting you talk to me? Why?" Furrowing her brow, she looked over at Aon, who was seemingly doing his best to ignore the conversation between her and Navaa.

"Only the servants could speak to you during your stay. He said it was to let you adjust at a more comfortable pace. He wished to limit his..." Navaa shot a pointed stare at Edu. "Undue influence upon you, and thought his more influential loyalists would be unfit companions. Although it did absolutely no good for him or you in the end."

Edu growled in response, and Navaa raised his hands as if to say he would go no further. But the grin on his features showed he wasn't remotely sorry.

Lydia sighed. How long was this fight going to go on? The debate over whether she was some meat puppet of the warlock? She was getting sick of being in the middle of it. "I'm going to ask a stupid question," she said to Navaa, lowering her voice so the others couldn't hear. "Because I'll level with you—I have no idea what the *ever-loving fuck* I'm doing."

Navaa grinned, a flash of white teeth on an otherwise dark background. He seemed amused by her honesty and matched her quiet tone. "By all means."

"Why're you sitting up here? Aon's awake."

"Ah. Yes, well. Aon is not allowed to weigh judgement up on his own crime for obvious reasons. But the House of Shadows is still invited to be involved. I sit here on behalf of the House for which he is king, so that he may have a vote in his favor."

"But you'd obviously vote for him, anyway."

"Yes."

"That's stupid, then."

"Yet, here I am."

"I hate politics."

"You and I will get along well, I feel." Navaa was still grinning. It wasn't a terribly friendly expression, nor was his tone, but she had seen a lot worse recently. Lydia figured it was probably the man's default mode. So she smiled back and took it as the compliment she figured he intended it as. She shouldn't be surprised that everyone in Aon's House was a little intense.

Their conversation ended as a figure entered the room. A man with a gray suit and a purple mask. Maverick brushed snow off his shoulders. The cane he carried was clearly for show, as was the derby hat he had tucked under his arm. He looked ripped right out of an old Sears catalog from the turn of the century her father had when she was little.

"The weather here is quite something, Edu," Maverick said as he approached, not apologizing for being late. Maverick likely apologized for very little.

"Master Edu says it brings his heart joy to see the fields turn white once more," Ylena said from where she was standing beside Edu.

"Yay for me dying, it fuckin' snows now," Lydia muttered sarcastically.

Navaa, the only one who heard her, burst out with a single loud laugh and had to quickly wave his hand away at the others to display that he wasn't mocking them.

"Are you this crass with Master Aon?" Navaa whispered to her once the others had looked away.

Flashing a grin, she leaned back in her chair. "You have no idea."

"I think I see why he is fond of you."

Lydia snickered in response and caught another broad smile from the man in return. All right, he was probably a bit much on most days, but at least Aon's regent had a sense of humor. If she weren't dreading what was about to follow and her role in it, she'd probably spend her time trying to get Navaa to laugh inappropriately during the meeting.

But this very much involved her.

Maverick climbed the stairs to take his seat at the table, and with that, they could begin.

"King Aon," Ylena began in an official tone. "You sit accused of the crime of murder of a man innocent of any crime, in cold blood, and during a time of peace. How do you plead?"

Aon shifted in his chair with all the air of a man bored out of his mind. "Guilty. Really, may we skip ahead to sentencing? This is a foolish waste of time." It was apparent how little weight he was giving to the proceedings.

Edu's hand tightened on the arm of his chair. Ylena continued. "Very well. Do you wish to plead your case in an attempt to lighten your sentencing, as is your right? We are all aware you claim to have righteous motives in your actions."

Aon tilted his head back slightly, light catching the reflection of his metal mask. Even when he was sitting on trial, he was an intimidating sight. "No," came his simple reply.

Lydia blinked, surprised. *No?* Why wouldn't he make his case as to why he had murdered Nick?

It seems Rxa wondered the same. "Brother Aon, all present are aware of the prophecy you received. You do not wish to plead for leniency in light of what inspired your actions?"

Aon let the moment hang in the air with nothing but the crackle of the fire before he spoke again. "No."

"Why?" the archangel pressed.

"Because it is a waste of my breath." Aon's reply was cold and terse. He didn't move. And somehow, that made him all the more eerie.

"What mean you?" Maverick pressed for specifics. But the Regent of Words narrowed his eyes and leaned forward. "What is your game, warlock?"

"I am hereby recalling my favors from the Houses so assembled. The ones given to me in exchange for allowing Ms. Lydia to go free." Finally, Aon moved. He lifted his clawed hand into the light of the fire. "Effective immediately."

Edu went stiff. His hands tightened into fists. "What?" Ylena stepped forward, inspired by the emotions of her king. "What *favors*?"

Aon laughed. Quiet, and cruel. "Edu, dear Edu... forever the fool."

Lydia knew she was missing something along with the King of Flames. "For the benefit of both of us. What are you talking about, Aon?"

He ignored her. "You all know very well I could have kept Lydia as my prisoner. But I did not. Edu, while you readied for war, I *bargained*. I would not seek to keep her as my prisoner then, now, or ever in the future in exchange for something simple. A favor for future use. And lo, here it is—you are all to recuse yourselves from this vote."

Lydia really wished she had half a clue what was going on. But judging how pissed Edu was and how pleased Navaa was, Aon was playing things very much his way.

He wasn't going to keep me prisoner, anyway. That's not what he wanted.

They don't know that. He used them like he was conducting an orchestra pit, and he still is. See why people don't trust him?

"I demand payment for the favors now. Rxa—Otoi sat in agreement with the others, and thus a bargain by a regent must be honored by their king."

"I know, yes," Rxa said with a heavy sigh. The angel moved to sit in the chair finally, and she watched in fascination as his wings shimmered and vanished, so he could do so without having to deal with their bulk. "Very well, Aon. I recuse."

Kamira sighed heavily and shook her head. "This is a farce. Nick was in *my* House," she insisted. "I should have a say!"

"You agreed, Kamira." Aon tapped his gloved fingers on the arm of his chair, one after the other in succession, clearly annoyed with her impertinence. "You all must stand down from judgement. Save for Lydia and Edu, of course. If you refuse, you are in breach of a contract and are to face your own trial. One over which *I* shall proceed. This bargain is now *law*. Or would you have me take her back into my protective *care*?"

Kamira began snarling obscenities, fuming and yelling at the warlock. But Aon merely laughed. Finally, with one last series of swears in a language that Lydia didn't understand, she sank back down into her chair and spat on the floor. "I recuse."

Ziza agreed next. After a long pause, so did Maverick. He sat back in his chair, looking wary and concerned over what was happening. Ziza looked as though nothing was happening at all, but then again, she always did. Kamira was still livid. She pulled her thick fur cloak up closer around herself, looking like a sulking angry cat.

Shockingly, Navaa snuffed and leaned back. "I recuse."

"What?" Lydia asked, stunned. Why would Aon give up a vote in his favor? If Navaa and Edu were both voting, their votes would cancel each other out, and it would be down to her. Right?

"If the other regents have stepped down from judgement, then it is only fair that I do the same. I merely am joining my peers." The smirk on Navaa's face said otherwise. He was following orders.

What the hell are you playing at, Aon?

Edu's hand finally loosened from the railing enough that his knuckles were a little less white. "You may have doomed yourself, Aon. You know how Edu will judge you. And it is her friend whom you stole."

"Then let her take her pound of flesh in exchange." The

warlock curled his hand under his chin as he propped his elbow up on the armrest. "Indeed, let Lydia judge me alone in this. For I would even argue, old friend, that you have no right to sit upon this council with your own crime of murder so recently performed."

And here we go. That was Aon's play—to try and get Lydia alone to judge him. Of *course.*

He didn't want their votes to cancel.

He wanted her vote to be alone.

This whole council was just a stage for him to play out their drama. To get her to either condemn him or forgive him and hold her to it in a way she couldn't then later change her mind.

"That's why you didn't just use your stupid favors with them to get them to pardon you." It was just starting to all come together. It was too late, but hey. Better late than never. "You don't want them to pardon you. You want me to decide what happens. You absolute *fuckhead.*"

He was using them to settle their far more personal score, like they were all just puppets for his own game of chess. She was not, under any circumstances, surprised. Pissed? Yes. Shocked?

No.

No, she wasn't.

Aon held his hands out in front of him palms up, as if to say, "And here we are."

"You utter douchebag." Now, she was trying to do her best to set him on fire with a glare. It only made Aon laugh.

Ylena interrupted. "Regardless. Master Edu rejects your motion to exclude him from this proceeding. Edu murdered a mortal girl who was at the time not one of us. Such an act is not a crime."

"You murdered a girl who was under my protection." Aon tapped a taloned finger against the wood of the armchair, still utterly bored and detached from the experience. As if he knew how it was already going to play out. "Ms. Lydia was a prisoner in my care. Killing her may not have been an infraction on its own, but that she was my ward makes it a felony, Edu."

"I love how you two are talking like I'm not even here." Lydia threw up her hands.

"Welcome to Under," Maverick replied dryly.

"Ms. Lydia," Ylena began and turned to look at her. Well, Lydia assumed she did, anyway. The woman's mask had no holes for her eyes. "Master Edu apologizes. When debating with the warlock, he can easily come to forget himself."

Navaa snorted at that, but kept his mouth shut.

Ylena continued as if nothing had happened. "What is your opinion on the matter of his guilt in your... transformation? Do you seek recompense, or do you pardon him?"

"I've said that I've forgiven you for that."

"That was in person. This is a matter of court and law," Ylena pointed out dutifully. "As much as it irritates Master Edu, it does make a difference."

Lydia watched the big man for a moment and sighed. "You were only doing what you thought was right. It wasn't personal. You got some stupid prophecy that said I had to die, so you had to do it. I get it." Lydia paused, unsure of what to do. But it felt right. She didn't want to hold a grudge, especially not this early on in her experience with eternity. "I forgive you. Or pardon you, or whatever I need to say for it to be official."

Edu bowed his head and put his hand to his chest, palm flat against the expanse of leather and fur that covered it. He was silently thanking her.

It wasn't until after Edu tilted his head back up that she realized what had just happened. Her eyes flew wide, and she glared at Aon, taken aback and angry. Aon merely laughed at her expression, clearly terribly pleased with himself.

"You son of a *cock-sucking donkey-fucking trash-fire!*" she hollered at the warlock.

Now, Aon was howling in laughter. "Oh, I do love it when you're angry."

Wailing in frustration, she slammed her fists down on the table and put her head down on the wooden surface.

She heard Maverick mutter his own, far more polite obscenity under his breath. He put it together a moment after she did, even if he was missing the details. He must have guessed.

In pardoning Edu of his crime against Lydia, she was forced to admit that murder, for the right cause, was excusable.

That murder, *in the instance of a prophecy*, was justified.

Aon's motives were exactly the same when he had killed Nick as Edu's had been when he had killed her.

"No." Lifting her head, she pointed at him furiously. "No! It's not the same!"

Edu tilted his head in confusion, not following along. The others, except for Maverick, seemed just as lost. But right now, she was too busy arguing with Aon to fill them in.

"How so?" Aon held his hand out, palm up, gesturing as if he were one half of the scale. "You died because the Ancients said the word." He held out his other palm to complete the invisible balance. "Same as the boy. I was given a prophecy of doom, and I acted to prevent it."

"It's completely different!" Lydia got up from her chair, needing to pace.

"Do explain! I am all ears. How is it different, save for that you cared for the boy who died?" Aon insisted.

Faced with having to come up with reasons, she found... none. Literally none. Both men may have been wrong, but they believed their actions to be righteous. She had pardoned Edu, and now Aon was asking her to do the same for him. Back and forth like an angry tiger, she paced behind the chairs, scrambling for anything. Anything at all.

But was coming up empty.

And it was just making the fury worse.

"Your selflessness and compassion are honorable and charming, my dear." Aon's words were likely meant to be soothing. But they were like salt on a wound. "But in this, they have ensnared you."

"Master Edu insists to you, Ms. Lydia, that you needn't listen to him. The crimes are separate occurrences. If you wish to condemn him for his actions, you may do so and sleep free of regrets. His argument that the crimes are identical is an opinion, not a fact."

Stopping in her pacing, she looked over at Edu. He was trying to pull her out of the catch twenty-two that Aon had put in front of her. It was a nice attempt, but she knew that he was wrong. If she claimed that the two crimes were different without any real reasons, she'd hate herself for it.

Worse, she'd become guilty of the same thing that Edu and the others had fallen into with Aon... hurting him for the sake of it.

Damn her and her stupid morals.

Damn Aon and his stupid games of chess.

Was this really going to be the rest of eternity for her? Being outplayed by a madman who enjoyed winning a little too much?

"You have options, Lydia. You needn't pardon him." Ylena interrupted her thoughts. "Simply that he argues you must do the other for your own moral high ground does not make it so."

"What are my choices?" She'd happily take the opportunity to stall for a few minutes to think this over.

"On one end, to be pardoned of all wrongdoing. Aon would leave here as he is now, with no expiation for his sin. On the other, there is a... process by which to render him not dead but gone." Rxa was the one who took over the explanation, as it was likely his job to see the task done. "It has never been performed."

"Let me guess. You all dreamed up the method for him, though." She jerked a thumb at Aon. Their stern expressions gave her the answer. "Do I want to know what it involves?"

Rxa shook his head no. "It is quite horrific. It would pain me to trouble your mind with such a—"

"They would remove all but one of my soulmarks with a burning firepower." Aon had no such a problem. "Then, using the same curse that removed Edu's tongue and my hand, they would slice my limbs from my body so that I could not free myself. They would remove my tongue so I could not scream. My eyes so I could not see. And they would chain me to the bottom of the Pool of the Ancients, where I would remain until our world ceased to be. Forever drowning with our damned gods." He picked a piece of lint idly from his sleeve. "Yet eternally denied death, lest Under be doomed to the void once more."

Her knees felt weak. She half staggered back to her chair and sank onto the cushion.

Shutting her eyes, she really wished she had something stiff to drink.

Clearing his throat, Rxa continued, trying to steer the conversation onto a cheerier path. Bless his heart for trying. "We may also decide to permanently or temporarily imprison him, exile him to the edges of the world and strip him of his title and powers, or force him to return to his crypt to sleep."

"Master Edu has longed to see Aon return to the Ancients," Ylena said coldly. "Perhaps today is the day we finally get to see him suffer."

"No. No. No, we're not—" Lydia rejected that option immediately, her stomach churning. "I'm not going to let him, or anyone, suffer that fate. And you need to get over this weird fetish you have to see Aon *suffer*. Your obsession for 'justice' went wrong a long time ago, Edu."

"Well said!" Aon exclaimed sarcastically through a laugh.

"And you're going to stuff it for a hot second, douchebag!" She snapped at Aon again. Her temper was starting to get the best of her. This was stupid, and she hated being played. Even though Aon was the one in the hot seat, he was still yanking all their strings like they were just marionettes.

Edu was watching her, although what he was thinking was a complete mystery. "Imprisonment, then," Ylena suggested. "Permanently lock him away."

That stabbed at her gut. The idea of locking him in a cement cell for the rest of time... she couldn't do it. She just couldn't. But the reason why wouldn't bode well with Edu. She had to come up with an excuse. "Give him enough time and he'll get loose. Do you really want to see what would come out of a cement block after a thousand years?" She rolled her eyes. "You think he's insane now? Can you imagine what kind of a giant 'fuck you, future self' moment that'll be when he digs his ass back out? The dude is several cards short of a full deck already, let alone after a thousand years of being stuck in solitary confinement. Maybe you don't plan to live that long, but I for one don't want to deal with that."

"She has a valid observation," Rxa commented.

Edu seemed to consider it for a long moment and looked over the table at Aon. The warlock and the warrior. Maybe he was trying to imagine what Aon would look like, coming out of that prison. With a weary sigh, he seemed to concede her point. "What would you have us do, then, Ms. Lydia?" Ylena asked her.

That left pardoning and forced sleep. Putting the man back into whatever weird stasis they lived in for a hundred years before trading places or letting him walk out, absolved of his crime.

Neither sounded great.

Lydia shook her head and leaned back in the chair. Forcing Aon to return to his crypt might be the best option. A hundred years wasn't so long when you thought about the whole of their history.

Then the other half of her mind spoke up. Send Aon to his crypt? Even if she had just pardoned Edu for the same thing? That was hypocrisy at its best. Even with her own self-interests aside, she couldn't pardon Edu and condemn Aon for the same crime in the same breath.

"I don't know," she admitted. "It feels wrong to send Aon to his crypt when I just forgave you for the same thing. But it also feels incredibly wrong to let him get away with this." Something dawned on her. "Edu. Your vote is still in the game because I pardoned you of killing me. So, if I agree to pardon him, and you don't, what happens?"

"A split decision always goes to the reigning king," Ylena explained.

"So... what's the point in all this?" Lydia pondered out loud, trying to figure out Aon's game for what it was and failing miserably. "Even if I decide to pardon him, you won't, and then it doesn't matter. So, why do I even need to make a decision?"

"Ah. Yes." Aon sat forward, suddenly sounding very pleased with himself. "Ms. Lydia, there is another favor owed to me in this room. Yours. I am now calling it in."

FIVE

Lydia's instinctual reaction was to laugh. She looked at Aon, confused and flabbergasted. Now he was trying to force her hand? "You're kidding me."

Aon shrugged. "Why not?"

"What favor does she owe you?" Maverick asked warily.

"I absolved the girl Evelyn of all her crimes at Lydia's request. In return, she granted me a favor that we agreed I could specify at a time of my liking."

"What does this have to do with anything, though?" She couldn't wrap her head around what possible fucked up four-dimensional chess move he thought he was making now. "That doesn't get you anywhere. My vote doesn't matter anymore."

"Ah, but it does. I hereby declare that I will void this agreement between Ms. Lydia and I, unless Edu also recuses himself from this judgement." Aon sat back in the chair once more, crossing his leg to place his ankle on his knee. He was very pleased with himself. "Checkmate, old friend."

Edu let out a roar of rage and stood from his throne, shoving the wood chair back so hard that it screeched on the floor. Everyone recoiled in their seats away from the man as he paced from the table. He reared back a fist and punched one of the massive stone columns. The whole of the building shook with the blow.

"Somebody want to fill me in?" Lydia murmured.

"If I void our arrangement, darling," Aon answered her plea for help, "then I void the clemency that was paid unto dear Ms. Evelyn. Her freedom would therefore become immediately revoked, and the glorified barmaid would have to stand trial for her previous guilty plea of attempted murder."

Edu snarled and pounded his fist into the column of his home a second time.

"My, my, what a passionate reaction, Edu!" Aon laughed as he teased the big man mercilessly. "Do not tell me you have grown fond of the redhead? I *had* heard a rumor she had taken up residence here of late. How... *sweet.*"

"Leave him alone, Aon." Her hands were now also balled into fists. "That has nothing to do with this. Don't—" She stopped before finishing her sentence. *Don't look down on him for something of which you're equally guilty.*

Sensing her discomfort, the warlock pressed. "Don't what, my dear?"

"Don't belittle the man for having the capacity for something other than hatred." Lydia shot back at him coldly. Let the room think she was insulting him. Let Aon know it for what it was.

Aon laughed, genuinely amused at her retort, and leaned back in his chair. "Edu is merely facing the reality that he must choose between his new darling lady and exacting revenge upon me. How is it that we have found ourselves in this scenario twice, old friend?" Aon said to Edu, amused.

Lydia looked back to Edu. Twice? When was the first time? Damn it all, they had way too much history for her to catch up on. Thousands of years would do that, she supposed.

Edu growled again in his throat. "Enough, Aon," Ylena

snarled. Edu walked back to the table and sat back down in his throne. "No more words from you, or else you may find the need for your own empath in short order."

Aon snickered but obediently fell silent. Edu was brooding, his large hand placed over his masked face. He sat there silently for a long time before finally lowering his hand to the arm of the chair. "Ms. Lydia," Ylena addressed her. "We are to assume you do not wish Evelyn to face charges for her crime, correct?"

"Of course not."

"Then... Edu concedes. He recuses himself from this judgement. It is now up to you alone, Lydia, to judge Aon for his crime of murdering your friend Nicholas. He... hopes you judges well."

"This is stupid." Wincing as if she'd been slapped, she put her head in her hands. She couldn't believe the asshole had won. "This is fucking ridiculous!" No one argued otherwise. He'd outplayed them all.

Edu had previously been holding Evie prisoner before Aon took possession of her—she never even stood trial. To have Edu immediately turn around and dismiss the charges would be viewed as favoritism. Well, it *was*, but she was sure that "because politics and reasons" would be the answer to why he couldn't just immediately free her, anyway.

Aon was going to get away with this. She was going to have to forgive Aon for his crime. She had to... she had pardoned Edu of the same thing. And now Aon had cleared the stage and made sure that only her opinion counted.

That son of a bitch.

What do I do? she silently asked Q, who had gone invisible shortly after arriving.

You're on your own on this one. I don't do feelings or politics, and that's all this is.

Lydia pinched the bridge of her nose, wishing her headache would go away. "Y'know what?" The heat of her anger had started to cool off, and what was left behind was a kind of poisonous spite. There was no small amount of resentment built up toward the warlock over how all this had transpired. "Fine. I'll pardon you, Aon. But only if you agree to two things."

"Oh, do tell," Aon said in a purr.

Lydia didn't know exactly where she got the balls. But sometimes getting pushed too far could do funny things. "First, the House of Shadows is no longer allowed to take or hold prisoners. Ever. Any of the people you're holding in your sick torture chambers are to be let go immediately. If you want to keep doing your messed-up experiments, you find *volunteers*."

Aon was silent for a moment and tilted his head back just barely. "Very well. It is not so hard to find those willing to submit to me..." The insinuation was thick in his words.

Lydia tried not to blush or throw up. She had the urge to do both. Instead, she found shelter in her indignity and just glared at the man.

"And the second?" he asked, unaffected by her scowl.

"You tell us all the truth of what you wanted with Qta during the Great War. You tell us what happened to him and why you killed him, right here and right now."

For the first time, he reacted with anything other than sheer boredom. And it happened so fast, it caught her by surprise. Aon jumped to his feet, his clawed hand flexed in such a way she wondered if he was going to leap at her and try to rip her face off.

His words were a hiss. "Do not *dare*."

Now, she knew she had touched a nerve. She met his anger with her own. "I won't spend the rest of eternity watching my back, wondering what you're after. And I want the truth. Not this 'I wanted to be the King of All' bullshit lie you keep trying to push." She held his stare. "If you want this pardon of yours? You tell the story. All of it."

"Then I will tell you in private. Not in front of *them*." Aon spat out the last word with such hatred that she was surprised nothing in the room exploded.

"No." Lifting her head, she held her ground. "They've suffered because of your war more than I have. You're going to tell all of us, once and for all, why you started this in the first place."

Aon snarled, his hands flexing and squeezing as if he wanted to throttle her. "And if I refuse?"

"Then you go into your crypt and sleep it off. For a few centuries." She grinned. "I'm sure I'll be perfectly safe and get along just fine without you, don't worry. I'm sure the Dtu, Vjo, and Ini won't have a problem with me at all."

Now, she was being vindictive. She knew Aon would never be okay with leaving her unguarded and unprotected while he slept in his crypt.

The warlock growled loudly in rage and began to pace back and forth in front of the fire, trying to find a way out of this. She was proud that she had managed to catch him so clearly off guard. He was a good actor—but he wasn't *that* good. It was his turn to pace like an angry caged animal. And if he was mad, it meant she got a move in that he hadn't expected.

The table was watching her with a mix of reactions that ranged from impressed to confused. Navaa had the strangest expression out of all of them—half fury, half awe. She'd take it.

"Well?" Lydia asked Aon, for once feeling almost haughty. "What'll it be?"

Aon stopped pacing and grabbed the chair he had been sitting in. In a roar of fury, he hurled it into the giant fire pit in the center of the room. He stood with his back to them, his fists clenched at his sides, watching the chair catch and begin to cinder.

"He will never agree to this." Maverick shook his head.

"A clever ploy, but a useless attempt," Ylena agreed. "He will return to his crypt, then."

"A shame." Kamira huffed. "I, for one, think we deserve to know why he—"

"I wanted a queen."

The room went silent at the sound of Aon's voice. It was quiet and strained. All sound stopped, save for the crackle of the fire. Aon cut an imposing silhouette against it, even as his hands loosened from their fists in acceptance of what he was about to say. He kept his back to them as he talked, his dark hair glinting in the amber light.

"I have spent… every moment of my life alone. Every day of five thousand years I have lived with no one by my side. I have watched as all my brethren found love. I have seen it bloom and wither like flowers in their seasons. But never once for me. Loneliness is my poison. After so long, I thought no one would ever come to this cursed place who could see me as anything more but the gargoyle that I am. The fetid warlock. The shameful and dangerous madman.

"And so, I decided that if none could be found, then I would, as I always have, take matters into my own hands. I would fashion for myself someone who could love me. But mine is not a gift that can create life. That power belonged to another. For Qta's dreams could create a soul—or close enough for my needs, at least. If his dreams were worthy, why not mine?"

Aon's clawed hand clenched into a tight fist as he continued to speak. "I knew he would never agree to help me. He despised me, just the same as all of you. I would not suffer his refusal and let him speak of it to anyone. I would not bear the shame for what I hungered to be made public. And so I found reason to take him prisoner. I engineered a war. If all of you died in the process? So be it. I care little for any of you.

"I took Qta as my hostage. At first, I merely asked him to

help me. As I suspected, he refused and said that it could not be done. He said that what I asked for was impossible. That his creatures had no souls. I was certain he was lying, and I would prove him wrong. For in that manner, my talents would be useful... very useful indeed.

"And it was then that on Qta, I plied my trade. I secured him into my machines. I tortured him. I drained him of his marks until there were none left but those that remained upon his face. I left him a shrinking, shattered, weeping thing. I drove him insane. I did not care, because I had what I desired from him. I stitched his power onto my own flesh. I inscribed marks in turquoise upon my skin. If Qta would not wield his power for me, I would do it myself. His power would not last in me for long, but it would be long enough for what I needed."

Aon paused, pulling in a long, wavering breath and letting it out. For the first time, his shoulders slumped. "It would be simpler to say that I failed. But with the power of a dreamer and my will, I created a bride. For the first time in my long life, I knew joy. This world had a creature within it who said that they loved me. She looked upon me, and in her mismatched eyes, I saw what I had desired for so long. It worked, and I knew happiness... but it did not last.

"What I fashioned was a broken thing... a twisted and monstrous homunculus. Weak, warped, mangled, and too mutilated to live. I am no dreamer... and she was not meant to be. I held her in my arms as she pulled in her first and last labored breaths. And as she did, still she pledged her love to me. It was then that I knew she had no mind, no soul, no heart of her own... merely love for me. I would have kept her and loved her until the day I was dust had she lived.

"In my grief, I knew only rage. For if I could have come so close... surely, Qta could have succeeded. I turned my loss and my agony upon the ruined king—empty of his essence and too afraid and left desolate by the agony I paid him to even look upon me. He cowered like a spurned dog as I burned the marks from his face and tore his heart from his chest."

Aon finally turned to look at them. "That is why I fought my Great War."

Lydia had sunk into her chair, looking at the man in shock. The story he had told left her feeling empty and overfull at once. She wanted to weep. For Qta, for the world, for the monster Aon created.

And for the warlock himself.

For the kind of pain a man had to be in to go as far as he had in a quest to stop it.

"Have I met the conditions of your pardon, Queen of Dreams?" Aon tilted his head back slightly, and the firelight reflected off the metal of his black mask. His voice was as cold as ice. Cruel and mean.

"Y—yes," she stammered weakly.

"Good."

And with that, he was gone in a swirl of black smoke.

Lydia bent over and put her head in her hands, resting her elbows on her knees. She heard people stand and move around, but she didn't care. She didn't want to look at any of them. She didn't want to talk to any of them. She wanted to go home.

She stood to do just that and was surprised to see Edu was standing there near her, watching her. Ylena was at his side. All the others were gone, save for Rxa and Lyon, who stood by the wall talking in hushed tones.

"What do you want now?" She couldn't keep the dismay out of her voice.

Edu rested his hand on her shoulder, and the gesture made her jump. "Master Edu wishes to convey his respect. You have earned it. It is clear to him you are not the warlock's puppet. For what you took from that cretin in payment is a worse fate than mutilation."

That doesn't make me feel better. "Thanks."

"Master Edu wishes to tell you that he asks his forgiveness in thinking you a foe. He needs... some time to think over the magnitude of what he heard. But, perhaps, you and he should speak in the future. If you are amenable?" Edu shook his head, and his body language was strange. Tense.

"Yeah... same. And sure. I'd... like to start over." There wasn't even enough left in her to be happy that Edu was giving up his theory that she was the warlock's slave. All her emotions were too busy trying to sort out what the warlock had said.

Edu patted her on the shoulder and then walked away. He raised a hand in farewell to Rxa and Lyon as he passed. Rxa and Lyon were clearly waiting their turns to talk to her, and she let out a weary sigh as the two men in white walked up to her.

"I can't. I'm sorry, I really can't," she said as they both approached.

Rxa bowed at the waist, his hand pressed to his chest. "If you are in need, you know where to find us. Come to the cathedral and see me, when you find the strength."

Lydia nodded, sighed, and forced herself to smile at them, as best she could. She was sure it looked as strained as she felt. "Thank you."

Can we go home now?

Thought you'd never ask. And in a swirl of feathers, she left. All she wanted was a stiff drink and to go to bed.

She made it two steps toward her home.

She wasn't alone.

"Finally—" someone said close to her ear, and an arm banded about her waist. She was yanked back into the shadows and flush up against someone's chest. A hand clamped over her mouth, keeping her from screaming. "I would like to have a word with you!" The voice close to her face was a furious hiss. The feeling at her back was a frame she recognized—Aon.

Her home disappeared as fast as it had come, as it disappeared in a rush of black smoke. When they rematerialized, he threw her from him. She staggered and smacked into the wall. Before she could even get a sense of where she was or what was happening, he had spun her around and pinned her against the surface.

Lydia went to strike at him, but he grasped her wrists in his human hand. He pinned them overhead without any effort and leaned into her. He would always terrify her—always intimidate her, the way he could loom over her—the metal mask glinting in the darkness.

And it was clear he was furious. His body was tight in anger, and the grasp around her wrists stung as he squeezed.

They were in his library. With the flick of his hand, the fire roared to life, illuminating the dark room, at least allowing her to see.

"Aon, what—" she started, but he cut her off when he clasped his metal hand over her mouth.

"How *dare* you!" He drew his hand away to ball it into a fist and slam it into the wood by her head. She cringed at the impact as he punched the wall again and again, splintering the wood. He kept ramming his fist into the surface, clearly wishing it was her face. Lydia stayed perfectly still, afraid to move, afraid he might change his mind and attack her instead.

Finally, he seemed to have calmed down long enough to stop wailing against the wall. Instead, his clawed hand snapped around her throat. "What a little insufferable *brat* you have become! What a vicious, vindictive little Pandora," he snarled, his voice seething and dangerous. "Do you even comprehend what you have done?"

"You agreed to the terms, you could have—"

"And left you here in this world alone while I was forced to slumber? Leave you to the devices of a world that has already successfully killed you once before?" He was still rocketing back and forth between screaming at her and hissing furiously through his teeth. "I think not."

Lydia was shaking; she couldn't help it. She had never seen Aon really and truly angry before, and she wasn't so glad that now she had. "Aon—stop, please."

"No!" Aon whirled from her suddenly, storming away. He picked up a book from the table and hurled it against the wall on the other side of the room. A glass decanter met a similar fate a moment later. It fell to the floor in a shower of shards and shining splinters.

It was clear all he desperately wanted was to throttle her. To hurt her. But he was destroying the rest of the room instead.

Want me to eat him?

No, we've got to work this out on our own.

Suit yourself.

Carefully, she stepped away from the wall. "Are you just mad that I won? That I talked you into a corner?"

"I am *just mad,*" he hissed as he whirled around on her, his clawed gauntlet snapping around her neck once more. He squeezed down hard, and she gasped, her hands going to his wrist. "Because you chose to force me to tell the world that which I have never spoken of to anyone! Not even the damned Priest knew what transpired that day!" He shoved her backward, sending her staggering a few steps. "He knew why I imprisoned Qta. He knew that I wished for him to make for me a companion. But he did not know..." Aon's anger wavered.

"About her."

With that one word, his rage collapsed, deflated in on him, and all that was left was pain. He pulled his mask from his face and put it down on the table next to him with a clink.

All that he wore instead was sorrow, regret, and shame. His obsidian eyes that looked like spilled ink were filled with agony, pleading with her for mercy. And they were filled with tears.

HIs voice was a whisper. "I would have told you... I swear I would have in time."

Lydia cringed at the look on his face. It was her fault it was there. She took a small step toward him, and when he didn't fly into a fury or strike at her, she took another one. "How long did she live?"

He shrugged, as if he struggled to recall at first. "No more than minutes. She was in great pain... her body was mangled and could not survive. But her suffering was brief."

Tears stung her eyes again, for more reasons than one. She watched as the torment on his face emptied and turned into a void as he spoke. There was desolation in his voice and a hollow expression in his eyes as she drew that memory back to him.

It was killing her. Twisting a knife in her gut more than if he had taken out his rage on her like he had clearly wanted to. "You killed Nick. You were playing us all like fools. I... I'm sorry. I shouldn't have made you do that. I just... I got so mad at how you were *using* all of us."

"You were beautiful, dragonfly." Aon smiled, his expression like a man watching his own funeral. "A blazing fire. You were magnificent. To outplay me so perfectly—to use my own protectiveness of you to ensure that I would tell you all the truth? Brilliant. Even I did not predict it. You were marvelous in your wrath. You tore to the very heart of me and hurt me in a way I did not know was still possible. I applaud you."

"That wasn't why I—"

"Wasn't it? To take your revenge upon me, for murdering your friend? To make me feel the betrayal you did that night?"

"I—but—" She stopped. No. That *was* why she had done it; he was right. She had wanted him to pay for what he had done. Payment and revenge were the same action by different names.

All she wanted to do was apologize for dragging him out in public like that. For hurting him. The empty expression on his pale features cinched something around her heart that threatened to stop it entirely.

But that wasn't why she'd done the deed in the first place.

"I deserve your hatred. If she had lived, I would have kept her." He took in a shuddering breath, almost as though he were about to cry. Lowering his head, his dark hair curtained off his features. He lifted his gauntleted hand and pressed it against his chest. "She was mindless. Soulless and empty. She only knew of one thing—love for me. I would have cherished her until the end of my days. She had no business living on this world. No creature that loves me can call this place home, after all. Someone had to die for my pain. Qta was the logical choice."

Lydia heard a quiet tap-tap sound on the floor. Looking down at his feet, there were drops of blood by his shoes. He had taken the blades of his hands and driven them into his own body.

Instantly, without thinking, she walked to him. Turning him to face her, she yanked his hand away from over his heart. "Stupid man." She put her hand to the wound. His dark clothes barely showed the blood. "Why the hell did you do that?"

She began to undo his shirt buttons to see the damage he'd done. The blood was flowing quickly from three deep cuts in his pale skin. Her worry was silly—he'd heal—but old habits were hard to break.

"I blamed Qta for my failure. I was alone. I have been alone all through my damnable and cursed life. All the others find love when they wish it. They may find another to see value in their souls. None have ever paid me such a gift."

"I meant hurting yourself," she grumbled at him as she summoned a cloth to press to the wound. "Idiot."

"Ah." He fell silent for a long time and let out a weary sigh. He moved to step away from her, but she put her other hand on his side and pulled him back to her.

"All this, because you were lonely." Lydia could almost feel her heart crack in half. The pain was visceral. He had suffered—caused so much suffering—just to end the emptiness. "Why didn't you tell me before?"

"It is a weakness in myself I do not care to admit. It is easier to pretend the stories of me are true, that I am nothing but a soulless cretin upon the face of this world." Aon tilted his head back slightly as he looked down at her, where she pressed the cloth to his chest. "And why would I tell those worthless, idiotic wretches of the tormented, mangled corpse I made in my efforts to fill the void that consumes me?"

"I didn't ask why you didn't tell the others. I asked why you didn't tell *me*." She shot him a look. "Stop being obtuse."

He flinched. She forgot how expressive he was. "I did not wish to frighten you. I did not want you to think so little of me. I suppose I enjoyed the fact that you look upon me differently than all the rest. I did not want you to think that my desperation was the reason why I—" Aon paused, shook his head, and started his sentence again. "I did not wish for you to believe that I loved you only as the answer to my loneliness."

Taking a second to think it over, she nodded. That made a strange kind of sense. If she had known the whole story, about how long he had worked and the depths he resorted to, she might have run for the hills the moment he confessed his feelings.

That didn't change the fact that he had tried to kill everyone and everything so he wouldn't be alone. That took a unique kind of madness. But here she was, tending to a wound on that same man's chest. "How long does a man have to suffer before he tries to destroy the world, just so he isn't alone anymore?"

"Roughly thirty-five hundred years, if you are counting," he quipped down at her.

"It was a proverbial question."

"I am aware. But I have the literal answer, so why not provide it?"

Keeping her hand holding the handkerchief to his wound, she tried not to laugh at his dry comment. Looking up into his sharp, beautiful, and sorrowful features, she could see in him the pain she heard masked behind his sarcastic comment.

"Tell me this is the truth. Tell me you aren't lying to me. Promise me there isn't some other scheme—some other reason behind all of this," she nearly begged him. She couldn't handle it if this turned out to be another game to him.

He traced the back of his finger gently down her cheek. "I promise." It was so quiet she felt it as a rumble in his chest more than words. "I cannot lie to you. I never will."

When she pulled him down to kiss him, he wrapped his arms around her and held her to him. Damn this man. Damn this fiendish, evil, beautiful man. She pressed into the kiss and silently begged Nick, wherever he was or if he could even hear her, to forgive her.

"Aon..." she whispered to him as she broke the kiss. "I love you."

SIX

Aon stepped away from her so unexpectedly that she staggered and barely caught herself. He took two paces back, and his dark eyes were wide in horror. They flicked between hers, back and forth, in complete and utter disbelief. Fear began to creep over him, and she watched it warp his features in an unfamiliar way.

"No," he whispered. Suddenly, the fear snapped and was overtaken by something else. Something worse. His face twisted in fury, his eyes wild and unfocused. His voice was ragged and low before twisting into an angry shout. "She is *dead!*"

Before she could react—before she could even try to understand what was happening—he threw himself at her. He tackled her against the wall, harsh and unforgiving, his hand tight around her throat. He clenched down harder than he had earlier when he was angry about the trial. This time it was clear he wasn't just venting—he meant to seriously hurt her as he cut off her air.

"Aon!" She struggled against him. But it was hopeless. He was stronger than her by a factor of ten at least.

He pulled back his clawed hand, threatening to tear her face to shreds as he raged at her. "What final dagger would the

Ancients twist in me now? Be you demon, or are you a wraith from my own mind, sent to torment my waking breath?" He shook her by the throat. "She must now even still lay dead in that pond, and what comes to haunt me is *you*!"

"Please, Aon—" she squeaked out and put her hand on his chest. She didn't try to wrench out of his grasp. There was no point. She turned her head to try and gasp for air and could only get just enough to speak. "I'm not dead—I'm right here. Look at me. I'm right here!"

"No!" he screamed, his voice cracking. "You are a lie. A fallacy in my own mind. The final shattering of my broken soul has finally come. You are nothing but a shadow—a nightmare sent to torment me!" He drove his hand down to rip her open.

Squeezing her eyes tight, she only waited. When there was silence, she turned her face back to him and reopened her eyes. She let out a small noise of fear as she realized the blades were hovering barely a half an inch from her skin, maybe less. He had stopped himself. But only just.

The frenzied madness had not left him. Now, the rage mixed with uneasy astonishment—horror at his own inability to kill her.

Aon's hand left her throat, and he staggered backward away from her, as if the floor had tilted out from under him. "Anything but this. No, please—" he whispered, muttering to himself, and turned his back to her. He took two steps toward the fireplace and gripped the armchair that sat there. "Lydia is *dead*!"

In one motion, he hurled the chair into the fire, the second chair he destroyed in one night in his rage. She flinched and reflexively ducked as it smashed into splinters, the wood giving way instantly under the force of the blow. It made her immediately aware how strong he really was and how much he must have been pulling his punches with her all this time.

The falling shattered pieces of silver-painted wood and

upholstery sent embers rolling out from the black stone hearth, glowing red against the dark surface and skittering across the wood floor. Some made it as far as his feet, though he didn't seem to care.

He dug his hands into his hair, his back to her, head lowered. His shoulders were tight and raised up to his ears. He let out a low moan. It was a strange keening sound she had never heard from him before. One of pure and utter pain.

Before she could react—before she could do anything but stand against the wall in wide-eyed shock—he collapsed hard to his knees. He sat back on his heels and doubled over at the waist, his head still tucked low, fingers grasping painfully at his dark hair. Fisting at it and yanking as if that would right what was unbalanced in his mind.

Aon was mumbling to himself, but she couldn't make out his words. Slowly, she crept forward from the wall, worried that at any moment he might snap and attack her. He was a wounded, rabid, and dangerous tiger.

But why?

What just happened?

Carefully, slowly, worried he might attack at any moment— she walked up to him and knelt at his side. Reaching out, she hovered her hand over his back. For a long moment, she was afraid to touch him. She feared what he would do when she did. He could disembowel her before she had the chance to fight back. He could rip her face to pieces, destroy the marks that kept her coming back and send her back to the grave.

And yet, somehow, as nonsensical as it was... she trusted him. Even through his madness, she knew he wouldn't hurt her.

That was probably why Q hadn't shown up. He wouldn't kill her. Not really. Not in any way that mattered. At least, not any worse than he already had. She let her hand fall against his back.

He jolted in surprise but didn't move. His hands tightened in his hair. His body was tense and locked tight. "You are not real..." He was arguing with her like a child might with the malicious shadows in the corner of his room. "You are a lie."

"I'm not dead, Aon." She scooted closer to him, edging closer like she would with a cornered animal. "I'm right here." She tried to coax him into calming down. But honestly, she had no idea what to do or any clue how to handle this.

She finally realized what was happening. He must think that what she had said to him was so impossible—so far out of his reach—that he believed she was a hallucination. That this was a vision of his madness and nothing more.

In Aon's shattered mind, it was the only logical option.

He was unlovable. Therefore, he must be crazy.

"Look at me." She carefully wound her hand into his metal gauntlet. The warlock let her pull his hand away from him, though he did not look up.

This damnable metal prosthetic with its knife-like claws. Lydia had spent what felt like years terrified of what he could do with it. What he wanted to do with it. But it was a perfect symbol of the man himself. Aon, the monster. The dangerous fiend. The warlock and necromancer. But in its twisted form, was immense beauty. The details and curling, esoteric etchings in the metal that matched his home. It was elegant, sophisticated, wicked, and deadly. Just like him.

And all of this, to hide a wound. Forged to hide what was missing beneath. It wasn't a lie. It wasn't a cover. It wasn't a front to protect what had been taken away. All that danger, all that darkness, all that torment? It *was* Aon.

Lydia leaned down to place a kiss against the metal of his palm and shut her eyes as she did. The metal of Aon's hand was chill against her lips. A tear slipped loose from her eye and slid down her cheek.

It was a tear for Aon. For how many miles of tunnels Aon's

loathing and madness must have dug through him, for this to be the only possible option left in his mind.

It was a tear for Nick. Because no matter how hard she tried, she knew she couldn't escape what she felt. She knew she couldn't escape the fact that she loved the broken man who had killed her friend. Who had done it to protect her.

She bent her head to place her cheek into his metal palm and held it to her. She let Aon rest his clawed fingers against her temple and her jaw. The point of his thumb was dangerously close to her eye. Right now, she didn't care. It was the first time she had ever really touched the gauntlet of her own volition. It was as much of a part of him as anything else.

Broken-hearted, she whispered, "I love you, Aon."

As much as he scared her—as much as she would jump in fear every time he moved too quickly—there was no running from it. True to her very being, she loved him. Loved her monster in the darkness. Loved him for his bleeding heart of stone.

She had to forgive him for what he had done, only because her heart wouldn't survive it if she didn't.

The words as they left her sounded different this time. She felt somehow raw and exposed. She was begging him to believe her. Begging him to realize she was here with him. That she wasn't an illusion.

He shifted, and she squeaked in surprise as he leaned against her unexpectedly. It pushed her from her knees to sitting as he slumped down into her lap, nearly falling there. His hand dropped from her face as he did. When he settled, he was curled on his side, his back to her, his head on her thigh. After her moment of confusion passed, Lydia tenderly began to stroke his hair away from his face.

The second chair he had trashed today was now crackling and burning, the fabric and material of the chair turning to cinders quickly in the flame. *Better the chair than me.* Glowing amber dots of charred upholstery were whisked upward in the rising hot air. His dark eyes were trained on the blaze, but they were tired, unfocused and unseeing.

Draping an arm over his shoulder, she gently held him to her and continued to slowly stroke her fingers through his hair, combing through the black strands.

For over five thousand years, he'd been alone. Five thousand. Lydia couldn't even wrap her head around the magnitude of that number. Older than the pyramids of Giza. Older than most of recorded history. Had he been on Earth for all that time, he could have watched the rise and fall of entire empires.

It was impossible to comprehend what that was like. To understand what it meant to live that long. To endure eternity. Maybe now, Lydia would have to learn. Maybe she had five thousand years of life ahead of her. What would become of her own mind, after all that time? Edu had become consumed by rage and lust. Aon was swallowed whole by madness and loneliness.

For all those years, he had been devoid of love and spent alone, with only the adoration of servants and liars to fill the gap. No wonder, when he had heard the words leave her lips, he couldn't grasp that they might be real.

So, she held him. Stroked his hair. Did her best to comfort him. As she began to hum to him quietly, his eyes slipped shut. The crease in his forehead smoothed. They sat like that for some time, minutes maybe, listening to the chair burn in the fire. She was lost in thought, watching him, and wondered if he was asleep.

Craning down, she pressed a kiss to his temple, and as she did, he let out a small sigh. He was still awake, just lost in his own mind.

"Into the darkness of my mind, my soul, I stare. Nothing shall gather within the shadows. In the twisting nettles, the briars, the thorns, I feel the pain that makes me whole. Balm not the biting sands that sting my flesh, for in that sorrow is my joy. To suffer is to live."

Aon recited it like it was a quote. His voice was quiet, barely audible in the crackle of the fire. It sounded almost like a poem with the cadence he gave it.

"What's that from?" Lydia stroked his hair tenderly again.

"A past long forgotten."

The Ancients, she guessed. She knew they were cruel and hateful things. Lyon had hinted, and so had the book she read, that they made Aon look like a saint in comparison. He may have chosen to forget what they had done, but he still bore the marks of it, even after all this time. They had taken something from him, and she was starting to understand what it was. They had made him into the man he was now.

"Dragonfly?" he asked her quietly.

"Yeah?"

"I love you."

She smiled faintly and leaned down to kiss his cheek again. "I love you too, Aon."

He seemed to be fighting sleep. "Each time I shut my eyes, I wonder if when I open them, you will be gone." He sounded a million miles away.

"I'm not going anywhere," she promised him.

"We shall see," he argued, but it was a mumble and too distant to have been cognizant. He was falling asleep. She watched as his breathing slowed, as the tension in him began to ebb away.

Aon always had to have the last word. She smiled to herself, watching him as he slept. She rested her head against his shoulder. Soon, her eyes drifted shut as well. He was warm, and the heat from the fire was lulling her away as well. There was no escaping this man—this beautiful, broken, tragic monster that, now she had to admit it, she loved so deeply.

SEVEN

Love.

She had spoken of *love*.

There was little else that he could remember after that. At least, not after she said to him the words he had so longed to hear. It was as though someone had pulled the curtain over his mind, although he knew better than to think he had merely passed out.

Madness was an insidious disease.

Bits of a chair were burning in the fireplace, and he could see shattered pieces of glassware sparkling from the wood floor nearby. The proof was, as the saying went, in the pudding.

Aon had awoken on the floor on his side, his head in Lydia's legs, sprawled on her like an overgrown house cat. His dragonfly was sitting on the ground cradling him like a child in her lap. Her head was leaning on his shoulder. When he turned his head to look at her, the delicate waves of her blonde hair were obscuring her features, serene in her own exhausted slumber.

His poor dear. He had put her to task in court. And as always, she had outperformed his expectations. Even as he had cornered her into excusing his crime of murdering that boy, she had in turn dug the knife into his ribs and forced him to speak the truth of Qta's death. He had been furious—oh, he had been *beyond* anger—but he had been at the same time immensely proud.

This dragonfly had fangs and would not hesitate to defend herself. Not even from him. She would not allow him to tread over her dignity.

Good.

Such had been the point of his entire endeavor in that damnable cage in which he had placed her. While keeping her as a toy would be amusing for a time, he had no desire to crush such a spirit as she possessed.

He could have a pet if he wished it. No, he had always sought an equal. Such had always been his curse.

Smiling sadly, he lifted his hand to gently tuck a strand of her hair behind her ear. Never would he tire of the azure marks upon her face. He found himself, as he was frequently wont to do, marveling at her. Her fortitude, her passion, her undying adherence to her own morality and level-headed ideals. But, most of all, he marveled at her compassion.

Judging by the state of things, she would have had every right to abandon him to his fit of violent madness and spared herself the chance of grievous injury. Or worse.

Or, perhaps, she trusts that there is a line that even my shattered psyche will not cross.

Someday it would be the end of her, he knew. The tenderness that filled her heart would cause her more harm than good and would destroy her in time. He could only pray that day would long wait in its arrival. And that it was not at his hand that it did.

She had looked him in the eyes—gazed at his features, something no one had ever done since the Ancients walked free— and told him she loved him. How such a thing was possible, he did not know. Yet he did not doubt the truth in her words. She was not one to say what she did not mean. If anything, she was too honest with him and too quick to betray her feelings.

He had known, from the moment he set eyes upon her, that she was fascinated by him. From their very first interaction in his dreams, he knew she was terrified and caught in his web all the same. How he had delighted in tormenting her, in twisting her desires and her uncertainty to place her in his palms. Indeed, that she still went wide-eyed and pale in his darker moments brought him no small amount of glee. He would continue to haunt her like a devil on her back until the moment he returned to those damnable creatures who made him.

Now, things had changed. With those words she had spoken, things were very different. Before, if Lydia had chosen to part from him, Aon would have taken the blow and mourned her loss in silence. But he knew now that he could no longer accept her rejection.

If she were to cast him away—if she were to tell him to leave her side—he could not persist. Let him die, consumed by worms, before that day may come.

Oh, my little dragonfly... You know not what you have done. Curling his fingers, he brushed his knuckles over her cheek, careful not to wake her. His poor darling had not even had a moment to catch her breath, let alone rest upon her laurels and adjust to the world around her. She had spent every waking moment since becoming marked entirely under siege by the demands of others. Himself included. The chaos around her would have consumed many in its rampaging inferno, yet she stood strong. Tired, yes, but who would not be so?

The fact remained—she would not rid herself of him now. Not until he was once and truly dead. He could hear her voice echo within his mind. *"Aon... I love you."* The words he had yearned for, all his life.

She was his. His! And he was hers equally in return. Perhaps doubly so. He had her heart; she owned his very soul.

Let all the stars in all the worlds burn to dust; he would have the void swallow them whole before he would let her go. Let time claim him if nothing else.

On that topic, now that he thought about it...

How long had they been laying here on his floor?

Damn his faltering mind.

At times, it felt as though he were gazing into a shattered mirror and could not make sense of the image that looked back at him, fragmented and incomplete. Recognizable as himself, perhaps. But sometimes if barely.

The fire was burning low, and he distinctly recognized the leg of his chair sticking out from the embers.

Ah.

Yes. He remembered the chair. He had seen that already. Shutting his eyes for a moment, he put the pieces back together.

It was highly doubtful she had been the one to throw his chair into the flames. He could not remember doing the deed himself. Therefore, the evidence left one option as to how, precisely, he found himself cradled in her lap with his favorite armchair devoured in ash with no recollection of the preceding events. The option that he had merely rambled harmlessly was succinctly eliminated.

"Hey, Nutjob. Welcome back."

Aon had to struggle not to jolt at the unexpected voice. Such a sudden movement would be sure to wake his dragonfly, and she seemed so peaceful. He glared at the small winged snake that appeared curled up on the floor in front of them, glowing wings folded at his sides, casting a faint glow of turquoise across the lacquered wood surface.

"Be quiet," he muttered. There was little else in this world he could desire less than to engage in repartee with the phantasmal reptile.

"Do you even know what you did?"

"I destroyed some furniture."

"You lost your goddamn motherfuckin' mind, you raging psychopath."

He glared at the snake, who seemed utterly unimpressed by his angry display. "I am *aware*." He could not abide by others reminding him of his own fractured psyche. He was far too well acquainted with the issue, after all.

How can she love me? How can she come to value a shattered cretin such as I?

Aon felt the pull—the tug of strings on the back of his mind—asking him to join the sharp-edged fragments of self-reflection that lay scattered about his soul once more. No. He had done so enough of that for one evening.

"'You're a lie,' 'you're dead,' 'you're not real!' Wah, wah, wah. You finally get what you want, and you decide to go berserko? Ugh. What a little dirty diaper bitch baby you turn out to be." Q—the name Lydia had given to her spirit familiar, as far as he could understand—huffed and swished its tail irritably.

"Do not taunt me." He decided he had enough of the creature's contempt and foul mouth. Carefully, he shifted, lifting himself out of her lap in such a way she nestled instead against his chest. He scooped her up into his arms and stood from the floor. She was light in his arms, a welcome presence against him. She let out a small sleepy sound in her throat and tucked her forehead up against his neck. "You best not wake her," he warned the snake in a whisper as it flew up from the ground to settle down onto the crook of her lap.

"What're you going to do now?" Q asked, its tone sarcastic. **"Now that you have the *one* thing you've wanted your entire life? What now? 'Be happy?'"** The snake snickered in incredulous disbelief.

Aon disappeared in a swirl of black smoke, taking Lydia—

and the snake, unfortunately—to his chambers. Walking to the grand bed, he commanded the sheets to pull back, and he laid her down gently upon the silk sheets.

With little more than a flick of the fingers of his right hand, he shooed the glowing, ghastly reptile away from her. Q hissed at him but flitted to the nearby nightstand and sulked. Another silent command of his power and she was in a nightgown and nothing else. He would not chance waking her by stripping her of her clothes, no matter how much he would care to do so. Desire flared in him, and he smirked to himself as a wicked idea played itself through his mind. But he would save it for the morrow.

"Aren't you going to ask me what happened?"

"I do not care."

The snake slithered up along the headboard, weaving around the gaps in the intricately carved frame like his relatives might do in a jungle vine.

"Fine. I'll tell you, anyway. You were a total crazy. Like, dime-bag, crackhead crazy. And a douchebag. It's one thing to be nuts. It's another thing to be a dick about it at the same time. You somehow manage to be *both*."

He glared at the snake viciously, and it fluffed its feathers.

"Just sayin'."

He removed his own clothes and, when he remained in his britches, carefully climbed into bed with her. As his weight settled, she, in her sleep, tucked herself up against his chest. It was a simple, unexpected gesture—guileless and honest in her unconscious state.

He laid a kiss gently against the corner of her mouth. She smelled like wildflowers, like jungle rain. Like dreams. Her snake may be the outlet for her power, but the strength beat within her. He was no fool and could see it plainly.

Her conscious mind, it seemed, was doing a great deal of

filtering for the subconscious ranting that was going on if that creature was what lived in her mind if left unabated.

Fighting a quiet laugh, he pushed that thought away and found himself once more in awe of the young woman in his arms.

She loves me.

Doubt gnawed at him, chewed at his soul, whispering second-guesses and lies. *It was a lie. She is fooling you. They were words of pity or inspired by spite. She does not love you. No one does. No one can. You do not deserve her.*

He willed the doubts that plagued him to be silent. For her damnable little familiar had taunted him with such things already. Goaded and mocked him for what would surely follow; that he could not believe the words that she had said. The phantasm had sarcastically asked if he could now find "happiness."

She will leave you for another, as soon as the opportunity presents itself.

Lydia curled into his chest further, a faint smile on her sleeping features. For a moment, he held his breath and felt a crackle spread through him of what felt like electricity. How he relished in her touch, how he would wallow in her presence.

For as long as it lasted.

No, snake. Happiness shall not stay with me. For others shall come for her. He let his head settle into his pillow and held his beloved against his chest, cradled now in his arms. *Either to take her or to destroy her. This is but a momentary interlude.*

The Ancients did not give anything without consequence or cost. To provide him with this beautiful creature—to finally find a soul who could love him—was bound to carry a hefty fee.

They were *never* benevolent.

This was merely the calm before the storm.

He knew it in his bones.

That knowledge had been what filled him with dread, even

as he was overflowing with joy, the moment he saw those turquoise marks upon her skin. Nothing in this world ever came free.

Others would ensure that he paid dearly to have that which he had sought with such vehement obsession.

A dreamer was alive once more. Their world was spared from the void that threatened to consume them so very slowly.

It was only a matter of time before the other Kings and Queens made their plays. He considered the players on the board, one at a time, as he always did. There was comfort in the games of old.

Edu was, in his own foolish way, too kind-hearted and gentle to ever truly be a real threat. His behavior at court had shown as much. He may be an idiot, but he was not imperceptive. Surely, he suspected they may be enamored with each other, even if he could not comprehend the depth of it.

If there was one thing for which Edu may put aside his obsession with violence, it would be for his fascination with love. In the matters of romance and his saccharine need for such cloyingly naive things, he was a child, cradling a butterfly in his hands.

So much so to excuse Lydia for her compassion. Edu had been lenient. He would not seek to control or influence his dragonfly. No. Edu's time for working against Lydia had come to an end, he suspected.

Rxa... his old friend was a threat, however. Perhaps not one to harm Lydia. But to steal her away? Most definitely.

Who would not love the golden-haired, glowing angel over a twisted and deformed soul in the shadows? She was so young, so new to this world. If she had said the truth—if she really did love him—then it must be naivety that was the inspiration. A lack of other appropriate suitors was clearly to blame.

And suitors would come.

She would be a joyful playmate for any, even before the

marks of a queen were gifted to her. And Rxa was *renowned* for his capabilities as a lover.

Aon shut his eyes at the thought and tried to push it away with all the rest. Sleep was coming for him quickly, and for that, he was grateful.

Yes. Rxa may try to win her heart. He would tear the angel's out before it came to that. Jealousy burned in him like an eternal flame, and he knew his darling dragonfly would contend with it many times in her life if the Ancients were kind.

But, in all honesty, it was not over Rxa's flirtatious nature he truly worried. It was a nagging thought, but none that he could not handle.

There was another thought that gave him real dread. For if Rxa was awake... the others would soon follow. And it was their reawakening that kept his dreams and thoughts troubled as he sank into the darkness that called for him.

The other three would soon wake and make themselves known.

Then, the true cost of his love would be made known.

May the stars be kind...

For I know the Ancients shall not.

* * *

Lyon rose from his bow at the foot of the stairs leading to King Edu's throne. While Aon had been excused of his crime, the abdication still stood. Not until all seven were awake would they all reign together as they had so long ago.

With the rise of Rxa, the rise of the other sleeping three were inevitable and short in coming. But for now, the law that deemed a single king would rule remained in place.

Edu was leaning heavily back into the hewn wood chair, roughly carved with the heads of beasts. The creature adorning the end of the armrest on which the King of Flames was currently tapping a finger, Lyon could never quite decide if it was a dragon or a lion. He doubted it mattered and considered that it was likely both.

Edu had requested his presence after all had departed. It did not come as a surprise. Often Kamira would tease him for being the errand boy of greater men, but he knew his role was more profound than that. He was, in his own right, trusted in a fashion that no other found themselves.

It was a double-edged sword.

"Master Edu thanks you for attending him," Ylena said from beside the throne, her hands neatly folded in front of her. She wore a long, flowing crimson dress with a fur stole about her shoulders. Even in the warm fires that blazed within the castle hall, the chill was pervasive. Lyon, devoid of body heat of his own, barely felt it.

"Of course, my king," Lyon responded. The room had even been cleared of servants and footmen. It was to prevent any gossiping ears from sitting in attendance.

Well, perhaps except for Evelyn who was standing by one wall, smiling cheerfully at him. Lyon wondered where she could summon such infallible optimism. It was both envious and quite impressive. But Evelyn called herself a friend to Lydia, and he doubted the girl would act in any way that might put the Queen of Dreams at risk. He had no question in his mind over what topic he had been summoned.

"Master Edu wonders your opinion over the tale that Aon recounted for us."

Lyon's opinion was complex at best. He shut his eyes and lowered his head with a sigh. He had known that Aon had sought Qta over his desire to have a companion. But he had not known to what lengths the warlock had gone to do so.

His heart wept for all involved. For Qta who suffered and died so needlessly. For the creature who Aon had made who only knew of love and suffering. And for Aon, to seek to mend a wound with such fervor only to have his efforts redouble his pain.

"Did you know, Priest?"

"I knew only for what reason Aon sought the dreamer king. I did not know of his... attempt." Lyon sighed and looked up at the King of Flames. Edu had seen through his veiled expression. Edu had a great deal of age and experience in dealing with his subtlety.

"Why did you never speak of what you knew?"

"With all due respect, you would not have believed me."

Edu huffed a laugh and leaned back in his chair. He nodded after a moment, conceding the point. "The Great War was over his selfish... need for love. Not power." Ylena's tone was thoughtful, reflecting Edu's own confusion. "He nearly destroyed this world—he was responsible for the death of millions and the murder of Qta—for the sake of loneliness. You say that this was no lie from him? You say that this was the truth?"

"Yes, my king."

Edu sighed and put a large hand over his masked face. "And he touts my ignorance? One cannot build *love*." Once more, poor Ylena was laid aside and talked as though she were the king himself. Her tone was that of a frustrated parent whose child had just attempted to fly by leaping off the roof with a bedsheet attached to their back as wings.

Lyon smiled faintly. "With no experience in the matter, he believed he could."

"Arrogant madman."

Lyon could not refute the insult. The warlock was many things, but both of those things were undeniable facts.

Ylena struggled to regain herself. "Master Edu must admit, he did not know that the warlock could feel pain. He thought the man was beyond the capability to feel such suffering. To see him so overwrought as he did tonight was... eye-opening. To see him so debased, and brought so low by Lydia, makes him wonder what is truly transpiring between those two. She knows how to hurt him in a way that it seems no others could."

Lyon kept his face successfully empty this time. While the mutual affection between the warlock and the dreamer was hardly a secret, it was not his place to share such knowledge with the King of Flames.

"What do you know of them, Priest? It is clear she and the warlock have lain together. But what more, past those poor choices on her part, do you know of their relationship?"

"It is not for me to say, my king. Forgive me."

Edu considered him for a long time. "You know, but you will not say." He growled, even as Ylena talked for him. "Your loyalty is to Aon, then?"

"My loyalty is to Lydia in this matter. She has been under siege since the moment she arrived here. I do not wish to further break her confidence—I have done poorly enough by her already."

"Very well. Regardless." Edu tapped a heavy finger against the arm of his chair once more. "She is not his thrall. That much was made painfully clear, even to Master Edu's thick skull."

Lyon smiled at Edu's rare self-effacing joke. "I am glad to hear you have come to believe so, my king."

"Edu will continue to remain watchful. He will never trust Aon."

He nodded. "It is of my opinion that there is little that could make Lydia do anything to which she did not agree. But I do not see in the warlock the desire to control her. He could if he wished. It was to protect her that he killed the poor boy, after all."

Edu was silent and nodded once slowly. "Master Edu is of the opinion that if Aon has become somehow—unlikely as it may be—*attached* to the girl, it may cause a war unlike any we have ever seen if he was to attempt to take Lydia away from him."

"I feel similarly, my king." Lyon was relieved to hear Edu speak some sense. "I will keep a close watch upon her. If I feel as though Master Aon is bringing her any manner of duress, save that perhaps which is inevitable due to his nature, I will inform you."

"We thank you, Lyon," Ylena responded.

We? Lyon questioned silently. It was scarce that he heard Ylena speak of or for herself. Then he saw the gentle smile on her face. The empath—so perceptive of the emotions of her king—may see more than the warrior could believe to be true.

With a faint smile of his own, he bowed low at the waist once more.

"It matters little, besides." Edu waved his hand dismissively. "The warlock is not of the temperament or selflessness to maintain any small amount of affection. He will tire of her, and they will go their separate ways. Perhaps if that cretin is finally given someone to play with until he winds down, we may have some damnable peace and quiet in this forsaken wasteland of ours. For a time, at least." Edu huffed a sarcastic laugh in time with the words of his empath.

Lyon highly doubted that Aon would ever tire of Lydia's presence. The reverse may not be true, but that would remain to be seen. Lyon was still not sure how Edu would react to the knowledge that the two were in love, and so he kept it to himself. "We may only hope."

"Master Edu hopes that this may all work out in favor for all. But he is, as always, one to worry where matters of the warlock are involved. If it is not by Master Edu or Aon's hands that trouble shall arise, then it shall be by others."

Lyon had come to a similar conclusion as his current King. With the reappearance of a dreamer and the salvation of their world, the return of the remaining slumbering Royals was nigh.

Rxa was a peaceful soul and never caused conflict with those around him. He preferred to pull his strings from afar, with influence and counsel.

But the others were not so restrained.

And when they arose, chaos would surely follow in their wake.

EIGHT

Lydia woke up to the sound of bickering. Quietly, two voices were insistently arguing. Hushed in an attempt not to wake her up but squabbling nonetheless.

"You're just going to ignore what happened?"

"I do not answer to you, vermin."

"That's a yes."

"Any apology I may wish to make will be to her, not you."

"She said the three magic words, and you lose your gad-damn mind. You need to apologize."

"My actions offend you, and it seems little I may do can be done to prevent this."

"Yeah, you're right. Everything you do offends me. You're just generally offensive."

"As you have said. Now be quiet."

"Dickwad."

"That is the best you can manage?"

"I can be more colorful if you want. What about this one? You're a platinum, top shelf, donkey-cock-sucking mother-f—"

"Both of you can feel free to shut up at any point," she

murmured. She was lying with her head on Aon's chest. They were in a bed, and lifting her head and blearily squinting, she realized it was his bed. He must have brought them here at some point during the night. Last she knew, she had fallen asleep on the floor with him in his library.

Aon was arguing with Q, who was curled up around the curved sections of the headboard like it was a tree branch. She reached up a hand and patted the creature on the head, who nuzzled happily into her touch.

"He started it."

"I did no such thing."

Laughing, she looked down at Aon with a smile. He had slept without his mask on and was looking up at her both annoyed and trying not to show his amusement at the same time. But the mischief glinted in his jet eyes, dangerous and sharp.

She leaned down to kiss his cheek. "Something tells me you're both to blame."

"Your 'familiar' is irritating at best," he complained.

"He's a little much at first. He's kind of an asshole, but when you get to know him, he grows on you. Sound familiar?" She poked him on the end of his nose.

He growled, and she squeaked as he flipped them over. She was suddenly on her back and he was over her, pushed up on his arms, caging her in. "You think to provoke me, do you?"

"Ugh. Yeah, I can't watch this. I'm out." Q vanished in a puff of turquoise, leaving her and the smirking warlock. **_"Gross."_**

"Are you all right?" She ignored the snake's comments.

His fiendish smirk faltered and faded as she reminded him of what happened last night. Turning his head away, he tried to hide his expression behind a curtain of black locks.

Reaching up, she tucked the strands behind his ear and ran

her palm over his cheek, trying to remind him she was here, and she wasn't going anywhere.

"I am now, yes. Forgive me for my moment of weakness." He sounded reluctant as he leaned into her touch, his features smoothing. Just this level of contact seemed to bring him comfort. "Did I scare you too terribly?"

"You worried me, but I knew you wouldn't really hurt me. I've never seen you that far gone. Do you remember what happened?"

"Not much of it. Did I... harm you in any way?" He winced. "In my madness, did I strike you?"

"You stopped yourself. You broke a bunch of things, said some weird stuff, and fell asleep. But you never hit me."

A look of relief crossed his face, and he nodded. She felt the muscles in his jaw twitch under her hand. After a long pause, he finally broke the silence, the pain thick in his voice reflected in his dark eyes. "I have yearned, all my life, to have someone say they love me. And when I do, I—" He sighed, and he moved to climb off her.

She pulled him back to her. The unexpected movement knocked him off balance enough he had to catch himself on his elbow. She pulled his face to hers and kissed him, deeply and passionately, trying to silently convey to him that which she didn't know how to put into words.

She loved him for all his insanity, for all his cruelty and his kindness, his darkness and his shattered mind. She understood why he had descended into a pit of his own self when she had told him how she felt. He had come to believe that either he was not capable of receiving such a gift or that it would never come to pass. That he had lost the rest of his sanity was the simpler and more likely solution.

When she broke the kiss, he looked down at her with a muddled expression of admiration and hunger. He was forever her tiger in the darkness.

"Do you forgive me? For what I made you do?" She had to know. After what she did, after what she made him say. *How couldn't he hold it against me?*

He flinched and sighed, and his bare hand wandered to her face to stroke the backs of his fingers against her cheek. "I intended to ask you the same."

"I'm always going to miss Nick."

"As is your right."

"But I..." It might be wrong. It might make her a bad person. It might make her amoral, and empty, and horrible. But he hadn't killed Nick for the joy of it. He hadn't done it to be cruel. The memory of Nick's death would haunt her for a long, long time. Maybe forever—now she'd have a chance to find out.

Raising her hand to his own cheek, she traced a single line of the dark writing that ran down his face with the tip of her finger. The pain that echoed in his eyes warred with the pleasure at her touch, and it looked to consume him as he slipped his eyes shut. He was clearly preparing himself to accept her condemnation.

Damn her to the hell she had found herself in. "I love you, Aon. So... for now, his loss hurts. And it will hurt for a long time. But I can't lose you too."

He leaned down, resting his forehead against hers. After a long pause, she realized that her fingers were damp. He was silently crying. She lifted both her hands to gently wipe them away and tipped her head up to kiss him.

At first, his kiss was gentle. Seeking comfort and confirmation. But then something in him seemed to snap like a cord pulled too tightly. He pressed down harder against her, his embrace becoming insistent, bruising and hungry.

Aon sank down closer, leaning his weight on her, and began to return her kiss in full. When his hand slid up her thigh, scooting the nightgown she was wearing up her leg, she let out a small *"mmh!"* against him and broke the kiss for a moment.

He eyed her scrupulously, clearly wondering why she interrupted his path. He cocked an eyebrow at her in the silent question.

"I'd like a shower before we go any further," she said up at him and kissed his jawline. "If you don't mind."

"Would you now? Well... ask, and ye shall receive," he purred with a fiendish grin and a dark mischief in those spilled-ink eyes that was her only warning of trouble.

The world tipped and whirled around her. She had become used to teleporting around the world, but she had gone from lying horizontal to hurtling through the air. That was not something she was accustomed to. She screamed as hot water surrounded her abruptly, and she panicked. Disoriented, it took her a few seconds to learn which way was up.

Floundering and splashing, her feet found a stone bottom to the pool of hot water. As she managed to stand, her head broke the surface. She was reeling. The water was incredibly hot, and it didn't help her confusion.

She pushed her hair back from her face. Coughing, she cleared the water out of her mouth. It was only after she managed to pull in a breath that she realized that someone was laughing. Aon.

Wiping water from her eyes, she looked up and recognized where they were. His hot spring. He brought them here and he had thrown her in!

"You jackass, what do you—" she snapped but couldn't help but break off as she was distracted by the image of him climbing down the steps into the water, entirely naked. He sank into the water up to his waist as he walked up to her, grinning like a demon.

"Do you forgive me now?" he teased. So quickly the tender moment had vanished, replaced by his dark humor and hunger.

"You're an asshole." Her insult lacked weight.

"Noted. But I hear creatures of such disposition tend to grow on you, so I am not concerned."

"Hah, hah. Why did you throw me in?" She wiped more water out of her face.

Catching her blush as she couldn't help but stare, Aon grinned wickedly in the clear enjoyment of Lydia's attraction to him. "Well," he began leadingly, as he walked up to her, fingers trailing on the surface, sending ripples out from him, "seeing as last time we were here, you interrupted my plans... I thought it was only fair."

Right. The last time. "You weren't seriously, last time..."

"Oh, believe me, I was *quite* serious, if you had been willing."

"You just like to torment me." She glared at him half-heartedly with her accusation. Something about seeing his face as he talked—as he walked up to her like a monster about to eat her whole with that wicked glee so clearly written on him—made him all the more intense. Made her stomach twist in both fear and delight at what was about to follow.

"Oh, my dragonfly," he said through a deep exhale. "When has that ever been in question?"

She held her own breath as he finally approached her.

Reached out, he gently stroked a piece of her wet hair back from her face. His hand trailed down her cheek and then to the strap of the nightgown which was now soaked entirely through and clung to her body. It left nothing to the imagination. "By the Ancients, you are beautiful..."

She went to reply to the compliment but didn't get far. His lips against hers silenced her, and she let out a small *"mmh"* at the embrace. For a man who had never kissed a woman before her, he was damn good at it.

His tongue demanded entrance to her mouth, and she granted it. He tilted his head to the side to deepen the embrace, his metal hand wrapping around her lower back and pressing her to his body. The feeling of the strength in his arms would never cease to make her melt against him like butter.

When he broke the kiss, they were both breathless. Slipping her hands up over his chest, she took a moment to explore him. Leaning her head down to his shoulder, she ran her tongue along one of the lines of dark ink that decorated his pale skin. "This wasn't what I had in mind for bathing."

"Then go ahead and, ah"—Aon moaned low in his throat at the touch of her tongue against him— "stop me."

She would never get over how responsive he was and how everything she did seemed to affect him. She knew he wasn't used to this kind of thing—being touched—and now she could watch his face as he reacted to all that she did. It was amazing, being able to find his buttons and watch as they played out across those sharp features.

Wandering one of her hands between them, she gently ran it against the already impressive proof of his passion. He pulled in a sharp breath through his nose, and she felt him twitch at the sensation of her touch. "Now, I don't think I want to." Wrapping her hand around his quickly growing hardness, she began to stroke it slowly, taking her time. Teasing him.

He let out a low noise deep in his throat and tilted his head back, those dark eyes of his locked onto hers, as if trying to burn straight through her soul.

God, what a handsome man. The cut of his jaw, the way he tasted, the way he moved. So dangerous and so vulnerable at the same time. She slid her hand up to Aon's neck and pulled his head down to kiss him again. It was hard not to forgive him for throwing her into his hot spring when he tasted like that.

When she broke the kiss, she paused her exploration of his body to take his hand and pull him toward the side of the pond, and the bench that was just beneath the surface, half as a step and half for seating like in a hot tub.

He followed curiously and eagerly, his dark eyes flickering in lust and mischief both. As they reached the underwater step that acted as a bench, just below the surface of the water, she turned to face him. "Sit on the edge," she said quietly.

He crooked an eyebrow at her. "Is that a command again?" After what had happened during the last time she had instructed him on what to do, she was surprised he was teasing her.

Rolling her eyes with a half-laugh, she leaned in to kiss his chest, letting her teeth graze along his skin. "A request. I can't breathe underwater."

"Well, far be it from me to turn down such an offer." Chuckling quietly, he stepped up onto the bench, turned, and sat on the edge. The water now only reached up to his knees, and... *ungh*. She would never get sick of that sight.

Pulling the soaked-through nightgown off over her head, she balled it up and tossed it aside. He let out a small sound as she did, and when she looked back to him, the expression he wore was one of pure hunger and fascination. Unguarded lust and desire burned away on his features.

As she walked up to him, his hands were quickly upon her, gliding up her arms and down to her chest, cupping her breasts in his hands and kneading them, the metal claws of his one hand digging dangerously into the skin. Her eyes drifted half-shut at the sensation, and she let out a small sound of her own of pleasure at his touch.

"I cannot wait until the day I see your flesh decorated with ink. Ah. Yes. I should ask. I *assume* the same rules do not apply as last time..." Aon teased her again, grinning, even though his voice was raspy and ragged.

"No games this time. At least not from me." Last time, she'd demanded he not touch her, and that had lasted until the moment he decided taking control was more fun. She smirked at him and moved to kneel between his legs. She slid her hands up his thighs and felt the strength in them. Lines of the archaic, esoteric writing ran down them to his knees, then tapered off. He was one-third writing, two-thirds pale skin.

She decided at some point, she was going to lick every line of ink on his body. Sitting back on her ankles, she slipped her hand around the base of his length, she found it still hot and slick from the warmth of the water and steam. God, how she wanted to taste him again. How she wanted to feel him again. She *loved* this. More than that. She loved *him.*

Leaning down, she let her tongue run up along him, base to tip, slowly. He moaned and settled his metal hand between her shoulder blades at the bottom of her neck. Not pressing down but instead tangling into her hair and twisting and curling the strands between his fingers.

"Yes, my dragonfly," he purred down to her, as she explored him, her other hand leaning against his thigh for balance. "Ah— oh, I think a man could become addicted to this sight…"

Taking him into her mouth, she ran her tongue around him in a lazy circle, tasting him. She began to make slow pulls against him.

Gasping, he lifted his hips up toward her as she did, instinctually starting to press himself deeper into her.

Impatient man! It was obvious what he wanted. Taking a few moments to just enjoy him in her mouth, rolling her tongue around him and tormenting him with the gentle suction, Lydia took a breath through her nose and pressed him down her throat. The feeling of Aon filling her made her moan —a sound that was matched by his in turn.

His ended in a throaty growl. "Yes, that's it… *ngh!*" His hand in her hair slipped to the back of her head, and he pushed her down further onto him. Not forcing her, not yet, but encouraging her enough to take him the rest of the way.

Aon lifted his hips into her, pressing himself up to the hilt, her nose against his body as he filled her throat to the brim. His girth challenged her control every time. When she went to lift her head from him, he allowed it, and seemed content this time to let her drive the pace.

And she wasn't in any hurry. He was throbbing in her hand as she pulled away until he just filled her mouth. She lingered there for a little while, bobbing her head on that part of him alone, catching her breath, before slipping him back further into her and holding it for as long as she could.

"You are a demon and a succubus... I think you mean to end my life." His voice was raspy and breathless. Moaning and gasping, encouraging her and seemingly basking at the worship she was paying him. "Do not stop."

She shut her eyes and sped up, letting her hand stroke what part of him was not in her mouth. She had teased him badly enough, it didn't take long before his hand tightened in her hair, grasping it hard as he let out a broken cry. The taste of him filled her mouth, and she found she didn't mind it in the slightest. It wasn't hard to take, and when he stilled, she pulled him out of her mouth and began to slowly lick him clean.

"Ah—" his whole body twitched in an oversensitive after-shock. When she glanced up at him, the look on his face was one she would never forget. It was bliss—ragged pleasure and pure ecstasy, mixed with a strange kind of awe as he watched her. His eyes were lidded and dark. "You are... a miracle."

"I know I'm good, but that's going a bit far," she teased as she finished her task, and sat back on her heels.

"I mean it in far more ways than one, my love."

That made her cheeks go warm. Standing from the bench as he shifted toward her, she thought he wished to join her in the water. Instead, he sat on the underwater ledge, submerged halfway up his chest. He grabbed her by the wrist, whirled her around and with a squeak she was sitting on his lap.

Aon pulled her by the shoulder back against his chest, and his hands slid down her thighs. He pulled her legs apart and put her knees on the outside of his. As he spread his legs, hers followed.

He buried his head in her neck and kissed her there, hot and passionate, his tongue rolling slow circles around the skin. Lydia moaned and tilted her head away and back, resting against his own shoulder to give him more room.

One of his hands left her—the flesh-and-blood one—and she watched through half-shut eyes as he seemed to summon an ornate, red glass bottle of some kind out of thin air. Magic. Right. He flicked the top of it open with his thumb, and she watched, wary and not sure what it was, as he poured it down over her chest.

She jolted as the substance touched her. But it looked like only oil of some kind. Her reaction made him chuckle, and she felt him smile against her skin.

"It is not *acid*," he chided as he put the bottle down on the edge of the hot spring.

"With you? Who knows?" She laughed. The laugh ended abruptly in a moan as he took both of his hands and began to slowly rub the substance onto her. He seemed intent to cover every inch of her with it, slowly and deliberately kneading it into her skin as he worked.

He was now kissing his way up toward her ear, and trailing wet, sultry kisses up to the lobe that he took hungrily into his mouth and bit down. Lydia gasped and arched, and he pressed her back against him firmly as she writhed in his grip.

"My beautiful darling... look at you." His words were a dark whisper as he pressed his claws dangerously into the tender skin of her breast.

She arched again in pain, trying to wrench out of his grasp. She'd worry about marks, but now she healed too fast for it to matter. She knew that meant he was only going to push her harder.

She really wanted him to push her harder.

"Yes, that's it. Just like that." His words of praise sent shivers through her that mirrored the twinges of pain. "I will never tire of watching you *squirm*..."

His voice was low, breathless, caught and tangled up in his own pleasure and desire. His body was hard and taut against her back. She could feel the muscles of his stomach ripple against her as he kept her pinned to him.

Turning her head, she caught his lips with hers and kissed him deeply. She wound her hand into his long hair and grasped it to give herself some leverage. Running her tongue along his lips, she found him eagerly slipping his own past her lips to explore her mouth.

He was still ruthlessly kneading and caressing her body, his touch setting her ablaze. She could feel he had recovered and was hard against her lower back once more.

His hand trailed lower, down her stomach, delving down below the waterline, and finding her core. She arched again further, and her mewl bloomed into a moan as he let his fingers probe and explore her, rubbing at her sensitive nub, sending her twitching in pangs of pleasure that stabbed through her unexpectedly.

"Ah!" she exclaimed breathlessly and broke the kiss as she did.

He allowed her some air and went back to kissing at her neck and shoulder, hot and sensual, in sharp contrast to the metal nails that were still dangerously exploring the rest of her.

But the fingers within her core did not linger there for long. Aon pulled his fingers away from her, and she let out a small, disappointed sound in her throat as he did.

He tutted her quietly, and she felt him lean to slip his hand further down and around her—between her legs and—she let out a startled, frightened squeak as he pressed a finger to an entirely different entrance to her body. She grabbed onto his arms, her body going rigid in nervousness.

He paused, the metal hand that had been kneading ruthlessly at her breast stopping in its ministrations. "Hm?" he said curiously to her, lifting his head just barely from her neck and shoulder. "What's this?"

"I—I—" she stammered. "Wait—"

"Oh, my... Tell me you lie to me, my pet." His voice was a heady mix of rapture and bliss. "Tell me that you cannot be so inexperienced in such a manner of lovemaking?"

"I've never—" she managed to let out of her lips before suddenly his were on them, silencing her against his suddenly feverish and overexcited kiss.

He broke it off to trail more along her jaw, up to her ear. He was suddenly tense in anticipation. "My poor darling thing, you should not have told me that. Now, there is *no* dissuading me." He released his metal hand from her breast to gently wrap his arm around her and hold her. Not forcefully, but instead as if he were trying to calm her.

"To think I *alone* can have this part of you? To watch your face slip from pain to pleasure for the *first time*... Oh," He took in a wavering, shuddering breath. "It is divine! Please, let me have this. Let me take this part of you."

"I—" Swallowing the rock in her throat, she tensed at the feeling of a finger pressing against her again. Aon swirled it slowly about her entrance, slicking it with oil, his hand still covered in it.

"Sssh," he coaxed her, his voice a low rumble. "Be calm. If you are so tense, it will hurt needlessly. Relax... *Trust me.*"

Shutting her eyes, she took a deep breath and held it before letting it out in a long rush. Oh, hell. Well, she'd enjoyed everything else he'd done to her so far. Maybe this would be the same. Fear was the only thing stopping her, and she was sick of being afraid.

Besides. He tore out my heart with his bare hand. This isn't going to be worse than that. She took in another long breath, held it, and slowly let it out, trying to command her body to relax. Willing her muscles to loosen. Trust him. Did she? In some, suicidal way, she really did.

"Good..."

And with that, Aon pressed until his finger slid inside her. Just barely, pressing into her where it felt impossibly tight. She let out a squeak and a gasp, and her body locked up tight once more. The moan that left him ended in a low growl.

It took Lydia a long time to remember to breathe, and when she did, she tried to force herself not to grasp at his arms like she was drowning in the ocean. When she successfully made herself relax again, he pushed his finger just barely further, easing his way in.

He was gentle with her. He wasn't a gentle kind of man by far, and she could hear his heavy breaths as he slowly withdrew his finger until barely anything remained. In incredibly patient, careful, meticulous movements, he began to slowly inch his finger further deeper each time. Each time he pushed in just a tiny bit more.

What Lydia had not expected was the small gasps that she made each time he reached a new depth. Each time he stretched her out just a little further. The feeling was entirely foreign. It hurt, but it was so intensely arousing that she leaned her head back against his chest and could only just surrender to it and to him.

He spread his legs wider, taking hers with them. "Yes, *yes*, just like that," He urged her along, his voice deep and desperate, as if he were walking the high wire with her. As if watching her were just as pleasurable as the act itself. "I think you are ready for another..."

When a second finger joined the first, she jolted at the unexpected shift in sensations and then moaned loudly at the result. Pausing before he resumed his careful, methodical movements, he watched her face, as though he could see her experience and understand it better than she could.

Once he seemed satisfied, he began to move again, pistoning his fingers in and out of her body almost maddeningly slow. Each time he pressed into her, she moaned, biting her lower lip. Her body tensed, then relaxed, as it adjusted to the new invaders.

It continued on for what felt like minutes like that, and slowly, she sank into the sensations, letting them overtake her, letting him have his way with her as he kissed and nipped at her neck.

A third joined the two, this time without warning. Lydia gasped and her back arched, and she threw her head back as a pang of pleasure and pain both ripped through her unexpectedly. She knew why he was doing this. She knew why he was tormenting her. He wanted to prepare her for what he was going to do to her next. She moaned in unbridled pleasure and discomfort both, and his voice joined hers, relishing in her abandon.

It felt so foreign, so intense, she couldn't help it. Her body felt like it was on fire, electricity arcing through her at his touch. With three fingers working into her at a frustratingly slow pace, she could barely breath.

She realized she wanted more.

Needed more.

It seemed he knew she was ready.

His fingers slid from her body, watching her where her head rested against his shoulder. Her lips were parted as she gasped for air. She felt his metal hand move to grasp her hip on one side and lifted her up—an easy task in the water.

When Lydia felt the tip of his length press against her, she twitched nervously, jolting in fear.

He shushed her gently and leaned his head down to nuzzle

into her hair and kiss at her earlobe slowly, trying to calm her. "Let me take you... Let me ravish you."

That shouldn't turn her on as much as it did.

But here they were.

She let out a wavering breath as she felt him press her body down onto his. As the first part of him slipped inside, her cry was drowned out in his loud moan of utter explicit pleasure.

It felt like he was splitting her in two. He had done a careful job of preparing her, but it hadn't been enough for this. Her hands had flown to his arms, and she was digging her nails into his skin, desperately needing something to hold on to.

There were broken sounds of sheer ecstasy coming from him, as he lingered in her without moving.

Slowly, the shock of it began to fade and as it did, she let her muscles unclench. Let her grip on his arms loosen. At the sign that she was adjusting, he lowered her just a little further, nudging himself only ever slightly more into her body.

Squeezing her eyes tight, she felt him press his length farther into her, delving inside only to retreat. He was moving with precise discipline. Careful to take two steps back for every three steps forward. Sliding slowly deeper and deeper into her, letting her adjust each time.

His strokes were gradually becoming fuller and deeper as he pulled her hips closer down toward his. Through it all, he kept the measured pace. Under her hand at his neck, she could feel his racing heartbeat. He was making hitched, gasping, broken sounds as he worked his way into her.

It must be taking extreme and careful control on his part to keep from simply ramming into her like she knew he must want.

After minutes of the slow and creeping progression into her, it no longer felt like she was being torn apart. Sensing the tension start to leave her legs, he lifted her hips almost all the way off him. This time, he did not stop, and instead drove deep, pushing inarguably into her. Gentle, slow, but firm and unstoppable, he slid to the root inside of her.

She had no words, no sounds for what it felt like, to have him impale her like that. To be so entirely full of him. It felt so vastly different than usual, and she could only lay in his arms and gasp for air.

His body was shuddering, convulsing in waves as if overcome. He began to lift her again—slowly, never quickening—until just the first part remained. He then slid back into her without a pause in between a second time.

When he started to speed up, she realized she had been letting out small, timid cries of pleasure each time he reached his end inside of her.

He pushed himself to the hilt once, harder than before, and it sent a wave of sheer bliss crashing over her unexpectedly. Her body arched against him, spasming in ecstasy as he forced her over the cliff's edge from that one movement alone.

"There—*ah*—" he gasped and groaned in pleasure. "There is the change. And it is as wonderful as I had hoped—" he bit out through grunts of pleasure. He lifted her hips and drove himself in deep once more, and she let out a startled cry that was all at once begging for more, and for mercy, as he assaulted her already overwrought body. Each time he drove into her, it felt like she was going to forget how to spell her own name. Her body was on fire, every nerve alight.

She wrapped an arm behind his neck to hold on for dear life as he used both of his to lift her hips and pull her back down onto him. His thrusts became harder, needier, and he was moaning and letting out harsh, broken sounds as he began to hammer into her.

"Oh god, Aon—" she cried, breathlessly, arching her back.

He thrust his hips up to meet her body as he pulled her down onto him in a stiff jerk once, twice, and then let out a broken, ragged cry as Aon buried himself down into her as far as he could go. It was brutal, it was amazing, and it sent her over the edge into another wild cry of ecstasy.

Wrapping both his arms around her waist, he held her to him so tight it was nearly painful. He nuzzled his head in her shoulder, and she felt him convulse beneath her and inside of her as he spilled himself into her.

They clutched to each other in their mutual loss of control and gently fading pleasure. He was twitching and each time he did, he pulled in a gasp of air through his nose. His arms were still cinched around her, hugging her to him as if she might vanish into thin air.

When he had the ability, he pulled himself from her body and sat her down on the bench. Lydia was still dazed as he moved to kneel over her, caging her in with his arms.

He began kissing her, again and again, as if begging her for something. He looked worried. What was he asking for? Forgiveness? Acceptance? Was he concerned he hurt her?

She put her hands to his cheeks, and gently stilled his kisses. She smiled at him, and kissed him back once, before whispering, "I love you."

"And I you, my dragonfly," he murmured back to her, the worry fading and blooming into a genuine smile.

"Even if you are a sick pervert." She jabbed a finger in his chest.

He grinned, the fiendish mischief returning to his dark features. "Oh, I am that without question. And you believe that was perverted? My dear, naive child, you do not even begin to comprehend. But, these things must be done gradually." He straightened up and smirked down at her, wiping a hand through his black hair and slicking it back away from his face, damp in the steam. "Now, didn't you come here for a bath?"

NINE

Kamira sniffed as she walked into the Great Hall of the House of Fate. It was raining outside, it was chilly, and she was damp.

She hated being *damp*.

Kamira never wore more layers than she needed, and this time she was mildly jealous of those who had a coat to remove in such an occasion. They might find it easier to rid themselves of the persistent drizzle that seemed both ineffective at watering the plants and annoying in how it clung to her.

Rain could be delightful, but she decided she preferred it in absolutes. Let it either pour in a deluge or not at all. This halfway spitting was just abysmal. She flicked her furred tail, brought the tufted end to her hand, and combed her sharp nails through it to straighten the clump that had formed.

It was not often that she set foot indoors. More often in the recent few months since the arrival of Lydia—or Lyd the Queen of the Dreams, as she was now—than in the past several years combined.

Still, it was never by Kamira's own volition that her bare feet touched smooth marble or polished wood. If she were to desire someone for a discussion or otherwise, she would call them to a clearing or her home in the deep woods. Never to a building or a city. *Peh.* Useless constructs of silly minds.

No, today she had been once more summoned here to this place. This time, yet again, by Ziza. She found herself irritated by the frigid woman. Although it had entirely the same result as being annoyed at the weather. The rain and Ziza cared for her opinion in an equal manner to the other; that was to say, not at all.

As she swiped some of the remaining droplets off her arms, she walked further into the Great Hall. The stone floor was cold against her bare feet, but she minded it little. Kamira was used to it. While she may don furs in terrible weather, she would never put on shoes.

"Lady Kamira, thank you for coming," Ziza greeted from where she stood across the hall from her, an austere figure in blue. The stony, immovable woman was standing beneath the orrery of which she was the caretaker. It twisted and moved in its silent dance over her, glinting in the candlelight of the ancient hall.

It could tell the secrets of all the world and all that was to come, if a person knew how to read it.

Kamira couldn't care less.

"The Oracle calls once more, and I must answer," she said tiredly as she approached the other woman. Ziza did not move or react as Kamira approached. She stood a good six inches taller than the Oracle who was diminutive in size at best.

To think that Ziza had been Edu's consort before the Great War still was incomprehensible to Kamira. Ziza was so... small. Weak. Calm. *Breakable.*

But, to be fair, she had barely known the woman before Aon forced the "sight" upon the Oracle and taken from her the capacity to love. Perhaps she was different back then. Yet Kamira always pictured Edu with someone with a bit more fire to them than the woman who made Lyon look so very emotive by comparison. At least someone with a bit more bulk to them.

The little redhead, for example. Edu's new favorite. The little girl was hardly a warrior by training but seemed quick to learn. She certainly was feisty.

"I will keep things brief," Ziza said. "I know how much you detest being indoors."

"I appreciate that." Kamira resisted the urge to shake herself off like a dog to rid itself of being damp. It would be rude. While she generally cared little for such things, there was no reason to pick a fight. "Tell me, what visions have you seen that I must know? I have never once been called here on my own."

There was the source of Kamira's acquiescence to the call of the Oracle. She was, even if she did not wish to admit it out loud, deeply curious. Every time she had been summoned to speak with Ziza, it had been as part of a pack. Never on her own.

"I do not have any vision to share with you, per se," Ziza responded, voice unemotional and flat.

"Oh, then what?" Kamira grinned. "Girly gossip, perhaps?" While joking with the woman was useless—Kamira would receive more of a rise out of the stone statues that dotted the hall—she could not help herself.

"Not quite." Ziza pointed at the grand orrery above.

Kamira turned her attention upward, and her eyes went wide at what she saw. A green glass orb upon its copper track—which had sat unlit for so many hundreds of years—was now glowing.

It meant only one thing.

Trouble.

* * *

Lydia did eventually get to take her bath. Eventually. Aon was incorrigible. It wasn't until she threatened to strangle him or down him in the hot water—with Q offering to help—that he finally let up and stopped interrupting her.

It was hard not to let him.

Not just because she found him so addicting, but because it just seemed to make him so damn... *happy.* The warlock had a joy around him she had never felt before. If it was possible, the man was beaming. He was basking in her presence. Occasionally, when he didn't think she was looking at him, she saw him with his eyes shut and a tender smile across his features. Like a man who was finally allowed to rest.

A man who was finally allowed to be loved.

Finally, she managed to shoo him away long enough for them to get dressed, and he donned his metal mask again. And just like that, he was once again the warlock that she knew.

Sarcastic and jaded.

He carried the same sense of dark and twisted humor when he was with or without the slab of metal, but his tone carried so much more nuance when she could see his face.

He had wished to see her home again. To see the Temple of Dreams—or at least, what she was making of it. Boston was slowly creeping over the Aztec ruins like moss, morphing together into a strange and twisted sense of architecture. It was eerie, it was bizarre, but more and more, it was starting to feel like it was hers.

It was starting to feel like somewhere she belonged.

He wanted to walk around the grounds of her home. He seemed fascinated by the blinking creatures that had taken up residence over the reflecting pool. The creatures that seemed so much like fireflies but came in every color imaginable.

"I thought you hated them?" Lydia nudged his arm as she caught him staring at the array of blinking bugs.

"Hardly. I adore them. I hate the false one that you wear. I hated that the merchant had the audacity to pretend it was real. It is only by your foolish and sentimental adherence to the little thing that I did not smash the necklace when I had the chance." His voice grew dark as he talked, and suddenly it all made sense. Now, she understood his hatred of the fake little magic ball she kept in the chrysalis around her throat.

His spite that day hadn't been pointed at the merchant. His spite had been pointed at himself. For he knew first-hand how useless it was to try to create something with a soul. She reached out and took his hand, wove her fingers in between his, and squeezed it tightly in hers.

"See? Such a sentimental thing you are." His teasing was to cover his pain, and she could see it for what it was now.

"Yup. And you love it."

"Hmf." He was set on walking in circles around the large reflecting pool. Something was troubling him, and he seemed unsure as to how to start the conversation. So she let him sort it out on his own.

She had had enough dire, world-ending, serious talks for the foreseeable future. She wouldn't mind postponing another one for a few more moments. She also knew he wasn't one to engage in conversation just for the sake of it. He always disguised any kind of discussion inside of something else. Her putting back the books in his library, for example.

Now that she knew Aon better, she could see that for what it had really been. He didn't want her to put his books back; he wanted to give her an excuse not to huddle in some corner and weep in terror. It gave her something to do. Something to hold onto. It also gave him a justification for having her around him. If he had just loomed near her with no other explanation, she would have panicked and wedged herself behind furniture to hide.

Clever asshole.

The city around them was still empty. Well, save for the two of them, Q, and the monsters she saw slipping in and out of the shadows. The creatures that were born from her subconscious mind were numerous and bizarre. She saw what might have been undead goats, grazing in the lawn before spooking at their appearance and taking off into the jungle trees.

All those nature documentaries she used to watch were going to come in handy. Lydia found herself smirking at the thought. Speaking of Q, she watched as he dove in and out of the reflecting pond. It was incredibly deep, and he was some twenty feet in length, announcing that he was hungry and that there were "fishes!"

Judging by Aon's angry sigh, he was not a fan of her snake.

Finally, she couldn't take it anymore. So much for postponing things—her curiosity got the better of her. "What are you avoiding, Aon?" The two of them had walked in silence for twenty minutes. That wasn't typical for a man who loved the sound of his voice as much as the warlock clearly did. "There's something you don't want to talk about."

"I am enjoying the moment. That is a rare thing for me."

Lydia lifted his hand to her lips and pressed a kiss to the side of his pointer finger before dropping their hands back to their sides. She couldn't argue with that. She might be a horrible person for being with him, but standing here at his side felt... right. It felt nice. She felt as happy as she could, all things considered.

It meant it couldn't last.

They walked in silence for some time longer, listening to the crickets and watching the blinking lights in the grass and over the pool, before she finally had the heart to break the moment. "You're trying to figure out how to explain to me that shit is going to hit the fan again, aren't you?"

"I... am unfamiliar with that term." She could hear the grin in his voice, now that she had seen his face to know what it sounded like. "That is immensely colorful."

"I didn't invent it."

"I can only grasp at its meaning, if I attempt to visualize what it is you said. That is... quite horrifying. You modern children have a truly grotesque and putrid vernacular."

Lydia snickered. He had no idea. She hadn't even gotten started. "I'll ease you in."

"Charming."

"It means you think that something is going to happen that's going to be a disaster."

"I gathered." He laughed and shook his head, still marveling over the disgusting phrase. Aon took in a breath, and she watched as his chest swelled with it, before he held it for a long moment and let it out. "Yes. You are right."

"You're just convinced that because things are finally Looking Up, Aon, someone's going to burst in and fuck it up for you," Q said from where he suddenly appeared swooping overhead, circling around them like a lazy, glowing vulture.

Aon couldn't hide his disdain for Q, not even while wearing a mask. "They always have. And with the rise of one royal will come the rest."

She sighed. "Green, purple, and blue, right?"

"Dtu, Vjo, and Ini. The King of Moons, and the Queens of Words and Fate, respectively." He was still so patient with her, explaining things to her like a tutor. She appreciated that, and honestly, he likely enjoyed having someone to teach. "One despises me, one dislikes me, and one... well. She is irritating at best. You shall see soon enough, I suspect."

Lydia snickered. "Threaten me with a good time, why don't you?"

"How am I threatening anything—ah. Another turn of phrase."

"Yeah." She smiled up at him and hugged his arm to her side. He responded by pulling her against him and draping his arm instead over her shoulder. There was a time, not so very long ago at all, that she would have frozen or recoiled at the nearness of him. Oh, he still had those moments. But this rabid tiger seemed to enjoy her company, at least. And it was mutual.

He turned his masked face to look down at her. "Tomorrow is the Festival of Moons. One of our holidays, in which all the moons appear full in the sky. It happens only once a year, and as such, we celebrate it. It is the purview of Kamira's House and will be held in a field like animals. We will be expected to attend."

It sounded like the very last thing in the world he wanted to do. But that something was inspiring him to go.

Her. As usual. Or at least, keeping her safe. Which meant there'd be trouble. "You think someone is going to pick a fight with me?"

"That is what I am preparing for."

Rubbing a hand over her eyes, she let out a beleaguered sigh. "This shit is going to give me a perpetual headache."

"Now, you see why I am always in such a mood."

"You're always in a mood because you're a dickbag."

Lydia elbowed Aon before he could generate a retort. "Stop it, Q."

"No-*pe.*" Q let out the last half of the word in a pop.

Lydia fought down the urge to get into a shouting match with the snake. Instead, she looked back up at Aon. "Do we go together or separate?"

"After the public blow you landed during my trial, and with the consensual nature of your participation in our relationship being largely suspect by others, I think some distance between us will benefit the situation. It is a public affair, and hundreds will be in attendance. They will not understand the... context should we appear together."

That was a long way of saying separate, but sure. She snickered. "Fair. Well. I'll try and keep Kamira from kissing me again."

"Again?"

There was such hatred in that one word, and he stiffened so heavily, she burst out laughing. "Aon! No. Don't start. Not over Kamira. I had nothing to do with it. She was being, well, her."

Aon growled low in his throat but then sighed, his shoulders slumping. "Very well."

"I'm not going to leave you for Kamira. Don't worry." Lydia tapped her finger on her chin. "Now, Lyon, maybe... or Tim. Or Maybe Rxa—"

Suddenly, she was slammed against the boulders that surrounded the reflecting pool. The top of the rough-hewn rectangular slab was just at the height of her lower back.

Aon had put her there, and he was now pinning her against it, her hands against the craggy surface. He was caging her in, his arms on either side. "Do not speak like that." His voice was a dark whisper. "Do not *dare*."

Watching him with wide eyes, she took a moment to calm her racing heart. Rabid tiger. Right. Don't poke the rabid tiger. "I'm sorry. It was just a joke. I—"

"For now." He shoved away from her and backed up. He whirled and paced a few steps away before stopping. His hands were fists at his sides. "It is only a matter of time."

"What the hell are you talking about?"

"I won your heart because you were my prisoner. You were under duress and knew no better. You had no one else to talk to but me. You are free now, able to make your choices and companionships as you may. You will choose another in time. I will value our time together while I have it."

"Oh, for fuck's sake. You were happy for ten minutes. Ten minutes! And now you start with this utter bullshit and—"

"No, Q. Stop it." She cut off her snake. *Go away. Now's not the time.* And with that, the turquoise ghastly thing sighed dramatically and obediently disappeared. "Aon..."

"He is right." He shook his head. "If it is not my paranoia that will consume me, it will be my jealousy. Forgive me. I still cannot believe that... what you say is true. Even if you do not mean to lie to me, it cannot be genuine. It will not stand the test of time."

She walked up behind him, circled his waist with her arms, and rested her head against his back. "I can't promise you anything. I can't promise what life will be like for us in fifty years—in a hundred—in a thousand. I don't understand what it's like to live that long. I'm a blip on the radar to someone like you. I'm a single blink of one of those insects. I can't tell you I'll be at your side for eternity. I don't know what eternity means."

"I would not expect you to."

"Then... believe me when I say that I love you. Right now, in this moment, I love you. As for how it happened? I don't care. It's not like you chained me to the wall. You never once tried to force me into any of this."

"Do not think for one second that I did not wish to. Do you know how hard it was not to wreak havoc upon you the moment you were in my home?"

Lydia felt her face go warm in a blush at the thought. "But you didn't. Why?"

"I have learned from my mistakes. I do not wish to love something that does not know of anything else. I do not wish for a shattered, mindless pet."

She placed a kiss against the middle of his back. "Do you trust me?"

"I..." He paused. "Yes."

"Then trust me. Trust me when I say that I love you. And try, maybe just a little less hard, to fuck things up along the way."

With a weary chuckle, he nodded. "Touché, my dear." He

turned around in her arms and hugged her back, pulling her into his chest and resting his head atop hers. "But like you, I fear I can make no promises."

"But hey, let's be honest." She smirked up at him. "Someone else is going to screw this up for us first, anyway."

"In that, I fear you are correct."

TEN

Lydia was a queen in a world of monsters. "Mother of Monsters," Aon had called her the night prior.

And still, she felt like a fish out of water.

They had spent the night in her home for a change, asleep in the pile of pillows that she called a bed. She could have changed it for something more traditional, she knew, but it was growing on her. After complaining about it for a long while, the warlock finally relented, and they had fallen asleep together. He had left to go tend to business, and as he had pointed out, it was better for them to show up separately.

Which left her with another burning question about what the hell she was supposed to do and how the hell she was supposed to act.

The sense of trouble kept nagging at her. Things were starting to become normal, to feel natural. And every time that happened to her, things were violently upended. She was even starting to feel more at ease around Aon—and she knew that couldn't last for long.

The other royals were rising. That meant someone was going to pick a fight. Which one? And when? And how?

She picked up Nick's mask from the shelf on the wall and placed a kiss on the forehead of the slab of carved wood, inked in green, that had belonged to her friend. She felt as though she had betrayed him. Maybe she had. Maybe she was a horrible person. Her heart wrenched, and she let the tears that wanted to fall roll down her cheeks. No one was here to judge her for them. She missed her friend. She always would.

She still felt torn in half. Propriety demanded she should hate Aon for what he did. But she loved the warlock, and no amount of denying it would work. Placing the mask back on her shelf, she let out a wavering breath. Grief was an awful emotion. It really did take the top of the list in things she never wished to feel again.

She couldn't hate Aon for what he did, just like she couldn't deny what she felt for him. But because of that, she questioned her own moral value. There was never a moment in time she had ever pretended to be a saint, after all.

Quibbling with herself about her own value wasn't going to get her anywhere. She had a party to attend, and she was already late.

There wasn't anything she could do about the sense of dread that pulled at the back of her thoughts, so she settled on a very real, very immediate, and very human problem—what in the ever-loving *fuck* was she going to wear?

Everyone else would be dressed up. She knew it. But she never was really one to get dolled up or anything of the sort. Standing in front of the silvery mirror in her bedroom, she tried her best. She had gone clubbing a few times in college—having been dragged out with a pack of girls—so she went with that.

She donned a turquoise silk halter top cut low in the front and all the way down to her waist in the back, black pants, and a pair of knee-high dark turquoise boots. Judging by all the stuff Q was trying to convince her to wear, Qta's motif had heavily featured gold. She put on as much of the jewelry as she was comfortable with. Q kept pushing for more, but she didn't want to waltz in looking like some kind of knockoff rapper from the nineties.

She looked down at the blinking glass chrysalis she wore. To her, it had come to represent her time with Aon before she died. Those few days that she had spent with him, happier than she had ever been before in her life.

But to wear it in public, with everyone there, watching her? She could hardly hide it beneath a halter that went well past the line of her bust. Sighing, she took it off and coiled it carefully on the nightstand.

To amuse Q, who was still whining about how human she still looked, she donned dark teal lipstick to go with the rest of her makeup. "There. Are you happy?"

Meh. You could do better. But fine. The snake was lying on the top of her dresser and watching her with a flick of his tail. **It's a decent start.**

"Can we just go get this over with? I hate parties. I hate being the center of attention, and I hate it when people stare at me. I get the feeling I'm about have to put up with all of that."

Can I make an entrance? I wanna make an entrance.

She rolled her eyes. She might hate the focus, but Q clearly ate it up. "Do whatever you want. But I'm not going to come busting in there like I'm some hot shit."

Spoilsport. Q whined, and flew to perch on her shoulder. She felt his tongue flick against her cheek. It tickled and made her twitch. She hated when he did that, and he knew it. **Try to have some fun, will you?**

In a swirl of turquoise feathers, the world disappeared around her. Traveling like that was starting to become normal to her. When she was in control of it, she didn't feel like she was going to throw up at least. It was like being on a road trip. If she were the passenger, she'd get carsick, but never as the driver.

Q was gone when she reappeared, standing on the edge of a

massive clearing in the woods. The trees loomed up around her, tall and ancient. The first thing she realized was how bright it was. Not only due to the giant bonfire in the center of the field, but because all the moons were high in the sky. There was easily a dozen or more, each in a different shade of color. They were gorgeous, especially with the full starlit backdrop.

Well, it was called the Festival of Moons, after all.

The clearing was ringed in massive upright rocks, roughly carved into rectangles, much like Stonehenge. Only these monoliths were somehow larger, reaching easily thirty or forty feet high. Each of the monoliths must represent one of the moons, as they were etched with a symbol and painted in a matching color to the glowing overhead orbs.

All the Houses had their own unique culture. The thought finally dawned on her, seeing this place. Each one looked like a piece of time from humanity's history. Kamira's House—shapeshifters—were primal and pagan. They felt and acted a lot older than the other Houses, even if it wasn't true.

Q at least had the presence of mind to materialize them somewhere away from the crowd. And it really was a party. People were playing music, mostly sounding like drums, and dancing around the giant bonfire in the center that reached up high into the night sky. The smell of burning wood was rich in the breeze. Other fires were burning around the clearing, with people looking like they were grilling food or just sitting around chatting.

The smell of cooked meat was pervasive in the air. There were hundreds of people here, wearing all the colors. Well, save hers. They were laughing, fighting, drinking, eating, and yes, off to the sides or right out in the open, engaging in... other activities. She tried not to stare or blush as it was clear that meat wasn't the only thing getting spit-roasted about thirty feet away from her.

She rolled her eyes. God damn it, people.

Oh, get over it, you prude. That's what people do here. Do you know how boring it gets being immortal? They've gotta do *somebody* to pass the time. Q giggled in her head from his lousy joke.

She tried not to shout at him.

"Can I just go home? I don't want to walk in there." She was muttering to both herself and Q. She was glad to be hiding in the shadow of a massive tree, at least. They were all going to stare. The moment she walked out from the shadows, she was going to have people breaking out in fits like when she went exploring through the cities. She didn't want to deal with people looking at her like the freak she was. It was bad enough when she had been mortal. Now, she might wear marks on her face, but she was still just as bizarre to them as she had been before. Even if she was a queen.

It still sounded stupid when she said it to herself.

You can't hide forever, you know. Just dive in. Lyon's over there by the main platform. She looked to where he was subconsciously pointing her. **Go say hi. Maverick's around here somewhere too. For some reason, you like that guy.**

"He's funny." She liked the abrasive, dry British doctor. He reminded Lydia of one of her college professors that everyone else had hated but she had gotten along with just fine.

You're literally the only one who thinks that.

"Whatever." Taking a deep breath, she let out a grumbling sigh and tried not to feel like she was walking into her high school prom all over again. Stepping out of the shadows and into the crowd, she did her best to avoid being seen. Did her best to keep her head down, hoping her long hair against her face might shield her from being recognized.

Not goddamn likely, but I can try.

There were a bunch of wood structures scattered around, looking like stages and set a few feet high off the ground. Places for people to sit that weren't the grass, rocks, or logs, she guessed. She hadn't seen them at first through the mass of people.

She made it about forty feet toward what looked like the main wood platform where she could make out Lyon's pale form standing high above everyone else before she was noticed. A man in a blue button-down and black dress pants. Ziza's House. The upper half of his face was hidden behind his mask, but it didn't do anything to stop his look of surprise. The fact that his mouth fell open had something to do with it.

He grabbed the person standing next to him—another man in blue—and pointed straight at her. As she caught his stare, he quickly lowered his head, stared at the ground, and stammered uselessly. They were just a bunch of mouth-noises and made no sense as actual words.

"It's fine." She sighed. "I'm a freak, I get it."

The man went to kneel, and finally words were intelligible in the stammering. He was begging for forgiveness.

"No! No, no, for fuck's sake—" She took his upper arms in her hands and pulled him back to standing. "No kneeling." She had only made his terror worse, and now the guy was shaking. Lydia let him go and took a step back. "I'm not a big deal. Stop it."

"You are," said his friend, who was apparently less jumpy but still wouldn't lift his face to look at her. "You're—"

"I know! I know." Lydia threw up her hands and resisted the urge to just go home right then and there. "I'm just—just don't kneel, you can just call me Lydia. Okay?"

The man made some blathering squeaking sounds before he finally got out a broken "okay" and that he was "truly sorry, mistress."

So much for just calling her Lydia. She tried. Shaking her head, she mumbled a "see ya" back at them and walked away. She needed the shelter of people who understood what was happening to her. More importantly, she needed a drink and some food. Now that Lydia could smell the cooking meat, she realized she hadn't eaten anything in days. At least not always needing food was a convenient side effect of her current condition.

The people she passed had two reactions to her. Either they staggered away in fear or they fell silent and stared. She was cutting a path through the crowd like she was a leper. *Or Aon.* They acted like this around him too. They were just as afraid of her as they were of him, if maybe for very different reasons.

This was hell. Every part of her hated being stared at. It made her skin crawl.

Finally, she reached the platform that Q had pointed out to her. Lyon was standing there, like a beacon in the darkness, his white suit looking amber in the firelight. There was nothing else to sit on but pillows and cushions. It was how she slept now, so she wasn't going to judge.

Kamira was lounging on the platform, a wood mug in her hand and a plate of food beside her. She was chatting up at Lyon and a shirtless man in a pair of green pants that she didn't recognize.

Pale, ice-blue eyes found hers. "Lydia." Lyon smiled upon seeing her.

Kamira sat up quickly, catching sight of her. Her expression bloomed into a broad and vicious grin. Her canine teeth—upper and lower—were pointed and too long, if not quite fangs. "I did not think you would come!" Kamira jumped up to her feet with the grace of a wild animal. The woman was nearly naked, as she usually was, save for a loincloth and a whole mess of jewelry. It seemed to bother nobody but Lydia, so she didn't bring it up. "I am so glad you are here. Come! Sit! Join us. You —" Kamira looked to someone near the edge of the platform and gestured her hand. "Fetch her some food and beer. The poor thing looks like she is in dire need of both."

"Thanks," Lydia said through a laugh and shook her head.

"I am. I think I just realized I haven't eaten in a few days." She climbed up onto the platform. Lyon walked up to her and extended a hand. She took it.

"It is good to see you." He looked at her ponderously, noting her troubled expression. "What is wrong?"

"People won't stop staring at me."

Kamira patted a cushion on the stage next to her. Lydia sat, and Lyon took a seat on the other side of his wife. "Well," Kamira said through a long breath. "I can tell you why they stare. You look utterly delicious." The sight of what color she must have turned at the feeling of warmth rushing to her face made the shapeshifter cackle in laughter. "Oh, I am so glad you have not lost that blush of yours."

The Priest was still smiling gently over at her. The man displayed emotions; she had to correct her previous beliefs. They were there, they were just so subtle they were hard to see at first. This time, he was looking at her with a look of knowing pity. "You know why they stare. And it is not for the reason my wife insists."

"I know. It doesn't mean I have to like it."

Kamira leaned on her husband's arm, still grinning at her devilishly. "Ah, do not worry over much. They will stare at their new beautiful Queen of Dreams for a time. They do not know who you are or what you mean to their lives." Kamira's wooden mask covered her forehead, temples, and the bridge of her nose and arched up into her hair to create wooden horns that went along with, well, real horns. That left her eyes visible—one of the few masked souls in Under who had both eyes exposed. They were green and had slits like a cat. They glinted in the firelight that made her look like nothing less than the predator she was. "They will come to learn you are fiery but mean them no harm. Perhaps they wonder if they will have another royal like Aon to contend with."

She looked out at the fire. "He'll be here late, I assume."

"I am surprised you did not come together."

She looked over at Kamira, startled.

"The smell of him is fresh on you, darling." The shifter smirked. "As of this morning, I think, he was with you. I take it you have forgiven each other your mutual transgressions, then?"

"That's creepy, disgusting, and weird." She tried not to look mortified. She suspected she failed.

"That was not a denial. I'm right."

"How do you put up with her?" Lydia asked Lyon pointedly.

"Carefully," came the deadpan response.

Kamira laughed and then let out a disgruntled snarl. "Where is that idiot boy I sent off for your food? Likely too busy gossiping about your arrival to do his damned job." Kamira shifted up to her feet and walked to the end of the platform and deftly jumped from the surface. "Must I do everything myself?" she yelled as she walked off into the crowd. She was giving Lydia time with her friend in private, and she appreciated that. Even if she had to do it in her overdramatic fashion.

"Is Rxa coming?" She finally broke the silence between her and Lyon. The Priest might like to sit in that state comfortably, and she didn't.

"He is on his way. He prefers to be fashionably late. I am glad you have come, Lydia. It is good for you to join in this world. And I am... glad you have forgiven Aon. And he, you. Even if it was a revelation made in my wife's typical less than graceful social fashion."

Laughing, she shook her head. "She's honest, I'll give her that." Her laughter died at the thought of the warlock, and she looked off into the crowd thoughtfully. "I couldn't hold a grudge against him. I tried. I just couldn't."

"Then why do you look so unhappy about it?"

"I feel awful. I feel like I'm betraying Nick."

"If he killed your friend out of callous hate, perhaps." Lyon reached out, and she was stunned as he gently ran his hand over her shoulder, consoling her. His touch was tepid against her bare shoulder. He had no body heat of his own. It was unusual but not unpleasant. "To forgive another is never the erroneous choice. And after what duration of grief would your acceptance of your love for the warlock become acceptable? A year? A hundred? A thousand?"

"I don't know."

"Then trust me, as someone who has lived that breadth of time. The passage of the clock does not heal wounds. It merely solidifies the scar. And even then, by what scale would you measure the propriety of your feelings? No, I think you have done the right thing. You taught him and the world that you are not to be trifled with during his trial. That you are both moving on so soon brings me hope for the future."

She couldn't help it. Sitting up, she hugged the vampire. Chuckling at the response, he hugged her back. The tall, lanky man knew just what to say, and it almost made her want to cry. "Thanks, Lyon."

Before the vampire could respond, she heard a laugh from behind her. "Well, well! I leave for one minute to fetch your food, and as soon as I turn my back, I find you in the arms of my husband. Sly creature, no wonder you have seduced the warlock."

Turning what she assumed was a shade of scarlet, Lydia jumped back from Lyon and sat back down on her heels. Kamira was climbing back up onto the stage, a plate of food in one hand and a mug in the other. Judging by the rakish grin on her face, she was hardly angry. "And you are not even drunk yet. My plans for the evening are working out already."

"I wasn't—that wasn't—" Lydia tried, and failed, to form words.

"I got you wine, not beer. I think you need something

stronger for this evening." Kamira handed her the wooden mug and the plate of food, ignoring her useless stammering. "Eat, drink, then you may have your way with my husband if you wish it."

"I... I was just grateful for something he said, that's all."

"Peh! You needn't apologize." Kamira sat back down between them, leaning back on her elbows and looking at her with a mischievous glint in her green eyes. "I understand attraction to the living statue, don't forget."

"I'm not—" Oh no. This was a trap. "I mean, I—it's not that he isn't attractive, but—"

Kamira was roaring in laughter, thumping her bare heel on the stage. "Oh, this is too much fun!" The shifter was closing in on the kill. "He is quite the lover, I promise you. I assume you like it violent and possessive, judging by your current bedfellow? Well, it may not seem like it, but once blood touches his tongue, he is quite the *fiend*."

"Darling. Be kind to her," Lyon said quietly down to his wife, watching the scene unfold with a mild kind of beleaguered patience that said he had suffered through this before. "If not her, to me, then."

"Very well. I'll wait until she's had a few mugs of mulled wine before I begin again. And perhaps when the menu has grown to better tempt her." The glint in Kamira's eye was one of pure chaos. She was clearly only *somewhat* joking.

Lydia tried not to think too hard about that. Instead of responding, she stuck a fork in a piece of sausage and took a bite out of it. It tasted fantastic. All her reservations about it being monster meat—or that it might have once been something that was a person—seemed less important than it used to be. Little by little, this was becoming home.

"Where is your companion, by the by?" Lyon asked after she had a chance to swallow.

"Oh, yes! I am dying to meet this creature of yours." Kamira was grinning still and was lounging back against the legs of the priest, half lying now in his lap. "Lyon has told me all about him."

"Q's gearing up for an entrance. He can't resist the temptation to be overly dramatic." Lydia's tone was as unamused as she felt. But at least maybe she could stop blushing, now that Lyon had changed the subject away from Kamira's teasing—or not so teasing—attempt to talk her into sleeping with him.

"I have heard." The shifter lifted her own roughly carved wooden mug to her lips and took a sip. "Edu, Aon, and Rxa have yet to arrive. Same with Maverick. Ziza is... somewhere, I am sure. I do not care." Kamira shrugged. "I have a hard time tracking that woman."

"Q'll wait until he can get the best reaction." Lydia lifted the glass of wine to her lips and sipped. Immediately, she nearly sprayed the liquid back into the glass. She barely swallowed it without making a mess or shooting it back out of her nose. "What the fuck is this?"

Kamira was once more howling in peals of laughter, entirely beside herself in glee. Lyon looked once more apologetic for his wife. "Oh, you poor thing! You really have not changed."

Looking down into her glass, Lydia swallowed again, trying to understand the aftertaste in her mouth. It was wine. But it was mixed with something else, coppery, slightly bitter, and undeniable. Slightly offset by the sweet red wine that it was paired with... was the taste of blood. "You *all* drink blood? I mean, I know he's a vampire."

"Yes, we *all* drink blood. Whereas my Lyon and his ilk need it to survive, we only desire it. There is pleasure in it. It is what joins us. We come from blood, and so we revel in it. Even you, now."

"So... who's in the wine?" Lydia looked down into the glass morbidly.

Kamira snickered. "You needn't worry. They are not dead for long."

Lydia took in a breath, held it, and let it out slowly.

I'm one of them now. I can fight it all I want, but it's not going to change. I have these marks on my face, and the Ancients aren't going to just let me cash them in for a T-shirt and a trip home. I know what it's like to die for real—and die like they do—and come back. Some part of her just gave up the useless struggle. She had plenty of ones to worry about; she had to give up the hopeless ones when she could.

"Well, when in Rome, I guess..." She lifted her glass and sipped it. Now that she was expecting the flavor, it wasn't so bad. She wasn't human anymore. Not really. The taste of the blood in her mouth confirmed it. It should have been revolting, and instead, she found herself sipping it again.

"That's the spirit." Kamira flopped back down in Lyon's lap, resting her head on his thigh.

"I'm not going to ask about the food." Instead, she set about just doing her best to enjoy it for what it was. Tasty. And she was glad for the wine. Filled with blood as it may be, she had a feeling she was going to need some liquid courage to survive the night

ELEVEN

Time had stretched on, and so had another glass of wine, before anyone else joined them on the platform. Ziza and Maverick with his wife Aria arrived within a few minutes of each other. She greeted them all warmly, and they did the same in return. Well, as warmly as Ziza could greet anyone, anyway. Maverick looked like a regular class clown next to the woman in blue.

In a burst of white light from over them, she shielded her eyes as Rxa appeared overhead. The first of the other "royals" of Under to appear.

His wings shone of a thousand colors as he dropped to the wood platform near Lydia, his bare feet touching one at a time. He looked so freakishly out of place as a glowing and ungodly beautiful angel surrounded by monsters and demons like them. But as he turned, an afterimage of him was left in his wake, wearing red wings. As the part of the spectrum of light that composed him broke off, it left the main, leaving Rxa's wings every shade but that tone of crimson.

The afterimage of the angel caught up a second later, snapping back to the whole like a ghost of a VHS tape that had been used too many times.

And just as quickly, his unearthly beauty was snapped, and she was reminded that he bore as dark a secret as the rest of them. The thin, barely there gold chains he wore around him swayed as he bowed to those already seated, a wing curled around the front of him like another arm. "Gentlemen. Ladies. My queen." His voice was soft and yet had no problem carrying in the din of the crowd and the noise. It was like a winter wind.

"Please just call me Lydia," she said with a faint smile. She couldn't help it. He was like looking into a summer sun. Even if he was incredibly eerie and... a hundred thousand people all at once. "Besides, I'm not your queen. You're a king also."

"A term of respect. But as you wish, sister." Rxa straightened, folded his wings behind him, and sat to the right of her. She was stuck between Kamira and Rxa now. Between a grinning, wild shifter woman and a glowing, breathtakingly beautiful, literal angel.

You're gonna complain you're stuck between those two? Bow-chicka-wow-wow.

Shut up, Q!

You know they'd both say yes if you asked.

Shut the hell up.

You know they would. Just say, 'Hey, guys, let's do it.' They'd jump right in. At the same time.

Holy shit. Stop already.

Make me!

Rxa noticed the look on her face. "Are you well, my lady? Ah—Lydia, forgive me."

Lydia laughed tiredly and downed the rest of her second glass of wine. She'd need a few more before the night was over. "The snake of mine that you met? He can talk in my head and does so frequently, loudly, inappropriately, and I can't convince him to stuff it."

"Stuff... ah. I understand." Rxa chuckled and lowered his

head, his blond hair falling along the sides of his face. "Lyon was correct. What a besieged creature you are."

"You don't know the half of it."

"I fear I do not." Rxa hummed thoughtfully. "I would like to know, perhaps, if you would be willing to share."

Another offer of friendship. Or something like it, she wasn't quite sure. She watched the angel for a moment, thinking it over, before the moment was interrupted.

"There is Edu." Lyon pointed. Sure enough, there was the man standing a full head above the rest of the crowd. "That means the warlock will not be far behind."

"Of course, he'd show up last." Lydia shook her head. Someone wearing green came over to refill their mugs. When she met his nervous, glinting eyes that were yellow like those of a wolf, she smiled and thanked him. He smiled nervously and managed to blather out a phrase that might have resembled something polite before scampering away.

What kind of major assholes were the kings and queens of Under to their people that had everyone so afraid of her? Maybe it was because Lydia just had no idea how to act regal. She had no interest in being bowed to or fawned over.

"You're late, you fat old man!" Kamira hollered at Edu as he approached. "Couldn't fit into your clothes again?" The big man's shoulders shook with laughter. It was clear the two of them had a long history.

"Master Edu says it is clear he is not last, so it does not matter if he is late," Ylena said as Edu helped her up onto the platform with the lift of a large hand. He ignored the 'fat' comments.

"The other one can stay home, for all I care. In fact, I'd prefer him to miss the ceremony." Kamira sneered.

"Ceremony?" Lydia felt dread well in her again. The last ceremony she attended didn't end well for her.

Seeing her expression, Kamira laughed again. She did that

frequently, and it was disarming and personable, if a little predatory. "It is nothing to worry over. We shoot off—what do you people call it? We light little rockets that explode into sparks in the sky." She snapped her fingers as if to try and recall it from her mind. "You have a word for them."

"Fireworks?"

"Yes! That's it."

"I love fireworks."

"As do I," Rxa added.

Lydia smiled at him and sipped the blood-wine. It was starting to grow on her. That, and she was starting to feel just a little bit fluffy from the alcohol.

"Bunny!" she heard yelled through the crowd as Evie bounded up onto the platform. She, uncaring for anything—pomp and circumstance be damned—jumped up onto it with a plate and a mug of her own and flopped down onto a pile of pillows between her and Kamira. Putting down her drink, she threw her arms around Lydia in a hug, nearly knocking them both back in the process.

Lydia laughed and couldn't help but smile at her friend as Evie pulled herself off her. Evie looked over to Rxa and waved brightly to him. "Hi, Rxa!"

Rxa bowed his head slightly. "Lady Evelyn."

"You two've met?" Lydia asked curiously. She was also impressed at how fearless Evie was around creatures like Edu and Rxa who clearly could squish her with a thought.

"He was hangin' around the keep for a while last week, yeah. I've already annoyed the hell outta him with all my questions." Evie flopped next to her and picked up her plate.

"It was my pleasure," the angel responded.

"You're just bein' polite." Evie cracked another grin. "But I appreciate the gesture. Lordy only knows enough people tell me to my face how annoying I am."

Rxa and Lydia both chuckled. Lydia was glad to have her

around. She really did cheer her up. Evie picked up her fork and began mowing into her food. "This stuff's amazing, isn't it?" The girl was beaming, piping cheerfully. The girl was so damn perky it was impressive. "I love barbeque. Your people make the best food, Kam!"

Kam?

As far as she knew, Evie and Kamira didn't know each other well enough to warrant the nickname. But then again, Evie had nicknames for everybody in about five seconds, as far as she could figure.

"That we do, little morsel. That we do." Kamira smirked at the girl.

Edu stepped up onto the platform finally, taking the stride like it was no distance at all. Even though it was two feet high, he took it like a stair. He looked down to Lydia and bowed his head to her. Not knowing what else to do, Lydia just... saluted him with two fingers to the brow.

Edu shook his head, as though reluctantly amused, and moved to sit at the end of the platform on a stack of pillows. Not too close to the others, yet not too far away. Ylena was in tow. "Good evening, all," she said. "Master Edu wishes you all a happy festival."

"Did he just say that? Really?" Kamira sat up from where she was on Lyon's lap.

"Huh?" Lydia asked, not getting it.

"I have long suspected that his empath Ylena does her best to fix what comes out of that man's head," Kamira accused with a playful smirk pointed at the woman in the long red dress.

"Well, somebody has to," Lydia quipped.

Kamira howled in laughter, and even Lyon couldn't help but smile. Rxa was chuckling quietly. Looking over at Edu and Ylena, she was surprised to find the empath smiling back.

"Indeed." The empath bowed her head. "He insists that it is better that you not know what he truly thinks of you all. The only thing a man accomplishes by reaffirming an idiot's foolishness is starting needless fights."

Lydia laughed in disbelief. Edu had just cracked a joke back at them. This was certainly a weird world with weird people with weird humor. Lydia lifted her mug in salute to him, and he nodded in response.

Here they were, a gaggle of freaks and monsters, interacting like people. Like real people, having a decent time. After swallowing a gulp of wine, she looked off into the crowd of partying people. This... wasn't so bad. This wasn't so bad at all.

Her enjoyment of the moment ended as fast as it had arrived, with the arrival of someone else.

A hush suddenly fell over part of the crowd. Groups of people were moving back from something that had appeared in the field. For a moment, she panicked, wondering if it was one of the other kings or queens. But seeing a man walking toward them, flanked by several others in black, she understood why.

Lydia sat up straight. Aon had arrived. She had just parted from him this morning with a kiss, but now watching him arrive with his gang of men and women in turn-of-the-century black clothing, she admitted he was as intimidating as he ever was. She was privy to a side of him that few others got to see. This was the warlock that they all knew. Dangerous and imposing.

Aon walked up to the platform and stepped up onto it gracefully. He tugged down on his suit coat as he did to keep it straight. He looked like perfection that had stepped out of the shadows. His mask glinting in the combined light of the fire and the overhead moons. Christ, he was beautiful and terrifying all at once.

"Good evening to you all," came his quiet, disingenuous greeting as he bowed dramatically to them all. He straightened and walked to the corner of the platform. With a gesture of his hand, a wooden chair appeared. It seemed he would not sit on the floor like everyone else. He sat on it and leaned back as though he were already bored.

Showoff.

Edu was watching Aon intently, and then he turned his head to look back at Lydia. Clearly, he was trying to figure out what was going on between them. Lydia just shrugged at the big man, not knowing what else to do or say. Edu shook his head and looked back out at the fire.

"How fare you two, might I ask?" Rxa was still sitting right beside her, and it felt like being near the bonfire in the center of the field. His wings radiated heat. "After what transpired at the trial, I cannot decide who owes who recompense."

"I think we're even. And to answer your question, it's... complicated." Lydia tried to make it clear how reluctant she was to talk about it.

"Oh, do not lie to the angel." Kamira huffed another laugh. "She was with him as early as this morning. I can smell the scent of dusty books upon her even now. Although that is not all of his scent I can pick up."

"Kamira—" Lydia hissed through her teeth at her. "That's *disgusting*. Stop it."

"Is it true?" Rxa asked her curiously, canting his head slightly to one side.

Lydia pressed the heels of her palms against her forehead, trying to rub away the ache that had formed behind her brow. "Yes. It's true," she finally admitted woefully.

"You have forgiven him and he you? Hm." Rxa looked to the brooding warlock in the chair briefly before turning back to her. "Your mutual bond must be strong, to survive such vehement weathering. I am... impressed."

"Judging by how strongly you smell of him, Lydia, I am impressed by other things," Kamira said with a fiendish grin. "I would love to hear the details if you would share them."

"Over my goddamn dead body, Kamira," Lydia grumbled at

the shifter. "Although, you already had your hand in that once already, didn't you?"

Kamira hissed in a breath as if Lydia had landed a blow, but she hardly looked offended. "And she finally bares her fangs. Now, I am truly jealous of the warlock."

"Speaking of," Lyon cut in. "At least we are all now in attendance." Lyon was dryly attempting to seek a way out of the awkward conversation.

"Not quite."

"Oh no." Lydia put her hand over her eyes.

"Who was that?" Evie asked, looking around to see who had talked.

The sound of a crowd becoming startled was a very particular noise. When four hundred people gasped in unison, there really was nothing else like it. Looking up, she saw why.

The massive bonfire in the center of the field—which was a burning pyre some twenty feet in diameter—was no longer red.

It was turquoise.

The drummers had stopped, and everyone was backing away from the fire slowly, pressing away from it in a ring as it burned and crackled. The unnatural color cascaded brightly out from the blaze.

Suddenly, Q arose from the fire, spreading his massive wings from the flame as he soared up from it, his ghastly smoke-like body resembling the blaze. His pale head glowed in the light of the overhead moons and the turquoise of the fire beneath him.

The crowd screamed. Everyone staggered back away from the fire, tripping and falling over each other as Q soared, about a hundred feet long, curling up into the air like the phoenix rising from the flames. The metaphor wasn't subtle.

All those on the platform with her stood—save for Aon, who remained seated. In fact, the warlock hadn't even moved, apparently unimpressed with the show in front of him. Reluctantly, she stood as well with a disgruntled sigh.

Q flapped his wings, briefly flattening the fire and sending embers skittering into the crowd. He swirled once, twice, and curled into himself and... detonated. A shockwave of turquoise light exploded out in a disk over the throng, shaking the trees. People covered their heads and faces to protect themselves.

When everything faded, the fire was burning orange once more. There was a murmur in the crowd as everyone looked to the platform and to Lydia.

Great. Now, Lydia had to do something. Q had forced her hand into taking the limelight. All she wanted to do was stay in the background and enjoy the party. "Screw you, Q," she mumbled under her breath.

The voice in her head was giggling. **That was awesome, and you know it!**

Walking to the edge of the platform, she looked out at the crowd. They were all watching her, some still picking themselves up off the ground.

What the hell am I supposed to say? Sorry, my snake buddy has a fetish for making dramatic appearances? Just a dreamer here, no worries, go about your day. Nice party! Weird wine, though.

Maybe this was her chance to get all the awkwardness cleared up, all at once.

"My name is Lydia." She tried to find the strength enough to project. "Not 'mistress.' Not 'highness,' not 'lady,' not anything except Lydia. I didn't want to be like this." She gestured to the marks on her face. "I didn't ask for any of what happened. But it did. And if it means I save this world from oblivion, then... it's worth it. That," she pointed up at the stars in the sky, "is worth it."

A familiar weight of a snake curled up on her shoulder. Q had appeared and done a few loops around her before landing, about the size of a raccoon, big enough that he needed to hold onto her shoulder with the claws of his wings.

There was a smattering of applause that caught in the crowd, and she was shocked, standing there, and felt her face grow warm as the people gathered clapped. She took a step back and bumped into Kamira's arm, who had walked up beside her.

Kamira let out a sharp whistle between her teeth and silenced the crowd. "We are gathered here as seven Houses for the first time in fifteen hundred years. The sky is once more whole, as we are as a people. This alone is cause for celebration!"

The crowd cheered, and the music started back up. And just like that, the moment was over. Lydia was shaking. Apparently, she had stage fright. She was learning all sorts of fun things about herself during her time in Under.

Kamira smiled at the look on Lydia's face and went to say something to that effect before she was instantly distracted by Q's presence on her shoulder. She reached out to touch the snake, beaming in excitement. "How wonderful!"

"Hey, Boobs. Nice to meet you."

Kamira laughed and shook her head. "What a cheeky thing."

"You have no idea," Lydia complained.

"I like it." Kamira grinned. Q flitted from Lydia's shoulder onto Kamira's and was weaving in and out of her hair. The shifter seemed to adore the attention and was already toying with the snake's tail between her fingers. "It is not shy, is it?"

"Can I teach her what 'motorboat' means?"

"No, Q."

"Damnit."

Rxa picked up her mug of wine from the floor of the stage and held it out to Lydia. The angel with the shifting shadows had correctly predicted she needed a drink. She walked up to him and took the mug and sipped it before sitting back down next to him.

Kamira was now lying half in Lyon's lap. Q was bouncing back and forth between Kamira and Evie like a contented cat who could not get enough attention from either woman. Lyon was watching his wife with a warm expression that creased the corners of his eyes with a fondness that displayed such love that it was captivating to watch.

The cold, stoic vampire and the fiery, predatory wild woman. "How did you two become a thing, anyway?" Lydia had to ask.

Kamira cackled.

The Priest slipped out from under his wife and stood. "I believe I have the need for more wine. Excuse me." He walked to the edge of the platform and stepped off, walking away.

Lydia looked to Kamira, worried that she had offended the man. "What'd I say?"

"Trouble not. He is painfully shy." Kamira sat up and moved to sit closer to her. "He could not tell the story without blushing more than he already was."

"He was blushing? How could you tell?"

Kamira chuckled. "It is subtle like the rest of him." She laid back and folded her arms behind her head. Slowly, Lydia was getting used to the fact that the woman was topless. It didn't help that Q insisted on calling the woman "Boobs" instead of her name.

Speaking of, the flying snake had made a fast friend in Evie. She was clearly fascinated by him, and all she wanted to do was shower Q with affection. Her snake wasn't about to complain.

As if by preternatural ability, the chipper redhead sensed there was going to be a juicy story told and moved closer to her and the shifter to listen.

And the shifter was eager for an audience. "When the Great War began, it was not clear at first whom the instigator truly was. It was not until the second half of the war that we even knew it was Aon who had masterminded it all. For the first seventy-five years, every House was at war with the other. Eventually, two factions arose. We in the House of Moons naturally sided with Flames. The priests, as they are prone to do, sided with the warlocks. And as always, Edu and Aon stood against each other."

"You and Lyon were on opposite sides?" Evie asked.

"Correct. One night, on the field of battle where many of us returned to the Ancients, he and I stood opposed." Kamira grinned, clearly enjoying the memory.

"Werewolf versus vampire. How cliché." Lydia smirked.

"I am no wolf." Kamira shot her a half-hearted glare. "That is a gross simplification. Regardless, we fought. As regents of our Houses, elders, and commanders of our respective armies. It was... spectacular."

The shifter breathed in as though she were looking at a beautiful piece of art in her mind's eye. "Naturally, I won. When I brought him down, I meant to take his life then and there. I found I could not bring myself to do so. I decided to keep him as a pet until I could bargain him off in exchange. Little did I know, Aon did not care that much for who he once claimed was his closest friend. Traitorous, worthless cur that he is."

"You realize that I am right here." Aon had been silent throughout the entire night, not speaking to anyone and barely even moving.

"I know," Kamira shot back at him. "And it is unfortunate."

Aon sighed.

Lydia tried not to laugh at the exchange, and Kamira returned to telling her story as if nothing had happened. "There I was, with a prisoner of war that carried no value. Dtu, my king, demanded I kill him. When I stood there to do so, I tore off his mask and... well, I could not do it. I found myself kissing him instead. I took him then as my lover, and he has not seen fit to complain since."

That was cute, in a twisted kind of way. Lydia couldn't help but smile. "What did Dtu think?"

"He was confused, to say the least. But he respected my wishes. Lyon stayed as our prisoner of war until Aon revealed himself as the mastermind behind the ordeal. When we all united against his fetid armies of the undead, he was released, but... chose to stay at my side."

"Armies of the undead." She had seen the mural in his library, but it was still hard to picture it.

"He does not fight with his own people on the field. He raises corpses to fight for him, for he is a coward."

"Again, I am still sitting right here." Aon was tapping one clawed finger against the arm of the chair.

Edu was chuckling, his shoulders shaking in amusement. It was odd to see Aon abused in such a way. They were picking on him, and the man in black was clearly both miserable and yet seemed accustomed to it at the same time.

Lyon was returning with a bottle in his hand, and he climbed back atop the platform. "Are we quite finished?" He filled everyone else's mugs before filling his own.

"Yes, darling. Fear not for your humility. I spared Lydia the sordid details."

"Awwuh!" Evie whined. "There were sordid details? I love sordid details."

"I fear Lyon cannot abide by my descriptions of our antics together." Kamira shot Lydia a wicked look. "Perhaps Lydia will share some instead."

"No, thank you." Lydia sipped her wine.

"Why not?"

"I don't like to kiss and tell. Not my style."

Evie nudged her leg, grinning up at her, and whispered loudly, "But is he any good?"

Lydia groaned and covered her eyes with her hand. "You're both worse than children."

"He must be, if she continues to let him into her bed," Kamira pointed out to the redhead. "Or perhaps it is you who are the talented lover. Come—why not take someone here and demonstrate?"

"Are you serious?" Lydia laughed incredulously. "Hell no, you freaking weirdo."

Kamira smirked. "You could have any manner of man, woman, or beast here upon this stage, right here and now. Every dark desire may be fed in this world. Anything you want, you may have. The most you might garner is a complaint from Edu if you do not allow him to join in."

"No."

"Rxa is quite the lover, you know. A far cry from your dark demon!"

"No, Kamira."

"Tender, gentle, considerate, and can you imagine what a man who can split himself into so many copies may be able to do? Think of all those hands and all those—"

Lydia swatted at the woman, desperately trying to get her to shut up. Kamira was howling in laughter at having goaded her that far.

"Oh, now she wishes to wrestle? Very well!" Kamira cackled.

A white wing snapped between her and the shifter, curling around them like a wall of opalescent light and breaking off the fight. "Enough, regent. Leave the poor woman be." The angel in question was chuckling despite his rebuke. "Forgive her. She merely does it to tease you. You are the new queen, and she must quickly find all your strings that she might pull to annoy you. I fear it is her nature. But I assure you, it means she enjoys your company."

Kamira shoved Rxa's wing away, and she propped herself back up on Lyon's lap, smiling smugly like a well-fed cat. She seemed happy with her accomplishment and, judging by the stern look Lyon was giving her, done with her game.

"I know. I get it." Lydia shook her head and looked back out at the crowd. "I'm shiny and new and exciting. It'll wear off. I can't wait."

They all left her alone for a little while, as the party continued, rightfully sensing she needed some time to chill. Rxa was chatting with Kamira and Lyon and Evie. Evie would occasionally get up to go see Edu. It was clear by the big man's posture how gentle he was with her. He would pet her hair, gently squeeze her arm. And Evie had lights in her eyes, every time she was near him. It brought her no small amount of relief to see that Edu could be that way. She hadn't ever seen it from him personally. But if Evie felt safe, then... who was she to judge? She was the one with the warlock, after all.

Speaking of, Aon was still brooding in his chair, talking to no one, staring off into the distance and, for all intents and purposes, could have been a ghost.

She couldn't help but stare at Rxa next to her. What else was she supposed to do? She was sitting next to an actual... angel. Opalescent wings, glowing, beautiful, androgynous. So utterly perfect he couldn't be real. It was fascinating but off-putting at the same time. She felt like she was looking at a living stained-glass window.

Rxa caught her staring. "You will make your warlock jealous," he warned, his tone playful and warm.

"If she ate a banana, he'd get jealous." Kamira cackled, and Lydia smacked the woman's arm, which only made her laugh harder. "Yes, yes, I'll be quiet."

Lydia's face grew warm all the same at her crude joke. Now, she knew how Lyon must feel, always being the butt of everybody's antics. She looked back at the angel again curiously.

There was a lull in the air between them again. Before she could stop herself, her hand was hovering in mid-air, reaching out to touch the feathers of his wing. He turned his masked face toward her slightly, and she froze.

"Go on, then."

"I'm sorry. I couldn't help it. I've just never seen anything like you before."

"You needn't apologize. I am quite accustomed. Go on, you may touch me if you wish. I do not mind at all. Quite the opposite, in fact." Rxa held one of his wings down and closer to her, the shimmering, opalescent feathers seeming to flicker in and out. Now that she could see them closer, they looked like they were made of razor-thin multicolored film. They glowed like a hologram in a movie. Flickered in and out like they weren't really there.

"You're made of light." That explained why he radiated heat. His wings were made of energy.

"Clever." Rxa took her hand in his and gently placed it against the apex of his wing that he lowered to her, zeroing the distance she was too afraid to break. "Yes. I am." He let go of her hand.

He was so *warm*. Like putting her hand on an electric blanket. It was soft and almost seemed to buzz. She brushed her hand along the feathers, and they moved and shifted under her fingers like a giant bird.

"All the other copies that you can split off. They're... points on the light spectrum."

"You truly are a bright one." Rxa stretched his wing out further and let out a small hum in his throat at her touch. "Too shy, perhaps. But wonderfully intelligent." She kept gently running her fingers through his feathers. Her best friend growing up had an African Gray parrot. It loved to be scratched at the base of the feathers, and she was too curious for her own good not to find out if he was the same. He let out another low noise in his throat. "And very good with your hands."

It was right about then that she realized what she was

doing. She had been lured into the moment, too fascinated by the feeling of the warmth beneath her hand, at the lightshow that was his opalescent wings. She pulled her hand back and was sure she was bright red by the burning in her cheeks. "Sorry."

"I certainly did not mind." Rxa chuckled.

Looking up, Lydia knew that someone *did* mind. Aon. He hadn't moved, but the claws of his metal hand were dug deep into the wood of the chair. So much for hoping he hadn't noticed. She sighed. "I'm going to pay for that later."

"I do not think he can stay angry with you. And I do think you may enjoy his wrath." Rxa folded his wings back again.

Lydia looked over to Lyon, asking for shelter from all this teasing, and he looked at her with an expression that simply displayed his years of having to deal with precisely the same torment. He was a partner in her suffering, but he had no shelter to offer her this time.

With a sigh, she looked back to Rxa. "You're all a bunch of children."

"I suppose we are."

She had another question. She couldn't help it. It wasn't like she ever had a chance to talk to someone like him before. "So, are you a vampire?"

"Yes."

A vampiric angel. Huh. "How does that work, with the mask and all?"

"I have my methods. Do you wish to find out for yourself what it is to be kissed by a vampire?" When her face grew warmer and her eyes went wide, he chuckled. "Another time. Your warlock would not abide and would see to it I suffered. I wish to keep my fingers where they are."

"He abides by little." She smirked and pulled a knee up to her chest and leaned her elbow on it. She looked out over the crowd. "Sometimes, I try to take a step back and look at all this, where I am, who I'm sitting here with. What's happened to me, what I am now... him. All of this feels impossible."

"You are unlike any creature I have ever met," the angel said to her quietly, his soft voice almost hard to discern at first. "At the very least, unlike any who have ever come to reside here."

"Why do you say that?"

"You are still so removed from our Ancients. Devoid of their influence or knowledge. You denounce your queenship. You say that you cannot believe the world around you. You wish to be treated as any other. You say you only accept your rule for you understand the value you carry by having it. You do not wish for power, child?"

"No. I just want to be left alone for a hot second to get my feet under me, that's all."

Rxa cocked his head curiously at her. "The allure of your stature carries no appeal?"

"None. Zilch. Zero." Lydia sipped her wine. "Actually, I don't want it. But I guess I have to take it. Like I have to take everything here."

"Like you have to take Aon as a lover?" Kamira snickered from where she flopped down next to her.

"Enough." Lyon wrapped an arm around his wife and pulled her against his side.

Rxa ignored the interjection and picked up Lydia's hand. She was stunned at the gesture and just froze, letting him turn it over, palm up, and trace the lines of her hand with his fingers. It brought a warm flush to her cheeks. "I did not wish to rule either, but I wished to serve the Ancients. And so, I do. Even as they say I am a king, I am a servant to them. Even as I hold their chains in their slumber. I am a king only by comparison. To them," he gestured his head out toward the crowd, "I reign. But to the Ancients, I am a child. You feel the same, don't you?"

"They've controlled every part of my coming here. They set

this all up. I'm not a child, I'm a puppet." There was no lack of bitterness in her voice.

"You rail against their guidance?"

"I don't like what they've done so far, so, yeah. I guess."

Rxa was talking quietly, his voice only for her. Evie and Kamira might be able to hear him, but no one else. "You have suffered. You have paid a price for what you now hold. But you are a queen. You have power beyond what any of those in the crowd may imagine. You are the Mother of Monsters—the savior of a world. You have not only spared Under from the void but given us prey to hunt that do not share our blood. Such suffering you have taken upon yourself, to save it from others tenfold. You have earned the heart of a man whose ability to feel anything at all was thought impossible. Do you not think all that was a worthy price to pay for what you now hold? A gift given to you by the Ancients? Nothing in this world shall ever come freely. And you have found the most valuable prize of all. Love."

Lydia hadn't thought of it that way. She felt her jaw twitch, and she sighed and shut her eyes. She let the angel keep toying with her hand. She didn't know why—it felt nice. Warm and comforting. "That was a good speech, angel."

He pressed a palm against his chest, bowing his head to her. "I do my best."

Finally, she pulled her hand back into her lap and looked off into the crowd. "You're right. I don't feel like a queen, because I feel like I'm just tugged along by someone else's grand design."

"Then you are wise." They sat in silence for a long moment. Q was still winding around Kamira, happy as could be, being petted by the wild woman. Everyone seemed distracted, happy. Save for her and the brooding warlock but for very different reasons. "Yet there is sadness in your eyes. Why?"

"I don't think this world is done with me yet."

A howl cut through the wind. A keening wail of a wolf. Silence fell like a fog over the crowd, and she knew she had never been more right.

TWELVE

The howl made Lydia's blood run cold.

Aon stood first. For the first time all night, he looked to be paying attention. He was rigid, his head lowered, his dark hair falling along the sides of his black mask. He was a terrifying image, and that was precisely what he was trying to accomplish, she was sure.

They all scrambled up quickly after that. Q vanished in a blink. He preferred the element of surprise, and she had the distinct sensation she was going to need his help in short order.

The howl that cut through the night silenced everyone and everything, leaving only the roar of the bonfire in the middle of the field.

It took Lydia a second to find where the sound had come from. There, on the other side of the field, perched atop a thirty-foot pillar of stone, was a figure. It was cut against the moons behind it like a silhouette. The creature was gigantic; its limbs were long and gangly and covered with fur. The ears of a wolf stood back from its head, ratted and torn. She could make out little else about the thing from where she was.

Unfortunately, she was about to see it a whole lot closer.

It vanished as soon as it had appeared. Blinked out of existence as it moved faster than she could track. Like a nightmare, like something coming out of the depths of her mind, it was suddenly in front of her, looming over her like a terror. Glowing embers flickered and curled away from a visage of bone, revealing that the wolf had gone *through* the bonfire to get to her.

Its face was rotted away. There was only a skull left—wolf-like and sharp. Its teeth were too long, jutting up and down through rows of teeth more like a crocodile than a dog. It looked as though a werewolf had died, but that its curse hadn't ended. Parts of its body were down to bone and sinew, black fur matted by sweat and blood and gore.

Its eyes stared down at her—large gaping black holes that were empty, save for two pinpricks of green fire that bored into her. As it breathed, its breath came out in steam, hot against the even warm night air. It stank of dog and rotting meat.

It loomed up over her, standing some eight feet tall, its body bent-backed and curled in on itself. Its legs were long, and even at its height, it was crouching. If it stood straight, the monster would be enormous.

Her heart was racing. Terror, instant and total, gripped her. Staring up, wide-eyed at the creature, she fought the urge to run. Her heart was lodged in her throat, and her pulse was thundering in her ears.

It talked, its voice a ragged, rasping hiss. And it's one word was full of hate, of rage, and of disgust. *"You."*

Its claw came down upon her, and her world went black. Everything upended, tumbling around itself, as she found herself sprawled down in the dirt. It had taken her and brought them somewhere else. The swirl in her stomach was telltale now. This thing had teleported them away.

She scrambled to her feet quickly and found them standing in another clearing. Smaller and more importantly... empty of anyone else. She couldn't hear the crowd nearby. Just the chirp of insects and the heavy breaths of the monster that stood in the clearing with her, cast in the light of the moons overhead.

The creature stood there and began to circle her like the rotted wolf it resembled. Its jaw was dripping like a drooling beast. Whether it was blood or saliva, she couldn't tell. She felt her hand crackle with power, and she knew without looking that her hand was sparking with that weird turquoise electricity she could summon when she was angry.

It eyed her and tilted its head up and to the side. One single green pinprick stared at her, a small dot against a vacuous darkness. She wouldn't be the one to speak first. This thing had grabbed her, dragged her off, and now was staring at her. She would let it deal with starting the conversation.

Besides, the longer she dragged this out, the more likely it would be that Aon would find her before things got too ugly.

The creature's voice came again, sounding like sandpaper rubbing on bricks. "You reek of him." Disgust dripped from his tone just as the ooze dripped from his maw.

"Oh for *fuck's sake*." Lydia rolled her eyes. There was no need to ask who he was talking about. "You must be Dtu. Nice to meet you. I'm leaving." She turned and pulled up her steps as the werewolf was standing right there, glaring down at her, his head far too close to her once more. Lydia held her ground and refused to let the monster have the pleasure of watching her retreat.

"You will go nowhere, broodmare scum."

Lydia levied her best glare up at him. "You don't get a goddamn say, Fido. Back off before I skin you and try to turn what's left of that disgusting pelt of yours into a rug. Although, never mind." She wrinkled her nose. "You smell awful. No wonder you aren't allowed indoors."

Dtu laughed, a horrid, grating sound that was bone on bone. When it talked, its mouth didn't move. It stayed shut.

"The warlock's bitch has bite. Do you talk to him like that, when he pins you down and mounts you?"

Before she could even second-guess herself, she rammed a dagger she hadn't realized she had summoned up into his neck, down to the golden hilt.

Dtu snarled and jumped back away from her, growling loudly as he pawed at the blade, knocking it away and skittering against the dirt. Blood, thick and black as pitch, oozed from the wound. But not enough.

She'd wounded him but hadn't taken him down. It'd take more than that to level a king, after all. "Watch it, fleabag. I'd threaten to fuck you up, but by the looks of it, somebody already beat me to it a long time ago."

"How dare you!" Dtu said through a deep growl. He took one step toward her, clearly meaning to maim her.

Q took the opportunity to appear, gliding up from the earth and blocking his path.

Dtu lowered down onto his haunches, snarling furiously at the snake. "Abomination!"

"Yuh-huh. Look, you—" Q reared back as Dtu swiped a claw at him. **"M'okay then."**

Dtu wasn't going to be calmed down. It was clear he was itching for a fight. Q was more than happy to give it to him.

The fight with Dtu went far differently than the one with Edu. Edu was, or so people kept saying, the greatest fighter on Under. Dtu wasn't. It was brutal, it hurt.

Several trees were destroyed, and it went so fast, she barely had time to think about what was happening. Something in her just took over. She had no time to realize she had no business knowing how to *throw knives* like she was doing. But there she was, *throwing knives* like a champ.

Under. Magic.

Whatever.

She wound up with quite a few gashes on her for her trouble. But when all was said and done, it wasn't her lying in the dirt. It was the werewolf.

Wiping the blood from the corner of her mouth, she coughed and did her best to catch her breath. All of Aon's attempts at hurting her, all the pain he had dealt her when she was in his prison, made sense now. She wasn't afraid of it anymore. She wasn't afraid of what Dtu could do to her if he got his claws into her. She already knew what it felt like to have her heart torn out.

Q was perched atop Dtu, pinning the King of Moons into the turf with the claw of one of his wings at the back of his skulled face. Every time the werewolf struggled, her snake would ram his head back down unapologetically. **"No. Bad dog. Stay. Bad, bad dog."**

"Release me!" Dtu was snarling, foaming at the mouth, claws digging deep into the dirt.

"I'll roll up a newspaper if I have to, Cujo." The wolf struggled again, and Q clonked his head back into the packed dirt. **"Down, boy. Leave it!"**

"Here I have come to aid you, and I find you have the matter in hand."

Lydia jumped at the unexpected voice from behind her. Aon had materialized from out of the shadows of a tree, stepping from the darkness. He walked past her, going straight to where Q had the wolf pinned down.

A roar of fire and a flash of white light and Lydia sighed heavily. This was going to get messy. All five royals were now in the clearing. She really hoped meeting Vjo and Ini didn't go this poorly. But she was putting her bets very low at this point.

"What mean you for this attack, youngest brother?" Rxa asked as he moved to stand by Lydia.

"She is an abomination! She should not live. Look at her!" Dtu was still raging, thrashing underneath the weight of her snake. "She is a mockery. She is not even a proper queen. Her power lives outside her own body! One that *he* clearly fucks at his leisure!"

Q, having had enough of it, began to throw coils around the wolf and squeeze. After a crack of a rib, the wolf let out a high-pitched yelp. **"Stop. Being. Stupid. *Fuckhead.*"**

A king will rise to destroy me. That was part of the prophecy Aon had been given by the Ancients. Lydia had assumed they had meant Edu. No. They meant Dtu.

"You should not insult a queen, Dtu." Aon stepped closer to the dog.

"You mean *your* queen," the werewolf snarled.

"She is not mine. Nor have I ever claimed her to be such."

"You needn't say the words. You are driven by your own needs and nothing else. You wanted a dreamer. You killed Qta. And now I wake to find her and that you have taken her as a mate? You have made her your slave!"

"I have done no such thing. Perhaps I have learned. Perhaps I have grown." Aon hissed down at the dog.

"Do not speak to me like I am an idiot. You are incapable of such things."

"I will speak to you as you are an idiot, as that is precisely what you are. I have been awake all this time, not you. You shrank into your tomb, whimpering and frightened." Aon's words were pure darkness. A threat of deep violence.

"She will die. She will die by my hand!" Dtu struggled again, but Q had him well and truly stuck.

Edu and Rxa were watching the scene silently. Rxa was at her side, his posture tense.

This was getting old. Lydia threw up her hands in frustration. "Why the hell do you want me dead, Scooby-Doo? I haven't done anything to you. I haven't ever met you."

"You are not him. You are a lie, a plague, an aversion against nature. Let me up!" Dtu snarled.

"Not happening." Q squeezed again to prove his point, and the dog yelped.

"What do you mean, 'I'm not him?'" Lydia shook her head, confused. "Do you mean Qta? No shit. He's dead."

"Don't remind me, girl."

"I fear," Rxa said quietly from beside her, "there is much history here you are not privy to."

"What's the short version?"

"Dtu and Qta were in love. When Aon killed Qta, he took from Dtu his mate," Rxa explained, keeping his voice low.

Lydia felt her shoulders drop. "Fuck."

"That is not your tale to tell. Do not dare speak of him!" Dtu howled angrily, struggling against Q with renewed fervor. "Do not speak to that slut—" Dtu yelped in pain again as Q squeezed again, and a loud *crunch* echoed disgustingly in the clearing.

"Each time you call Lyd a stupid name, I'm gonna break another one of your bones. And I'm gonna like it. Don't tempt me to do worse, doggo." Q flicked his turquoise tongue as he glared his own empty skull down at the werewolf.

"Let me get this straight, dog. You hate me because I'm not Qta? I'm sorry. I'm sorry that I'm not him. I wish he had come back from the dead instead of me. Trust me, I really do. I never wanted this. I never wanted these." She pointed at her face, making the point again for the second time that night. "But I didn't get to make that call. The Ancients did."

"The Ancients? Fah! No. Your rutting alpha was to blame. The warlock is at the root of this."

Edu let out a heavy sigh. "Master Edu believed the same, Dtu. It is not the case. Trust him on this." Ylena was thankfully at Edu's side.

Dtu was growling low, turning his head to look over at Edu. "He reeks of her. And she of him. You let this be?"

"Master Edu has made his opinion known to Lydia how he believes she is making a poor choice. But she is a queen. She may decide such things for herself." Edu shook his head. "Lest he be guilty of the same charges he would bring against the warlock."

"For once, Edu, I agree with you," Aon interjected.

"I care not." Dtu tilted his head to fix a green glowing pinprick of light up at Aon. "She is your whore. She reeks of you. You've painted her, mounted her, claimed her as your property! This cannot stand."

"I do not claim her. You are an outrageous fool. I am here to aid a queen who had been attacked. That is all." Aon's clawed hand was flexing and clenching at his side. He clearly wished to tear the other king to shreds.

"Never have you come to one of us in aid! You only come to plague, to hurt, to torment. You claim her as yours, by merely being here. By not laughing at her pain when I tear those marks from her face. She does not deserve to wear them!" Dtu sank his claws into the dirt, digging trenches in the packed surface with his large, black and jagged nails.

"If you dare to step near her, dog... I will make you learn the true meaning of pain," Aon threatened, his voice little more than a whisper, but seething with such a promise of violence that it made Lydia's skin crawl. "You will not lay another paw on her, insipid mongrel! Do you understand me?"

"Why do you protect her so?" Dtu jeered. "Because she is the only one who will let you fuck her? More proof she is your slave! No one would let you have them willingly. Or is she just that free? I will tell you what, warlock. I will promise no more violence on her, for a fee."

"Which is?"

"I get to mount and knot the whore while you watch me—"

That was too far. Q let out a squawk and flapped his wings

and recoiled to safety as Aon couldn't take it anymore. Black fire roared from his hand as he gestured toward the werewolf. Black spikes shot up out of the dirt—metal shards that grew into pointed, dangerous tips that were too small, too sharp to be seen. They hurtled through the air and impaled the wolf, sending him careening through the air and pinning him, skewering him to a tree.

Dtu cried out in pain, yelping and whimpering like a dog. He was thrashing, but it was pointless as his limbs were well and truly secured to the wood. Black ooze dripped from each spear that stuck through him at grotesque angles and splintering all the way through the tree at the back.

"I come to aid her, for she is more valuable than any one of you in this forsaken world!" Aon was shouting at the werewolf, pointing a claw at him that still licked in black flame. "You shall never again speak of her, or to her, in such a fashion. If you dare to disparage her in such a way, I will marry you to Edu in your silence! Or perhaps I should take that putrid organ that festers between your legs instead, for I see it is still the only thing in this world over which you hold value, *little* brother."

"Such passion I have never seen from you. By the Ancients... you love her." Dtu began to hiss his raspy laughter, although now it was thick with pain. "By the Ancients in their grave, you do, don't you?" The wolf tilted his head back, and his maw opened. More of the steamy breath curled out from his jaw. "Edu." Still, he didn't seem to use his mouth to speak. It was only for show, a horrible, morbid grin. His tone was suddenly gleeful and excited. "Edu, we may have our revenge! We can take from him what he took from us so long ago. Let us use her raw while he must watch. Let us kill her as he took Qta. As he took Ziza."

Lydia could only stare at the scene in wide-eyed shock. Ziza's name shook her back to reality. Edu and... what? There was a story there she would have to pry from the warlock—if she lived that long. She looked up at Rxa, and the angel shook his head down at her and placed his hand on her shoulder. It was warm and comforting.

"You will not touch her, brother," Rxa said before Aon could. "She is under my protection as well. She had nothing to do with the actions of the warlock so long ago. She will not be made to suffer your vile threats or actions for it."

"I awoke to the scent of a dreamer. I awoke thinking he had returned. That the Ancients had righted the sins of the warlock. But instead... instead I find *her*."

The warlock was shuddering in rage, his shoulders rising and falling in deep breaths. "If it would not doom this world once more, Dtu, I would grant your wish and send you to join him. I would throw your mangled remains into a pit, just as I did that worthless snake of yours."

"I am sure you would. You have not changed." Dtu shut his mouth slowly. "Rxa. You stand beside her. What of you, Edu? Stand with me in my revenge. Help me hurt that stinking corpse of a man now that he has something he cannot stand to lose."

Edu shook his head.

"You... will not?" Dtu seemed agog. "Time has changed you, friend."

Edu shrugged silently. Ylena did not add anything to help.

The wolf growled low and let out a long, rasping sigh. "Four against one. Very well." Without so much as another word, the wolf disappeared in a swirl of green fire. He just... left.

Lydia let out a breath she hadn't realized she had been holding. She was shaking. Partially in fear, mostly in adrenaline. The cuts on her arms that she had taken from Dtu had healed, but the blood remained. She put her head in her hands and let out a long, weary sigh. "Tell me Vjo and Ini aren't like that," she said under her breath to Rxa.

"They are unique in their own ways, and I am sure will find

reasons to irritate you. But they will… not greet you in such a fashion." Rxa tried to console her, running a hand gently over her hair.

When she looked up, Aon was still fuming. His head was bowed slightly, his dark hair loose, his hands still fisted at his sides. He was nearly shaking in rage.

"Master Edu asks you, warlock, is it true?"

"Is *what* true?"

"Do you love her?"

"It is none of your concern, Edu," Aon ground out through a furious hiss.

"Fine." Edu turned to look at her. "Master Edu asks you instead. Lydia, has Aon removed his mask for you?"

"I—uh—" Lydia took a step back but was stopped by Rxa's arm. She glanced at him warily.

The angel gestured her to step back forward. "It is fine. You are safe."

"Safe?" Lydia bust out in a sardonic laugh. "Safe! I just listened to an undead werewolf threaten to gang-rape me with the guy who's already killed me once before. You have a funny definition of 'safe,' flyboy."

"I am sorry for his threats. That is all they are. Disgusting words spewed in fury not meant for you. Besides… it appears you can handle him in a fight. Trouble not. The wolf is, pardon my pun, far more bark than he is bite."

Ylena spoke up again. "Master Edu insists. Please, Lydia. He means you no harm. But he must know. Has the warlock shown you his face?"

Both of Aon's hands were now curled into tight fists. He took a slow step toward the huge man. Aon wasn't short by any means, and yet the other man still towered over him, even more so in his full armor. "And I will repeat myself as well. This matter does not concern you. Begone, Edu."

"You do not deny it, Aon?" Ylena asked for Edu, who was

now standing to face him. Edu wouldn't cower from the warlock's fury. Probably never had. It was clear the two of them were still itching for a fight.

First Dtu, now this. "Screw this." Lydia walked in between the two of them. "First of all, Edu, it really is none of your business. Second, both of you, stop acting like children."

"I wish you the best of luck with this endeavor," Rxa flatly quipped from behind her.

"So... it is true," Ylena observed. Her tone was strange, and she realized it wasn't her own. Edu was over-emotional again and had commandeered the woman.

Lydia sighed and threw up her hands. She walked into it. It was clear though that Edu already knew the answer and just wanted one of them to confirm it for him. "Yes, and? I've seen his face. You see my stupid face all the time, Edu. Get over it."

"Say it, Aon!" Ylena snapped as Edu stepped toward them once more. Her face twisted in anger, and Lydia knew it was Edu's hatred showing through, not hers. "Speak this farce aloud."

"Why?" Aon's voice was a low hiss. "Whatever for? What do you plan to do, once I have done so? Kill her once more? Trap her in a crypt? What manner of revenge do you plan to take upon me? Dtu made his intentions quite clear. What are yours?"

"You took Ziza from me." Ylena's sense of individually was now fully gone.

"Whoa, whoa—" Lydia waved her hands. "Ziza's alive."

"She is a shell of the woman she once was. When Aon murdered the old Oracle, the power of the sight was forced into Ziza. It robbed her of her heart, her soul."

"Oh, Aon..." Lydia looked over at the warlock sadly. "You didn't."

"Our lives are long and storied, my dear." Aon stepped around her, brushing her aside as he advanced toward Edu. "How many others have you loved? Can you even remember them all by name? Their faces, even? How many souls have pledged themselves in devotion to you? Give me a number, if you can even do that much."

Edu growled in response.

"You cannot, can you? Five thousand years of love and lovers. Come and gone like seasons." Aon's voice was cold in its anger, cutting through the night air like a knife. "For your heart is as wide as the sea and as quick to change. But like a child, you can only remember the one you were denied."

"Do not speak to me of love. You have never known it once in your life."

"Precisely my point! And if I were not a stranger to such things any longer—if I felt such a bond with another—what would you do?" Aon tilted his head back slightly, dangerously, taunting Edu to make a threat. Begging him to give him a reason.

Edu's hands tightened, the leather of his armor creaking. He remained silent, fuming—his frame locked tight and ready for a brawl.

"Very well. Then I will give you the words you are longing to hear!" Aon paused, his voice wavering. "I love her, Edu. And for the first time, in all my thousands of years, I have heard the words repeated back to me. Now tell me, great King of Flames —what will you do?" Aon's voice was emotionless now, cold and exacting. "Will you take your revenge on me for a love you have already replaced with that redheaded child? Will you take an eye for an eye?"

Edu looked over Aon's shoulder to her. It was a silent question, asking her to confirm what Aon had asserted—that she loved him. She could only nod in response and swallow the dread in her throat.

The King of Flames seemed to shake with a fury, but then it

slowly ended as he let out a long sigh. He seemed to relax as he took a casual few steps toward Aon.

"A rare moment of intelligence." Aon struck out his hand as if Edu meant to shake it. "I am glad to see you have come to your—"

Edu hauled back a fist and planted the massive metal-clad object straight into Aon's face. The warlock's head snapped back violently. Aon couldn't even collect himself enough to catch himself on his hands before he was sprawled on his back in the dirt. Edu leaned down over him and grasped the front of the warlock's shirt and coat and hefted his back a few inches off the ground.

"Listen carefully, warlock—" Ylena snarled for her king. "Do not paint yourself superior for that I have the strength to ignore all that you have done. You are not the victor here. My armies could march against you. I could work with Dtu to destroy this precious thing you now have."

"Then why don't you?" Aon asked up at Edu blearily, still reeling from the punch.

"For I have faith you will destroy it on your own and in short order. Furthermore, if I were to take my revenge, I would be no better than you." Edu dropped Aon back upon the ground and stood. Without another word or even a look, Edu turned back toward Ylena. In two paces, he covered the grass back to his empath, and in another jet of fire, they were gone.

"I suppose it was about time he was allowed to have the last word," Aon groaned from where he lay. He placed his hand over his masked face, pressing his palm against his forehead with his fingers spread.

"You deserved that." Lydia walked up to him to kneel in the grass next to where he was sprawled out. "They might not hate you so much if you weren't such a dick all the time."

"Is that how you thank the man who defended your honor?"

Lydia laughed. "Yeah. Thanks for that. But I think you still deserved a punch in the head."

"I am not wrong in the things that I say."

"Delivery counts, y'know. For example, have you ever said you were sorry about Ziza?"

"Apologize?" Aon lifted his head slightly from the dirt. "I am sorry, have we not met before? Forgive me, for I am prone to bouts of madness." He extended his metal hand to her. "I am Aon, King of Shadows. A pleasure to make your acquaintance. You are quite lovely. Who are you?"

Lydia laughed and swatted Aon's hand away playfully. Aon pulled in a hiss of pain through his nose and let it back out as a groan. "Are you all right? Sorry. Stupid question. You got sucker-punched by Edu."

"I have had the dubious pleasure as well," Rxa said as he walked up to stand near them. "I do not recommend it."

"Noted."

"Your presence is no longer required, Rxa. I am grateful you joined us, but..." Aon grunted as he tried to stand up. He made it about halfway before he fell back down. "Oh, charming."

Lydia snickered and pulled him half into her lap. "Stay put, stupid."

"Are you able to take him home? Unless he wishes to heal lying here in a clearing that is covered in werewolf blood," Rxa noted as he looked around the trashed clearing. Looking up, she hadn't realized what kind of a mess she and Dtu had made of it in their quick brawl. There were trenches taken out of the trees by giant claws, and several sections of bark were scorched when her lightning had missed pay dirt.

"I think so," she replied. She hadn't ever taken anyone else anywhere. But she didn't know why it wouldn't work.

"Why? What is wrong with this place?" Aon mumbled sarcastically and laid his head down in her lap. "I love the smell of dead dog in the morning."

Lydia laughed at his joke again and shook her head. He was kind of funny when he was grumpy. "I guess the secret's out now, huh?" Lydia looked up at Rxa. "Is Edu going to be a problem?"

"No. I believe the fist Aon received is as close to a blessing as you two will ever receive from him. In light of Aon's forced confession at your trial and this... I think Edu wishes there to be peace."

"Note to self, don't get Edu's blessing. Ever."

"His wrath is worse," Aon grumbled.

"I still say you had that coming." Lydia smirked down at the warlock and stroked his hair. "Come on. Let's get you home."

"I would like a real bed this time. Not that mass of cutoffs that you foolishly insist are comfortable."

Lydia laughed. "Your place, then."

"Until later." Rxa bowed at the waist. "I bid you both *adieux*."

"Yes, yes, goodbyes and etceteras." Aon waved a hand dismissively at the angel. "Go, angel. Squinting at your irritating glow is exacerbating my sudden and *inexplicable* headache."

Rxa was chuckling as he disappeared in a flash of white light. After a few failed attempts, she got Aon to his feet, leaning heavily on her. A swirl of turquoise feathers and she took him to his bedroom. He flicked his hand and was instantly down to his britches. He almost collapsed into bed, and only with Lydia's fussing was she able to convince him to even get under the covers. She sat at his side, looking down at the clearly miserable man.

"Get some rest." She stroked his hair back gently. "I'll be here."

"Lydia." He reached his bare hand up to her. It looked like he was going to miss, his hand moving weakly. Poor thing was literally punch-drunk. She took his hand and placed his palm against her face. "I would never let that cretin touch you. He will never—" He choked off in a hiss of pain.

"I know."

"Tonight's escapades have not changed your mind?"

She knew what he was asking about. Her decision to be with him. "Aon, I love you. The disapproval of the family dog isn't going to change that."

Aon laughed weakly. He pulled the metal mask from his face and laid it on the sheets next to him. His spilled-ink eyes were unfocused as they turned to her. He looked feverish, and he clearly had a concussion. And a hell of a big one, her EMT training told her. Not like it mattered, she reminded himself. He'd heal.

"What's more, I think I really now get why you felt like you needed to kill Nick. Why you..." She trailed off, uncertain.

"Your heart will always bleed for the loss of your friend." Aon provided for her when she couldn't figure out how to say it. "But perhaps now you may see that he was doomed regardless of my actions. Even with no prophecy to defend me, think of this. Nicholas lived within Dtu's House. The wolf would not have hesitated to use your friendship to hurt or control you. If he threatened your friend's life, you would have sacrificed yourself for him. I know you well enough to see that."

Lydia hadn't put that much together yet. But now that he pointed it out, it was obvious. If Nick had been alive right now, he'd be a hostage. Dtu would maim Nick to hurt her, in order to hurt Aon. There was no doubt about it. Lydia cringed at the thought.

"No one will hurt you. That is my sole right." Aon's tone was dark as he looked up at her; even if he did seem disoriented and bleary, he was still threatening.

How a man could be so loving and yet so twisted about it, she'd probably never understand. But she also knew there was no small part of her that enjoyed it—the fear that he brought with him, whenever he was near.

She leaned down to stroke her hand through his hair and kiss his cheek gently. "I love you."

Aon let out a small, wavering sigh at her words. As if some great weight had been taken off him—as if every time she said the words, he felt bliss. The poor man. He had been the villain for so long, he had forgotten what it was like to be anything else.

Lydia grinned. "And if the other royals don't like it, I will happily tell them where to go sit and spin."

"Does that mean what I believe it does?"

"I think it's actually based on a kid's toy. But now it means exactly that, yeah."

"Another charming invective for the books." He turned her face to look at him, his fingers curled under her chin. "Lydia. Forgive me, for I still find it hard to believe when you say that you love me. After all that I have done, that I can do."

Lydia shook her head, frustrated but not surprised. "You think I'm lying when I say it?"

"No. I believe your words."

"Then what're you implying?"

"You question the value of your own soul for that your heart is mine." His voice was strained in pain and dismay both. She had never seen him like this. The concussion had knocked his barriers down. "I hear you when you speak of it to the Priest or to Rxa. You question your own value, for that you have forgiven me. Do what you must."

"What?"

"You are strong, my dragonfly. Should you decide to condemn our love because of who and what I am—I have faith you could withstand that suffering."

"Aon…" She shifted to take his hand in hers, and he clasped her fingers in between his.

Before she could gather her thoughts enough to form words, he began to speak again. His voice was thin, quiet, and honest. "Know that I am capable of far worse than the murder of a single boy. Know that I am a demon upon this land or any other. Know that I will do more to you to bring you grief than what I have already seen fit to pay you. But know that I will love you until the day that I am rendered unto dust. If you are to refuse me, show me pity and do so now. I beg of you."

Lydia had been wondering about her own morality, questioning what it made her to be with a man like Aon. She didn't bother denying it.

Yes, he was alluring, seductive, and intelligent, and she found herself drawn to his darkness and his violence like a moth to a flame. But it had become far more than that. It had grown into something far more than an infatuation with a villain and a monster. She knew how gentle he had been with her, all through her stay with him. He treated her with as much respect as he was capable of, even when she was a mortal girl. He had fought to give her some semblance of normalcy in her upturned life.

Even more than that, she had seen his vulnerability. His pain, his self-loathing. Aon was a man with an enormous ego and a penchant for inwardly turned hatred all at once.

He was a murderer. A torturer. A sadist. A madman. And he had promised with every breath to do worse. That he would, at some point in their continued thousands of years of life that lay ahead of them, find a reason to do far crueler acts. But she had seen from him a man capable of compassion in his own way.

Lydia loved him. She knew she did, and every time she thought about it, every time she debated it, there was no denying it. But what he was suggesting was that she could say that the love was not worth it. That she could not stand beside a man like him, even if she wept for her own loneliness.

It's probably what a smart person would do. Lydia never claimed to be smart.

"Aon," she began quietly, not wanting to speak loudly at a man suffering from a concussion and who was clearly a little delirious. If he hadn't just had his head knocked in, she had no doubt in her mind that he would never have brought any of this up. He never would have asked her to entertain the idea of leaving his side. "I have a question. And I need you to promise me that you're telling the truth."

"Mmhn," was all she got back from him.

"When I was mortal... did you know? Did you know I'd become a dreamer? Did you have any idea what was going to happen to me?"

"No." Aon opened his eyes finally to look at her. He reached his metal hand up and placed the palm of it against her cheek, with some help from her to help him aim properly. She no longer flinched when the blades touched her. "I thought you were merely a charmingly naïve girl with absolutely *abysmal* luck."

Lydia laughed quietly. "Then why did you keep me here?"

"The defiance in those beautiful blue eyes of yours. That through all the fear and the horror, you would not be broken. You would not succumb to hopelessness in the face of death and suffering, even when the queens and kings of this pathetic world could not say the same. They are demigods. You were human. And you shamed them in your resilience. You stood toe-to-toe with Edu and did not flinch. You stood strong against me at every turn. Me, a demon in the darkness, immortal and powerful, who could destroy you... and you chose to take it all in stride. You, a mortal girl. You were worth saving. Even if that was all you ever turned out to be. And because, even then... even before I saw it for what it was? I loved you then too."

Lydia held his hand to her cheek and leaned her head to kiss his metal palm. She had her answer. "I'm not going to leave you, Aon. I love you. And if that makes me a bad person, then so be it."

He was smiling weakly up at her, his eyes half-closed and his brow still creased in pain. "Lydia, I—" His eyes rolled back into his head, and his hand went limp in her grasp. The man had passed out. She resisted the urge to worry. Even if he stopped breathing, he'd just come back in a few hours. She let out a small chuckle and leaned down to kiss the corner of his mouth.

Lydia stood, careful not to disturb the bed too much. She put a glass of water on the table for him and teleported from the room and back to his library.

The room was darkly lit, the electric lights with their exposed Edison filaments set low. The library was still ungodly beautiful to her in its twisted mix of Baroque and Art Nouveau splendor. This room was Aon, almost just as much as the man himself.

Q appeared and swirled around her before growing to several feet in length and landing on the table. **You could've asked him all sorts of shit, and I bet he'd have told you the truth. We should knock his brain around more often!**

Lydia shook her head with a laugh and walked to the fireplace. She reached out her hand and, with a snap of her fingers, willed the wood to start burning. To her surprise, it did. She hadn't ever tried that before. Lydia snickered. All right, that was fun.

The warmth of the fire was comforting. She walked to Aon's nearby chair and sat in it, draping her legs over one of the wood arms and tucking her head into the wing of the back. It smelled like him, of old books, and it was as reassuring as the fire.

No snippy comeback? Wow. Q flitted across the room, shrinking to the size of a large cat, and curled up in her lap. Lydia petted his head and shut her eyes, thinking. **You okay?**

"Yeah, I think so. I guess I just expected he knew what was going to happen. It would've made everything make so much more sense. All that time before Edu killed me, Aon really had no clue what I was going to become. He just..."

Cared about you, even when you were a squishy little human. Do you remember the day he took you out on the town? I think that was the happiest he's been in a long, long time. He loves you. He did then, he does now. And you feel the same way. So just let yourself be happy. Morality be damned. Morality is useless in Under. You both deserve a good turn.

Lydia smiled down at the snake and scratched the tufts of the feathers at the back of his head. He purred and scuttled into her hand, going belly-up at her attention. "Q? All bullshit aside? I'm glad you're here. Thanks."

M'aw. You too, Cupcake.

Watching the fire, her thoughts drifted. It wandered to the former regents and elders, several of whom she had begun to think about as friends. This place really was her home now. Even if a portal back to Earth opened in front of her, right here and right now, she couldn't step through it.

With all that had happened and with everyone she had met, she couldn't go back to her old life even if that were possible. Slicing up murder victims and overdose cases, living her humdrum life. The pain and torment of this world were worth it.

It was worth it for several reasons. For the silly ghostly snake in Lydia's lap. For Evie. For Lyon. But mostly... for Aon. Under was her home now, and her life was with him.

One way or another.

THIRTEEN

The snow crunched heavily under his boots as he cut trenches in the newly fallen fluff in Edu's wake. It was deep. It had collected impressively over the course of a few days. It reached up past his knees as he walked. Edu adored the cold and the snow, despite the namesake his House may carry. His were the flames of warfare.

Ylena was behind him, bundled in a fur cape, hood drawn high over her head. She walked within the trenches that he left behind.

Edu cut a far more impressive swath through the snow than she did and made her passing through the thickness far easier. Edu had not come out here into the freezing night for his own enjoyment. He had come by request.

But Edu would not complain, even if Ylena may. This night was beautiful. The snowfall had only recently ended. His breath turned into mist in the biting temperature, and Edu welcomed it. The frozen air and snow had been gone from this world for far too long.

How he had missed it.

It was his love of simple honesty that inspired his appreciation for the brutal, straightforward and uncomplicated conditions that the cold weather would bring. Either you ate or you starved. You lived or died. Hunter or prey. Battle was similar in that you either won or you did not.

Perhaps it was his love of such simple honesty that he could not stand Aon and all the warlock stood for. The man played games with those around him, twisting them to his will. Manipulating them into serving a purpose of his design with little care for those he turned into unwitting pawns.

But when he had watched the warlock come to the defense of Lydia in front of Dtu, he had seen a different man. A creature bound in an anger that was not selfish—merely a man who wished to guard that which he *cared for.*

It was clear to him, now that he looked back upon it, that Edu had been a fool not to see what was so plainly there. Aon had doted on the girl when she was a mortal not for her secrets, but for that she had drawn flame from the spent candle that was his soul.

He remembered now, all the moments that lined up to form the completed puzzle in front of him. Yes. It had always been there.

The warlock had been in love from the very start of it. No wonder Aon had been so furious when Edu had killed her.

Edu could not help but shake his head. He counted himself lucky that he still owned his eyes. The warlock was not known for his compassion, after all.

"Yet I find you have found your own where it might have fled, my king," Ylena's voice was often in his head, he did not find it jarring to hear her there. *"To let them have each other. To give them peace now."*

"I know what it is to love. I know what it is to have it taken away. I swore I would never sink to his level. I am... hopeful for

them. This world may know quiet if that cretin is happy for once."

He huffed a laugh. Unlikely.

For even if Aon were not the one finding reasons to destroy all the world around them, someone else would come to take his place, certainly. And that was why he had come out into this blisteringly cold night, after all.

The silence that came with the passing of a recent winter storm helped him think as he walked. The chirping birds and chattering creatures that had returned to his woods had all gone silent under the weighed boughs of branches as they slumped with the heavy pack upon them. The white surfaces were glowing an eerie mix of colors in the overhead moonlight. Small specs of ice within the snow sparkled to match the stars overhead.

It was beautiful. But still, Edu's thoughts were dark.

Edu wondered what would come of this. While he hoped for peace, he knew it would likely not come. Their world was rarely quiet. While it was now saved from the void, and Edu slept more peacefully at night knowing the stars once more blazed overhead, he sensed danger.

They had merely been pulled from the jaws of one death to be thrown into another, he was certain.

He could only hope Lydia had played her part and was now spared of whatever other torment was to come. He knew his hopes were very likely in vain. He wished the girl no more suffering. She had endured enough, much of it his own fault.

Edu was, astonishingly, growing fond of the blonde Valkyrie. She had a quick mind and an empathetic heart and seemed to have no issues putting the warlock in his place when it was necessary. The girl had forgiven Edu of her own murder at his hands and had done so with little pause. Only a wary fear of Edu remained, over which he could not find the means to blame her.

But she was a child. Naïve and young and thrust onto the stage with players who had known their roles for over five thousand years. She was an infant to them, unaware of the countless thousands of wrongs that Aon had committed over his lifetime. And the others repaid in kind.

She was unknowing of the history of blood and lies he had trodden into the dirt behind him, so very much like Edu's path through the fallen snow.

Edu prayed she learned in the gentlest way possible.

"Warrior."

The voice stopped him. He walked deep into the woods of his home by request. For there was a king who rarely deigned to go indoors, and Edu's keep was no exception.

"Master Edu greets you, King Dtu." Edu turned to see the werewolf walking out from under the darkness of the trees. He did not sink into the snow, despite his massive size. The creature merely walked atop it as though he were weighed nothing at all.

The King of Moons moved silently and like a wraith in the darkness. No prey would ever hear the shifter king approach—not even Edu.

Dtu tilted his head back and to the side, peering at Edu with one glowing speck of green flame for an eye in his empty-socketed skull. "I apologize I could not greet you properly before, old friend." His voice was ever the raspy hiss. "And you, little empath. Are you well?"

"I am, thank you," Ylena replied fondly. Very few ever talked to her directly. Dtu was a rare exception. Dtu was very kind toward Ylena, and during battles would often defend her at his own expense.

Dtu was always watching out for the weak ones in his pack.

"Good. I am glad for it. I am warmed to think that most are well in my absence. We have lost shockingly few since I have slept and gained quite a few mighty new souls. Although I find Kamira and the Priest are now wed." Dtu huffed a single laugh and shook his canine skull. "I find the need for ceremony and the title pointless. But she loves him. They are suitable mates."

Edu chuckled and shrugged. "Master Edu says the Priest could not be dissuaded. He is stubborn in his chivalry."

"He must be stubborn to tolerate Kamira." Dtu sat on his hindquarters. "Now, with Rxa's return, at least Otoi is no longer regent. Perhaps the angel will finally let me eat the ball of fat. Though it may give me heartburn to do it." He laughed sharply, the jaw opening wider as steam curled out between his teeth. "To think you all survived Otoi as the white regent. What a miserable time of it you have all had."

"It has been a challenge not to drown the man."

Dtu snorted. "I also see Vidor is no longer Regent of Words. Who is this man called Maverick?"

"He is a proper regent, worry not. Vidor was ready to surrender his post and retire. Maverick is an honorable man, if as reclusive and cold as the rest of his ilk. He reminds Master Edu much of Vjo. They will get along well."

Dtu snuffed and looked up off into the cold night. "So much has changed, yet so much remains the same, old friend. I had hoped perhaps the world would be different, if I ever woke from my slumber."

Edu heard the sorrow in the wolf's voice. Heard the loneliness. It had been fifteen hundred years since the loss of Qta, but Edu knew the wound still bled in him as though it had been carved there yesterday. And upon seeing the new dreamer, and that she was bound to the warlock... he could sympathize deeply with the man's agony. And his rage.

"I have come to apologize to you for my actions." Dtu huffed and shook the snow from his shoulders. "To involve you in my row with the dreamer mare was a mistake. But I am shocked to find you stand in her defense."

"Master Edu shared your suspicions. Indeed, he took the girl's mortal life over it. It was the Ancients who saw to her rise, not Aon. Master Edu entreats you to listen to him, in that Lydia is no threat. Her choice in partners is dubious, he will grant you." Ylena paused as Dtu laughed cruelly. "But she is a fine soul. Strong. Killing her will doom this world back to the void."

"I know that," Dtu snapped, literally and figuratively, at Edu. "I am not a child. I was angry. Jealous that it was not Qta who rose. I was caught in a fit of anger. I did not mean to kill the girl. I wished to *hurt* her. To make the warlock watch. I still would, if—" The wolf broke off in a low growl.

"If what, Master Dtu?" Ylena questioned.

"Kamira. She is hideously upset with my actions. I have only just healed from the holes her claws put in me. I have caused great wounds with her due to my absence and now further by challenging the woman she calls a friend." The wolf's fur—what was left of it—bristled.

Edu tilted his head to the side. "Master Edu is surprised to hear this. Kamira has been your staunch defender in your slumber."

"She defends her alpha from all attackers. But when it is the two of us, she nips at my heels and says I abandoned her. That I cannot judge Lydia for what has transpired, for I was not here to see it for myself." His shoulders raised as he recalled the fight with the weretiger. Kamira was second in command to Dtu— but only barely. Often, fights between Kamira and her alpha were mere inches from ending in her favor.

Edu chuckled. He could only imagine that "nipping at his heels" had been far more dramatic and violent than how the shifter king downplayed it. "No regent loves their king as much as Kamira is devoted to you, old friend. She will forgive you. It has only been a few days. Give it time. And... ceasing your violent threats toward Lydia will go a long way to mend the damage."

Dtu laughed, hissing and dry. He nodded. "Perhaps. You know me. Emotion rules my tongue. It always has."

That was why Edu called the wolf his friend. Dtu was primal, honest, open. He was as quick to anger as he was to apologize when he was wrong. He felt no shame. "Master Edu has missed you, dog."

"And I you. Even if your head is filled with rocks for letting Aon have his way with the new queen." He paused. "Your little empath is shivering. Take her inside before the poor girl freezes." Dtu turned to walk back into the woods. "Good night."

"You as well, Master Dtu," Ylena called after him.

"These will be interesting times." The wolf's last words barely reached him as the shadowy creature disappeared into the darkness of the trees.

Yes. Interesting times, indeed.

* * *

Lydia must have dozed off in Aon's chair. She realized why he sat in it and brooded so often; it really was cozy. Especially in front of the roaring fireplace. She had left Aon in bed, and had gone to his library to relax. She must have just nodded off.

Q was the one who woke her up, nipping at her fingers like a playful cat. "Hm? Huh?" Lydia snuffed awake, sitting up. Man, she had been out cold.

"Company."

"I am sorry to intrude. I did not realize I would find you sleeping."

Looking up, she saw Rxa, standing by a bookcase, casting the room around him in a white glow. Well. More accurately, she saw five versions of Rxa, looking through several bookcases at once. Green, yellow, orange and fuchsia-winged duplicates of himself were poking around, leafing through the collections as the primary Rxa stood reading one in his hands.

Standing, she tried to subtly make sure she looked somewhat presentable. She was still in her clothing from last night, in the halter top and black pants. "How long've you been here?"

"An hour. I did not wish to disturb you."

That's creepy as hell. Lydia didn't know what to say to that, so she just shook her head. *He's five thousand years old,* she reminded herself. *That's going to make you a little socially awkward.* "Aon's passed out, if you're looking for—"

"I came to speak with you, in fact. Indeed, I assumed he would be too injured to intervene, which is why I have troubled you again in such short order and come into his home without his explicit permission." That perfectly smooth, white porcelain mask turned toward her. Well, the primary one. The other ones were still busy amusing themselves with other books.

Uh oh. "You want to talk to me alone?"

"Yes, I do. He hovers, forever at your heels. He spies on you, even when he is not near. Now that I think he has been... incapacitated, I would like to finally speak to you in true seclusion." Rxa folded his white wings at his back. His tone was still warm and gentle, but no less eerie than he ever was.

That made her nervous. Seeing the look that must have been plastered her face, Rxa chuckled. "I mean you no harm, Lydia. I assure you. I merely wish a chance to get to know the woman who has run havoc into this world and commandeered something that we all thought to be a myth—the heart of the warlock."

Don't worry. I can take 'em. If I could take Dtu, I can whoop the birdman. And there's a house full of people in black here to help you out. It was because of Q's words that she relaxed, not Rxa's.

"Sorry. My default state in this place is to suspect the worst." She half-smiled at him. Walking to Aon's bar, she poured herself a drink. "Want a—right. Mask. Sorry."

He hummed thoughtfully, letting the moment hang in the air as he paused. "I do not blame you for your suspicions, knowing what I do of your life in Under. Lyon has filled me in on the details." Rxa's other copies kept going about their business. She wondered if that was his normal state of being, scattered around like that. If it was like a guy sucking in his gut and this was him relaxed. Seeing her eyes flick to the other copies of him, he shrugged idly. "My condition is unique. If it troubles you, I can stop."

"It's okay. It's weird, that's for sure. But everything here is weird."

"I am a countless number of minds, joined into one. I am one, and yet, we are all. I suppose you could consider that odd." Rxa laughed. His voice was always so quiet, and his laugh was the same. But it had no trouble carrying in the room. When she looked over at him, he had folded the book he was reading and placed it back on the shelf. He was shaking his head, clearly amused. "It is for that reason I have come to talk, in fact."

"What, that everyone's weird?" Where was he going with this?

"Yes." The angel walked to stand opposite her from the table. His wings were no longer pure white. They glowed still, but sans the tones that were reflected in the other versions that were scattered around. Suddenly, his wings turned deep purple.

In that instant, a hand on her shoulder turned her to her right. Rxa was there, now without the purple tone, as he had left a piece of himself behind to move most of him next to her. Lydia tried not to jolt in surprise, but it was hard.

His hand drifted to her cheek, and he cupped her face in his gentle touch.

Feeling her face go warm, she took a step away.

He watched her with a thoughtful tilt to his head. "Do you enjoy his style of affection?"

"It's none of your business, Rxa." She took a sip of her drink. Luckily, it was just alcohol—no blood this time around. "If you're here to proposition me, go ask Edu how that went."

Rxa shook his head with a chuckle. "No. I am not here to ask you to sleep with me, Lydia. I know that would result in my being plucked like a goose by the warlock. I have come to speak to you of the fact that your mind is free of the influence of our Ancients. That while you are a queen, you remain curiously removed from us."

"I'm not free of them, Rxa. They pull my strings like I'm a puppet."

"I did not say you were not bound by them. But you do not seem to know them as we do." Rxa paused. "This... troubles me."

"Know them? What do you mean?"

"You do not worship them. Your power lives removed from your body, in that familiar of yours."

"As for Q, it was either compartmentalize what happened to me or go nuts." She shook her head. "I don't know if he's permanent or not, but I know I didn't have a better choice at the time. And as far as I can tell, Aon and the others hate them just as much as I do. So it isn't about my not loving them."

"To worship and to love are different things." Rxa lifted his arm, and a thin gold chain dangled from where it was wrapped several times around his wrist. "I am their devoted servant and their most barbarous warden. I hold the power that keeps the Ancients chained in their depths. I adore them, and yet I fear them deeply enough to keep them in the pit where they have lain for so long. I understand your distrust. I wake in the nights with nightmares of what they had done to us in the days before we overthrew their rule."

"Then what're you talking about?"

"You wear no mask. Your power beats outside your body. You have not yet come to accept what you are—what you have become. You should carry marks on your skin like a royal, and yet you do not. You should have known Dtu or myself on sight, and yet you know nothing of us. Nothing of our world that you have not been told." Rxa stepped forward, his hands trailing down her arms.

Lydia shivered and went to step back again, but he tightened his grasp and kept her from retreating. "Do you want me to say I'm sorry?"

"I understand why you came to be this way, when you first rose from the pool. It was too much for your mind to grasp, so you forced it away from you. But now... you are safe. You are cared for. Aon would help you in your adjustment. Your life is born anew in front of you. Why have you not yet embraced the Ancients?" Rxa's thumbs were gently stroking over her skin. His touch was soft, tender, and gentle, so far away from what Aon's was like. It wasn't threatening, and yet it still made her skin crawl.

"I can't control it. I can't just magically be different."

"Are you so certain? Come to the Pool of the Ancients. Stand at their altar and accept them. Come join me at my Cathedral, kneel at their altar, pray for acceptance. Worship them. Let us right this wrong together."

Every time she went to that place, something horrible happened. Like hell she was going to go back there anytime soon. Lydia narrowed her eyes up at the angel. "No."

Rxa tilted his head, just slightly to one side. "You refuse them?"

"I don't worship anybody."

The angel didn't move. Just like Lyon when he stood too still, like a statue, Rxa just... didn't. Even his copies all seemed to hitch in place.

She stared him down. "Kindly take a step back, Rxa."

The angel pulled his hands from her and obeyed. He bowed his head. "Forgive me."

"You come into my home unannounced and uninvited, angel?" The dark voice carried through the room like a blade. Aon stepped from the shadows, dressed and donning his metal mask. He looked as though nothing had happened. He moved to quickly stand beside Lydia.

"I came to call upon the lady. You were incapacitated. If she wished me gone, she could have sent me away." Rxa's multiple copies around the room all turned and vanished, and his wings were a pure white once more. "I merely wished to talk to her about the uniqueness of her condition."

"Call on her another time. It is late, and it has been a long day."

The angel took another step backward, folded a wing around him in a deep bow. "I have meant no offense. You are still unwell, brother. I hear it in your voice. Let the lady tend to you, and I will take my leave."

"I do not need tending to."

"Needs and wants are different, eldest brother."

Aon growled quietly, not appreciating the tease. "Begone, then. Let me return to my sleep that you disturbed."

"Then I shall say goodbye again. My lady, please call upon me at the cathedral when you can. Come and kneel in worship to the Ancients you serve. I... beg of you."

"I'll think about it." Lydia wasn't going to do anything of the sort, but it was the easiest way to end the conversation that she could see. Fuck the Ancients. Fuck Rxa and his religion. She didn't want any part of it.

"That is all I can ask. Farewell, Lydia. Rest well, brother." Rxa disappeared in a flash of white light.

The conversation had felt strange, disjointed, and odd. Rxa was trying to get at something about her that she hadn't really understood. It's not like she had picked her new state of being. Why was he so concerned about it? What was the problem if she stayed like she was now? Why did it bother him so much?

And why did the whole interaction give her the willies?

"Do not let him trouble you. He is a zealot, and your unusual state concerns him needlessly. He does not understand change. He will accept it in time." When he went to move, his knee buckled. She reached out to grab him, and he slung an arm over her shoulder for support. He wavered but used her for balance.

"You're still hurt. You shouldn't have gotten up."

"And leave you alone with Rxa in my home? No. He knows better than to come here unannounced. Yet, I admit, I —" He nearly collapsed, now both his knees giving out from under him. If he hadn't caught himself on the wall, there was little she was going to do to be able to keep them both standing. "I am not quite sure what I would have done had he been looking for trouble. If you ever tell him such a thing, I *will* make you pay."

"I can also protect myself too, y'know." She couldn't help but laugh as she held him upright. "Come on, handsome. Let's get you back to bed before you end up on the floor."

"Perhaps that is a wise plan."

"Perhaps."

* * *

She wasn't sure what drove her out of the house or what made her get up in the middle of the night and strike out of Aon's home and toward the forest. But Lydia was halfway across his front yard before she honestly realized she had even been moving at all.

She felt compelled. Pulled. Drawn out by something that called her—and needed her. She froze, shaking her head, as if coming out of a dream.

"Lydia?"

The voice behind her stopped her, and she turned to look at Aon. He came up close to her, his hand on her shoulder. His posture was tight, concerned. "What is wrong? Are you well?"

"I—" She blinked. She looked out at the forest nearby, and

she just felt within her a deep call that was summoning her there. "I think so. I just… I can't describe it."

"Ah. It has started." He gestured for her to lead the way. "Good. Let us go and follow this yearning that you feel."

"What's started?" She raised an eyebrow at him. "Should I be worried?" She didn't *feel* scared. It wasn't like when he had used his mind control on her. This felt different. More like a yearning.

"No. Not in the slightest. Go, lead the way."

"All right… sure?" She resumed the path that she had simply known she needed to walk, and he followed close beside her. "Want to tell me what's happening, though?"

"You have just born another creature into this world from your dreams. It has taken life. The more impressive ones… they call to you. Your soul wishes to see it for yourself. Dreamers are —pardon the horribly apropos choice of words—prone to sleepwalking. I have been calling after you for ten minutes now. Nothing I could do would rouse you."

"Oh." She had no memory of hearing his voice. "Well, that's just… great. Anything else I should know about?"

"Most certainly." He offered her his arm like they were a lady and a gentleman on a stroll. She put her hand in the crook of his elbow and couldn't help but smile. The night air was cool, like a crisp fall evening. "I do not think I could list it all if I tried. If you keep your power separate from yourself, you will have to discover it as you go, I fear."

"Thanks."

He ignored her sarcasm. "You are most welcome."

Creatures of every kind chittered and screeched in the darkness. Calls of monsters big and small as they went about their lives. These were not the human-born monsters that came from the Pool of the Ancients. These were hers.

The woods thinned, and there in the center of the clearing

was the thing that had been calling her name. There was what had pulled her out of bed and wished to say hello.

It looked like a shepherd's hook—something you would stick in the ground in your garden to hang a plant or a sign. From it hung a strange glowing insect chrysalis, shimmering and translucent. It resembled the necklace she adored so very much. There was no doubt it was the inspiration for what she saw in front of her. It let off a pulsing light that was hypnotic and stunning. There was a deep and luring humming that increased and faded in volume in time with the glow.

There was a form inside the cocoon, fluttering and squirming. Energetic in its youth. The hook was planted in the ground around it and looked as though it were made of twisted vines.

"How beautiful, my dragonfly. Come, let us get closer. Does it mean to hatch?" He walked toward the glowing pod, and she had to grab his arm and yank him back. He let out a grunt of surprise as she did and turned his masked face down to her to rebuff her. She raised her fingers to her lips to silence him.

For once, he listened.

Leaning down, she picked up a small branch. She tossed it toward the glowing chrysalis.

As the stick hit the ground at the base of where the hook of twisting vines met the field, the clearing suddenly changed. Massive jaws—like a steel bear trap—sprung from the flat ground. The illusion of the beautiful grassy clearing was gone. With a vicious and deafening *snap*, the jaws came up around the glowing hook.

Lydia and Aon were now both on the ground, having thrown themselves backward in shock. She had sensed the danger, but like a dream that she couldn't quite remember the minute after she woke up, she hadn't been *quite* sure of what she was looking at.

The glowing cocoon on the hook had been like the creature's tongue—or lure on the end of an angler fish. It was the bait. The monster was comprised of ninety percent mouth; the giant jaws that folded up around the lure were so thin she could see the light of the glowing lure, like a frog who had swallowed a lightbulb. Its teeth were long, thin, and cruel, very much resembling that of a Venus fly trap if it was made of bone.

The creature made an annoyed *"Scree!"* as it realized it had not caught prey, only a stick. It shimmied to the far side of the clearing from them, its little clawed legs splayed out around it to get as flat to the ground as possible.

Like a manta ray looking for a hiding place under the sand, it began to shuffle itself down low again. Scooting its big, flat body into the dirt and leaves. It swung its massive jaws open wide, and like someone laying down a blanket at a picnic, it folded itself out until it was once more unnaturally flat to the ground.

Even its teeth stretched out to lay flat. The inside of its mouth blended in flawlessly with the leafy ground. And just like that, it was now invisible to the naked eye. The perfect trap.

"Well," Aon said with an impressed air as he stood from the dirt. He offered her a hand and lifted her up easily to her feet. "That is... quite the creature you have made, my love. We will have quite the menagerie of monsters with you at the helm."

Chuckling, she plucked a few leaves off his shoulder and arm. "Thanks. I—"

Something grabbed him around the waist and yanked him suddenly and without warning into the darkness of the forest. One minute he was there, the next he was gone.

Just. Poof.

It had happened so quickly he hadn't even made a noise.

"Aon!"

Q was at her side in an instant, swirling around her, ready for whatever might come.

"My, my… what do we have here?" a female voice said from overhead in the trees. That wasn't good.

Nothing good ever came of somebody talking *above* anybody.

"Worry not for the warlock, he is unharmed. I have only meant to buy us a few moments in private. I simply had to come say hello."

Lydia looked up and screamed.

FOURTEEN

Lydia had a complicated relationship with spiders.

It's not that she hated them per se. It's not that she wanted them all dead. It's not that she was entirely afraid of them either. It was the fact that they were eight-legged, multi-eyed, *startle machines.* They were simply designed to sneak up on you in the worst ways possible.

Nick had always made fun of her, every time a spider would catch her off guard and she would shriek like a small child. Nick called them "spider-bros" and would constantly remind her that without them, she'd have more bugs in her apartment and so on.

If she saw a spider on her terms, everything was fine. She could look at it, acknowledge that yes, that indeed was a spider, and move on with her life. She was even okay with spiders indoors if it was where she wanted it and not somewhere horrible like the shower. But spiders, amongst all their other skills, were very good at sneaking up on her. It was then that she was very much not okay with their existence.

And this spider was no different. It had snuck up on Lydia. And that was really an impressive task, for one simple reason:

It was the size of a fucking house.

The gigantic spider was looming over her, long and delicate legs holding it up in the branches of the twisting trees effortlessly. It was covered in dark purple fur, with shining eyes that looked like amethysts in their faceted surfaces. She had to admit it was beautiful.

For a creepy-as-hell, giant, probably man-eating spider, anyway.

The creature was looming over with the front mandibles of its jaws flexing in and out as it watched her. "Oh. Dear. I am sorry, have I startled you?" It was also apparently able to talk, although the movement of its "mouth" seemed to have nothing to do with it.

She was starting to get used to creatures sneaking up on her and those that could talk by unnatural means.

It had been a woman's voice coming from the massive creature. The tone was warm and didn't seem aggressive. It seemed sincere in the question.

"What gave it away?" Lydia snapped from where she had wound up sitting on the ground again. Q had grown and was now coiled around her protectively and hissing up at the giant arachnid.

"You are not afraid of spiders, are you?" The giant monster sounded terribly amused by the idea.

"Not exactly. I don't like being snuck up on by them. And that's when they're normal sized. That's exactly what you did, and you're freaking enormous." Lydia picked herself up off the ground for the second time in ten minutes and began brushing herself off.

"My sincerest apologies, darling."

"Are you going to eat me?"

"Of course not!" She laughed. The spider began to move, lowering itself down from the branches to stand closer in front of her. As the monster moved, its form began to shift. It morphed and shrank, its body changing until it was that of a woman.

She was naked, at least for a moment until her fur changed into the lower part of a dress, held together with layers of black straps and buckles that shone in the moonlight and jangled as she moved. A silver chain wrapped around her waist and a large, elaborate key hung at her side. Four of her spidery legs shrank and curled around her upper body, doing at least something for the sake of modesty. Not much. But hey.

Honestly, Lydia was also starting to get used to people's questionable ideas of fashion.

The woman's face was covered fully in a purple mask. It was a rich, deep tone etched with symbols inked in dark gray. The visage was smooth, save for eight silver spikes. The lips of the mask were painted in the same dark gray as the writing. The eyes were blacked out, like all the others.

Her exposed skin was a warm chestnut color, setting off the amethyst-colored writing on her skin beautifully. Her long hair was black, woven into a braid traveling down behind her. She might have been of Indian origin, she didn't really know. Without a doubt, she was stunning. Creepy. But like her spider shape, beautiful in her own right.

"This form has become less natural to me over time, I must admit." The former spider was an inch or two taller than Lydia and moved gracefully. Unlike Kamira, who wore a great deal of jewelry and made no sound, this woman jingled as she walked. All the belts and straps of her dress made a noise kind of like a wind chime as she approached. "But I should have known you may react poorly upon meeting me in such a fashion. I did not mean to frighten you."

The woman held out her hand to Lydia with long and gray-painted fingernails. Lydia smiled faintly and met the woman's outstretched hand with her own. "It's all right. I'm starting to get used to how you people say hello. I'm Lydia, nice to meet you. I assume you're Vjo."

"Yes, indeed. I would have come sooner, but my new regent, Maverick, insisted on informing me of what had transpired recently before I arrived. He seems like a nice gentleman. And he has talked of you quite fondly."

Fondly. That means he didn't call me a complete idiot. Probably just mostly an idiot. "You two hadn't met?"

"I was asleep in my crypt when he rose as regent. I believe he may have been just as startled as you to see me." Vjo chuckled and lifted her fingers to the lips of her mask. "I fear he, too, wound up sprawled upon the floor in surprise. It is a pleasure to meet you, dear sister. I extend my apologies for the manner in which you arrived here. More again for the circumstances surrounding your rise as queen."

"Thanks. It's still all catching up with me."

"I can see." Vjo turned her head up toward Q where he was looming over her, some eight or so feet from the ground to the top of his skulled head. His turquoise wings cast the trees near him in a matching glow. "And what a beautiful thing you are."

"Well, shucks. Right back at you, Spider-tits."

"It talks? How charming." Vjo walked closer to Q and surveyed him. "Though its choice of language is questionable, I appreciate the candor. It seems, if I may be so bold to presume, that your power is largely bound up in this creature? That you keep it separate from yourself to lessen the burden upon your mind, likely due to the method of your making?"

"You got it." She was glad she didn't have to explain it. Again. "His name is Q."

"Yo."

"Q. How wonderfully fitting." Vjo seemed to have a better understanding of it than she did, to be honest. But if the House of Words kept all the scholars, it would make sense that Vjo was brilliant. "I can only imagine what damage the power of a king pouring into a mortal mind could have done. You would have gone mad, I am quite sure. It is enough that we must suffer one mad royal. I am glad we do not have two." Vjo tipped her head curiously as she continued to peer up at Q.

It was clear who she was referring to. From the sound of things, she wasn't overly fond of Aon either. Then again, it seemed Lydia was on a very short list of people who didn't outright despise the man.

There was a light giggle from behind her. "Oh, sister, you know he cannot help it. Do not mock the warlock so." The voice was sing-song, cheery and whimsical. "Especially when he is not here to retort!"

Lydia blinked. Who else was here? She turned, and her mouth fell open. There in the clearing, hovering over the glowing lantern that her dreamed monster used as bait, was floating the most beautiful woman she had ever seen.

She was literally hovering in the air, her long and flowing dress curling around her as though she were submerged in water. The layers of her dress were sheer and shimmering in the light of the moons. Her hair reached long past her waist and was a beautiful tone of sapphire blue. It, too, waved around her, floating as though suspended in water.

The woman's skin was a tone of pale blue. Her ears were long and elfin, protruding through her darker blue hair and accenting the Venetian-style mask that she wore. Her mask was full, decorated with pearls, diamonds, and sapphires, and they glinted in the light.

Everything about the woman was elegant, graceful, delicate, and perfect. She was floating over the monster's lantern and was reaching out to touch it. If Lydia had ever wondered what a real-life fairy would look like, that would be it.

"I, uh—" Lydia stammered, afraid she was about to watch her monster chomp off the woman's hand. "I wouldn't. That's a trap."

"I know!" The woman laughed again, musical and joyful. Her voice was higher pitched than Vjo's, but not unpleasantly so.

"Come over here, Ini, and greet our new sister," Vjo half scolded, half cajoled the other woman.

Ini sighed dramatically and turned away from the glowing lantern. But, upon seeing Q, she gasped in awe and flew up to the snake.

Q recoiled his head, startled by the sudden movement. **"Geh!"**

"Oh, my," the woman cried in glee and placed her palms against Q's face. "Look at you!" Ini stroked her hand slowly up Q's face from nose to tip, and Q seemed to want to draw back but was deeply conflicted.

"Lady? Could you not? I mean. That's nice and all, but I—oh, okay. Maybe just—all right—maybe just a little." Q leaned into the woman's touch, and Ini giggled, continuing to slowly stroke Q's head.

"It's... nice to meet you both, I guess?" Lydia said after a pause, not sure how she should feel about the gorgeous woman petting her snake into some weird kind of hypnosis.

"You guess?" Vjo questioned her, sounding a little surprised.

"Sorry. I'm sick of meeting people who're going to hate me." Lydia shoved her hands into her coat pockets like she always did when she wished she could hide.

"Hate you? Why would we ever hate you, sister?" Ini asked from where she hovered. Now, she was lying her head against Q's forehead and was petting the side of the snake's face.

Q was purring. Literally purring. She didn't even know her snake could *make* that noise.

"Everyone else does."

"Oh, you mean Dtu and Edu." Ini laughed. That seemed to be her default state. "Those *brutes!* They do not understand.

Pay them no mind. They can only think with one head at a time, and often I think betwixt the pair!"

"Ini," Vjo scolded the other woman for the crass joke.

Honestly, it took Lydia half a second to get it, and when she did, she couldn't help but grin up at the woman in blue. That only set the beautiful woman in blue giggling again in response.

"But why do you think Dtu hates you?" Vjo asked.

"Dtu hates me because of Aon," Lydia replied, dreading their reactions. "Trust me. He attacked me and made it very clear what he wanted to do to me." Lydia blanched at the memory of the threat. Even if it had just been words, it'd been damn colorful.

"Stupid dog." Vjo sighed heavily.

"But why because of Aon?" From Ini's tone, it was clear she already knew. Lydia cocked an eyebrow up at the woman, who only laughed and conceded the short game. "Oh yes, yes! Maverick told Vjo all about the rumors, and so I have heard as well!"

Ini broke free of Q suddenly—leaving the snake shaking his head as if to clear a fog—as the beautiful woman in the gossamer layered dress floated down to Lydia. Lydia took a step back reflexively as the Queen of Fate was now very close to her. Ini finally set her bare feet on the ground.

The woman in blue reached out and folded her hands behind Lydia's neck, standing close enough to have been a lover. Lydia froze solid, not sure how to react to the woman's nearness. Ini's sapphire hair flowed in the air around them. "Oh sister... you are gorgeous, do you know that? Look at these marks. I have never seen the soul of another royal before." Then, one of her pale hands was on Lydia's cheek, stroking the lines of turquoise ink on her skin. "No wonder Aon is besotted with you!"

"Besotted? Really, Ini? You think the warlock feels such things?" Vjo asked.

"Would *you* not be? Look at her." Ini kept gently stroking her hand over Lydia's cheek. Her touch was tender, and she could see why the snake found it so alluring. The woman had a pull to her. "The warlock has more in his heart than greed and death. I am one of the few who can see this." Her fingers were suddenly on Lydia's mouth, drawing a nail gently along the swell of her lower lip.

Lydia could only stand there, locked wide-eyed in shock, not sure of what to do. She pulled her head back just barely. "I, uh... I take it that you... started all the fairy myths?"

Ini burst into a peal of silvery laughter that sounded like bells ringing. She swirled up into the air away from Lydia, graceful and like a dancer. She hovered now a foot or two off the ground. "The tales of the fae folk? Of creatures that could bring wealth or ruin to any who were careless enough to cross us? Sprites who would lure you off the beaten path and take you to their world to never let them go? I am a touch of fate, wherever it is needed. I have played these parts before, though I am not the only one. We are far more than the stories that are told of us, my beautiful sister. I cannot wait to see what stories they tell of you."

A hand on her shoulder startled her. She had almost forgotten Vjo was standing there. Ini's speech had been captivating. The woman in the purple mask chuckled once. Her voice was warm. "We did not come here to make enemies. We came to meet you and to introduce ourselves. To say that we are glad you are here and not just for the fact you have saved the world from the void. And, if the rumors are true, and you bring that dread warlock some manner of peace to his cold heart? Well. You will do us all a service for which we could never be more grateful."

"What I feel in my cold dead heart is of no business of yours, Vjo." Aon's voice arrived a second before he did. There was a roar of black fire from the center of the clearing, swirling up in an angry pyre. Her new monster screeched and snapped its jaws shut, running off into the thickness of the jungle.

As the fire died down, the man in question was standing there in its wake. Aon tugged on the bottom of his suit coat to straighten it and brushed what looked like a piece of a cobweb from his arm. "That was *immensely* rude, Vjo."

"Oh, do not be angry, dearest," Ini cooed and swirled around Aon, who tried to swat her away like one might a mosquito. She withdrew obediently, but only for a moment. "It was my idea. I wanted to meet Lydia without you hovering so close. We have heard you are mighty protective of her."

"One of us saw fit to take her mortal life. Another has already insulted and threatened her. I will take no chances," Aon growled at the floating woman. "Will you stop circling me like a botfly? I have forgotten how irritating it is to be pestered by you, Ini."

Ini laughed, the musical sound leaving her effortlessly. She swirled back to Q, who watched her approach warily. "Very well. I will entertain myself with my new friend!"

"Seriously, woman, I—Ooh... okay. Okay fine..." Q leaned into her touch and gave in to Ini's petting, pulled in by her hypnotism.

Lydia put her hand over her eyes and sighed.

"Forgive my maltreatment of you, Aon. I hope I did not harm you." Vjo crossed the clearing toward Aon.

"Of course not," Aon defended indignantly. "I would not be so easily injured by your parlor tricks, spider."

"Perfect. No harm was done then, and as such, you have no reason to be angry." Vjo played Aon's ego against him flawlessly. It was apparently a practiced skill, judging by the disgruntled noise he made.

"This world has become crowded again," Aon complained. "I do not believe I am happier for it."

Vjo shook her head and looked back at Lydia. "It seems you

have found some manner of comfort. I would not be so quick to cast your displeasure upon this new state of being. Surely you must greet us with open arms if it means you have someone to share your embrace?"

Aon's clawed gauntlet twitched at his side. Lydia had never seen the man matched in a conversation before. Usually, he always had the upper hand, always twisting other people around his fingers and tugging on their strings. Vjo was clearly Aon's intellectual match, and he might not be so pleased to have someone on the board who could keep him on his toes.

"At least you have neither murdered her, propositioned her, threatened to ravage her to upset me, nor questioned her right to exist. I suppose I will place you one step above the other children." Aon sounded as though he might be on his heels in the conversation, trying to recover his ground.

This was fun to watch. Lydia found herself smirking. "I think Dtu wins the prize for threatening to gang-rape me to spite you, however."

"He *what?* Oh, that foolish mongrel. I will speak to him." Vjo shook her head with a sigh.

"I have not propositioned her yet! I would happily do so," Ini chimed from where she was still floating, petting Q into a state of complete bliss. "But I do not think you are one to share, dear brother of mine."

"I am not," Aon replied.

"You claim her, then?" Vjo asked.

His hand twitched again. "No." Aon's reply sounded deeply reluctant. There really was no point in hiding the truth anymore. "Lydia is of her own mind, heart, and soul. I am... merely stating my personal inclinations."

"If Lydia were to decide to take on another lover, what would you do?" Vjo continued her line of questioning. "If she were to leave you for Rxa or Ini? Or a night with Edu himself, perhaps?"

Aon's metal prosthetic closed into a fist. He had just found himself on the witness stand for the second time in recent memory. "Nothing. That would be her decision to make. She wears no collar. She is not my slave."

"Good," Vjo answered and placed her hand on Aon's chest, stepping in to look up at him. "I am glad to see you have grown during our long repose, warlock."

Aon brushed her hand off his chest irritably. "Yes. We are all met. Perhaps now my private life will be less in focus, now that you have all had your chance to goad and tease me for it."

"So sensitive, Aon!" Ini scolded playfully. "I think perhaps you protest too much. How much it tells me—how much I can see in your mannerisms, darling warlock." Ini abruptly darted from Q, blinking through the air nearly faster than Lydia could track.

"Do not pry into my mind, Ini. You know you are not welcome there. You may cut yourself up on the broken glass, remember," Aon warned darkly as the woman in the gossamer blue dress swirled behind him and draped herself over his shoulders, clasping her arms around him from behind. Aon snarled at Ini but did not strike at her and kept his repose as best he could. At least for the moment.

Ini was a psychic? *Well, shit.*

"Your mind? Why would I do that? I have seen plenty from hers," Ini purred to him, leaning her painted mask close to his metal one.

Yup. Shit.

"Ini," Aon warned, his voice turning into an angry hiss. "Do not dare."

"Hmm? Dare what? What might I say that would bother you so? My goodness," she teased him. Aon swiped at her with his black claw, but the woman in blue retreated too quickly. Ini disappeared.

The secret of where she went didn't last long as Lydia felt a pair of arms wrap around her, as Ini instead draped herself over her now. "I am jealous, sister dear. I had no idea Aon was such a *fantastic* lover. Aon, shame on you! Such talent, so wasted and selfishly kept to yourself for so long." Ini leaned her head into her ear, and she felt the lips of her mask press against the skin of her cheek. "And love, indeed, is what I find here. I am overjoyed. That pauper's soul deserves some happiness after all these thousands of years."

Ini vanished again, reappearing by Q, who now let out a squawk of dismay and shrunk to a much smaller size to hide behind Lydia. **"No! No more magic hands!"**

"Come, sister, I think we have tormented them enough," Vjo called to the woman in blue before turning to face Lydia. "It has been a great pleasure to meet you. I hope you will come to see me at my library in short order. I would love to show you the marvels we have collected."

Lydia nodded weakly, not quite sure what the hell was happening. These people were like runaway trains—just screaming through the station at breakneck speed with no care for the people who were standing on the platform.

Ini swirled up higher into the air and clapped her hands excitedly. "We are all awake once more. For the first time in fifteen hundred years, our people are whole. We should celebrate! Let us hold an event to commemorate this wondrous moment!"

Aon sighed darkly. "Charming. Another 'party.'"

"Oh pooh—" Ini scolded down at the warlock. "You are ever much the spoilsport."

"Listen to my words carefully, you vapid, air-headed excuse for an imp, I will not have you—" Aon began but was interrupted as Ini was literally blah-blah-blahing him. "Will you—" Aon broke off, frustrated. "Immature child!" Aon finally roared, which ended Ini's taunting into a fit of laughter.

"Ini. Let us leave before you send him into an apoplectic

rage not one day after we have woken," Vjo scolded the woman in blue far more firmly. "Farewell, Aon. Farewell, Lydia."

"Nice to meet you..." Lydia said, trailing off—still amazed at what she was witnessing. Ini treated Aon like a grumpy older brother, needling him for sport. And damn, she was good at it.

"Bye now!" Ini disappeared in a swirl of blue light. Vjo bowed and was gone in a twisting net of spider silk that came up from the ground, and when it retreated, she was gone.

Aon growled loudly in frustration and buried his head in his hands. His shoulders were tense and locked up to his ears. The man was furious at having been so utterly mistreated in two different ways by two different women.

Strangely though, they were kinder to him than Dtu or Edu. Kinder by far. It was clear they respected him, in their own ways. And Ini, in some messed-up way, seemed *happy* for them. She seemed to honestly *like* Aon.

Walking up to him, she gently grasped his wrists. For a moment, he did not allow her to pull his hands away from his masked face. "Why did I bother trying to save this world?" he complained quietly in an angry hiss. "Remind me."

She couldn't help but smile at his melodrama and finally convinced him to lower his hands. She wrapped them around her waist and stepped into him, clasping her own hands behind his neck. "Because you'd die with it."

"It might be worth it. At least the void is quiet."

Reaching up onto her toes, she kissed the spot of his mask over which his lips were. "Then you couldn't hear the sound of your own voice either." Instantly, she could feel the tightness in his shoulders grow slack. When she dropped back off her toes, he leaned down to rest his forehead atop hers.

"That would be a crime against the cosmos."

Running her thumb along the back of his neck, she smiled as he pulled her in tighter in response. The man really was incorrigible. And honestly? She couldn't complain. "I think I need a drink. C'mon."

"Another firm benefit of taking my mask off around you," Aon observed as he let Lydia lead them from the clearing back toward his home. "I am beginning to see your logic behind not wearing one."

"You should give it up."

"Hah! Never." That was apparently the most ridiculous thing Aon had ever heard.

"Why not?"

"And risk damaging my beautiful face?" It was a joke, overstating his own ego for the sake of humor. "Hardly."

"Mmhm. And you have no idea why the others don't like you." Lydia laughed.

"None at all. I am perfectly likable. It is their shortcomings, not mine, that are to blame."

"You're impossible." Suddenly, the ground disappeared out from under her, and she found herself upended, pinned on her back to a soft surface. She thrashed, startled. He was over her, pinning her to wherever he had dumped them. His arms had caught her wrists and had them pressed fast over her head.

"I am. And you adore it," Aon said, clearly quite proud of himself. He had skipped the walking, and the drinks, and dropped them back into his bed. "Say it."

"You know I do." She didn't even bother getting angry anymore. This was just Aon and his games.

"Say you will always be mine. Say you will never leave me for another." Aon's shoulders were abruptly tight again, and his demeanor changed without warning. His words were not threatening. They were not demanding or domineering. They weren't making her his territory.

He sounded... afraid.

Vjo's and Ini's teasing had honestly bothered him.

"Aon? What's wrong?"

"Tell me that the moment someone vies for your heart—someone kind, and beloved of others. Someone safer than me, and not the *scum of the ground itself*—"

"Aon, stop. We've been through this—" Pulling her hands out of his grasp, she reached up and gently took Aon's mask off his face before dropping it onto the cushions next to her.

His expression was exactly just as she worried it was—wide-eyed and verging on the edge of madness.

What could she expect? The man had spent five thousand years thinking that what they had was impossible. A few reassurances and pats on the head were not going to stop his paranoia. She braced herself for having this conversation with him many, many times.

"Stop." She cradled his face in her hands. "I'm right here. I'm not going anywhere. I love you for you and everything that comes with it. I'm not some idiot child hiding in your coat, afraid of the dark. I'm not going to jump into somebody's arms just because they offer me a safer harbor. Screw 'safe.' Safe is boring, and around here, it's a lie, anyway."

Without warning, he sank down and laid half atop her, half next to her. Burying his head into the crook of her neck, he clutched her close to him. His voice was a ragged whisper. "Forgive me. I have never had anything so worth taking from me. The mere thought of it—I could not withstand the loss."

Gently rolling him over until he was on his back and she was atop him, she kissed him, pouring into it everything she felt for him. Lydia felt the rest of the tension in him melt away.

When she finally broke the kiss, his eyes were shut, his face smooth and free of the pain that had been there a moment before. She kissed his ear and whispered to him. "All the rest of this world could burn away, and I would be here with you."

"Do not make promises you cannot keep..."

"What?"

He opened his eyes, his expression far away and distant. For a split second, she almost didn't recognize him. "I remember this world when it was nothing more than dust."

"I was just trying to—"

"I know." The moment was gone. He smirked sardonically at himself. "And I have ruined it, as I always do."

There was one way she knew to break him of his mood. She lowered her head to his ear again and whispered, "Then shut your mouth or use it for something better."

His arm banded around her lower back, and she felt him shift eagerly beneath her. His other hand tilted her face toward his, catching her chin between his thumb and forefinger.

Mischief glinted in his dark eyes as he accepted her invitation gladly and pressed his lips against hers.

FIFTEEN

Lydia felt the tips of Aon's claws slowly rake down her back. She gasped against his lips, arching, feeling four lines of stinging welts start to form against her bare skin.

He'd removed her clothes with a thought.

At some point, she'd be annoyed about that.

But she was too busy moaning to really care at the moment.

His other hand was tangled in her hair, keeping her from pulling away, as he trailed his claws down her back to her rear, before cupping one of the globes of her ass and squeezing, being careful not to break the skin with the pointed tips of his fingers.

With the pressure of his hand, he pushed his hips up against hers, desperately seeking friction. Their bouts of lovemaking were often about games. About exchanges of power. About new explorations.

But not this time.

Something about this time felt different, but at first, she couldn't put a finger on what it was.

His hand fisted in her hair, yanking her head back away from him, arching her back farther. She hissed at the stinging in her scalp—but the twinge of pain only tangled with the arousal that was burning in her like gas on the flame. It was rougher than he usually was.

Aon was usually *restrained*. Careful. Measured in his strength.

But that wasn't like him.

Then she saw it. There it was, in those smoldering dark eyes of his—the dangerous glint that she had seen a half dozen times since she'd met him. He grimaced. "You should go, dragonfly. I may not quite yet be myself in this moment."

His voice was husky and thick, clearly on the edge of losing control.

God. She didn't know if she had ever wanted to see someone lose control so badly before in her life as she did right in that moment. She knew Aon was dangerous when he snapped—she'd seen him trash furniture, seen him break things —but she wasn't so easily damaged anymore now that she was a queen.

Right?

"I'm not afraid of you." She relaxed into his grip, even just a little.

His expression turned into a faint sneer. But his eyes flicked to her lower lip. She saw the hunger there. The desperate need. "Oh, my poor, foolish little dreamer... what a silly thing to say."

The world spun around her abruptly as he sat up with such speed that she didn't even have time to make a noise. She finally managed to yelp as her shoulders hit the mattress, but she was still moving. She was now on her stomach on the bed.

Pain stung her scalp as he yanked her head back by her hair. When she cried out, he slung something between her lips, and tied it behind her head. A gag of some kind—fabric strap, but she couldn't tell what.

"I think I would rather do without listening to you when

you change your mind and beg me for mercy tonight, forgive the indignity."

Snarling, she went to pull the gag out of her mouth, but didn't make it far.

He caught her wrists, yanking them behind her back and lashed them together. "Ah-ah. Now. That's better, don't you think?" His human hand came down on her bare ass with a *smack* that sent her wailing.

The groan that left him was one of pure bliss. He kneaded the spot he had just offended. "You have been spared this part of me, dragonfly, haven't you? The stories that have been told of my *predilections.*"

His hand came down on her ass with another *smack.* She bit down hard on the gag and buried her face into the sheets of the bed, muffling the cry.

"No. I want to hear you scream into the silk." He yanked her head back up by the hair. "Scream for me, *little dreamer!*" His hand came down on her ass again, harder than before, and this time it stayed, and squeezed the spot where he had struck her, finding a pressure point.

She gave him what he wanted.

The weight of his body was on top of hers a second later, and he was kissing the back of her shoulder. "Beautiful thing... perfect thing..." His hand was stroking her abused skin, before slipping between her legs.

And finding that he wasn't the only one that apparently enjoyed this kind of foreplay.

Well, hell.

There was another thing she learned about herself in Under.

The laugh that left him would have made Satan himself blush.

"Lydia, Lydia, Lydia... I believe the Ancients must have

picked you out for me. There is no other explanation." There was a strange lilt in his voice. He was absolutely not really all there. "I will praise them until the end of my days if that is true."

He plunged two fingers inside of her, thrusting deep. She moaned as the sudden invasion sent arcs of pleasure ripping up her spine. But it seemed he wasn't content there, as he then used that leverage to guide her up onto her knees.

She whimpered, forced to go along with it, until she was face-down, ass-up on the sheets, unable to support her weight with her arms tied behind her back. There wasn't much she could see of him, and certainly nothing she could do as he shifted to kneel behind her.

Crack! His human hand came down on her ass again, this time on the other side. "Lest it feel neglected, of course."

The cries she made into the gag mixed with moans as he went back and forth between strikes and soothing touches. But he soon wandered his hand to her core, sending his fingers delving back into her body, pistoning lazily inside of her as his clawed hand began to trail over her body, the knifepoints digging into her skin to leave welts at random intervals.

Now, it was her turn to wonder if she was going insane.

His thumb pressed against the sensitive ball of nerves at her core and she twitched, wailing in ecstasy as she nearly peaked, but he backed off before she reached the crescendo. Keeping her just at that point, but not quite.

This was about suffering, after all.

And not all suffering was about pain.

"My beautiful, perfect little dreamer," he murmured down to her as he dragged a claw along her back, drawing a stinging welt along the skin. "My Queen of All, my chosen bride. How we could rule together, you and I..."

What?

"If you prove resilient enough, that is." He pulled his

fingers from her, both his hands shifting to grip her hips. "Shall we see? Hmm?"

That was all the warning she had before he yanked her back against him and rammed himself into her to the hilt in one fell swoop.

For the second time that night, he heard her scream against the gag he put between her lips. And it wouldn't be the last time.

He began to rut her then, his body impacting hers like a machine, relentless and unforgiving. Each strike of his body sent her to a new height that made her wonder if she would ever come down.

There was no pulling his punches, now. There was no measured, careful restraint. This was every ounce of power the King of Shadows owned, poured into every thrust of his body into hers, as if he were trying to ensure that she would never leave this moment.

As if he were trying to drag her down into madness with him.

And God, if this was madness, she wanted it to never stop.

* * *

Aon could not quite focus through the feeling of her. Like being lost in the darkness of an unfamiliar room, but with someone beside him.

He was fully lost inside his own mind.

Madness had claimed him.

But she was there with him.

She refused to leave his side, no matter how hard he tried to shoo her away. And now... now? Now, he felt the bliss of her, felt the ecstasy, heard her cries of utter pleasure and pain as he tangled them together as one.

He could see them, feel them. See her, lashed and gagged,

on her knees on his sheets before him. And he was rutting her like a wild animal, relentlessly teaching her what an immortal king of Under was capable of. Showing her what true strength was like.

Showing her how much restraint his sanity had been showing her.

And how she moaned in joy. In release. How her body tightened and spasmed around him in waves, accepting him— begging for more.

She had not only surrendered to this...

She had *wanted* this.

Wanted to embrace him in his madness.

Wanted to show him that there was no part of his soul that she would not love. Could not love. And the only regret he had in his fractured mind was that he would not be able to admire the bruises in the morning for that they would heal too quickly.

I truly am a monster.

He picked her up by the forearms, forcing her up off the bed, using her weight to pull her even harder back against his relentless impacts, finding a way to seemingly core himself deeper into her body.

The agonized, overwrought wailing from her as she hung her head was like the chorus of archangels to mortals.

Beautiful.

Perfect.

His.

He pulled her up into his arms as he could not take anymore. Ramming himself as far as he could go inside, he felt his own body tighten and surge as he buried his head into her shoulder and let out a roar of release.

Blissfully, everything went black for a time. He did enjoy it when his mind was kind enough to give him a reprieve. But, sometimes it could be quite inconvenient. For he had just done... a terrible and violent thing.

And now Lydia was likely to abandon him, having suffered it.

When he woke, he expected he would do so alone.

* * *

She wasn't sure what the make and model was of the goddamn sex truck that hit her, but she hoped somebody got the license plate so she could make a police report.

While she'd known kind of what to expect from making love to Aon-the-madman, she hadn't quite expected *that*.

Lydia groaned. That was the best she could do. Her arm was slung over her eyes, as she laid there on Aon's bed, and just... yep. Just laid there.

Aon had untied her, taken the gag off, staggered to the bathroom, come back with a warm washcloth, and then she'd honestly lost track of them.

Sex truck impact and all.

When she finally felt like she could form thoughts and *maybe* words, she dropped her arm and lifted her head. He was sitting on the edge of the bed, his back to her, head lowered.

"Hey."

He didn't answer.

"Hey."

Still nothing.

Fighting the urge to kick him in the back of the head, she sighed. Shifting to kneel behind him on the bed, cringing a little bit as she moved, she reached out and put a hand on his shoulder.

He flinched, but didn't pull away.

"Aon?"

Nothing.

"I'm here." She stroked his back. "I'm here, I'm not going anywhere."

"You'll leave me. You're lying." His voice was quiet, raspy. It broke her heart.

"I'm not lying. Right now, I'm not lying." She folded her arms around him and hugged him, resting her chin on his shoulder. "I don't know what'll happen in the future. But I'm not lying."

"I hurt you." His eyes were shut.

"Yeah but. Only in a kinky way, and not a lot. And." She paused, and wrinkled her nose. "I liked it?"

That made him laugh, just a little. Success.

"I love you, my little dreamer." He leaned his head against hers.

That phrase was strange to her for some reason, but she couldn't put a finger on why at first. "You've never called me that before."

There was a faint, strange smile on his face. "And maybe I never will again. I doubt I will remember any of this come the morning."

SIXTEEN

Edu looked down at his little Evie, who was doing her best to help fasten the buckles of his armor. Dtu had wished to spar with him, and he readily and happily accepted the challenge. Both he and the King of Moons felt woefully out of practice on the battlefield. Now that the wolf had risen, he had his old training partner once more.

Evie insisted on helping him as much as possible. She felt the need to be useful. It was yet another reason that his heart bloomed in the presence of the redheaded spitfire. He was reminded of a line from a human theatrical piece—*and though she be but little, she is fierce.*

The House of Words collected all written works that they could muster during their times where Earth and Under aligned. While Edu had little interest in attending the performances they staged, it was not to say that he had never been forced to go. He remembered that work in particular as being spectacularly dull. No one had died.

Evie was swearing and muttering to herself as she tried to fasten the buckle that was just beneath his shoulder blade. Edu couldn't help but begin to chuckle at her over-dramatic reaction to something so simple.

In truth, she made for an abysmal squire. But he patiently humored the young woman's efforts. He did not mind. After all, he sincerely enjoyed her company. A mis-buckled piece of armor or two was an excellent price to pay for her nearness.

"Stop laughing!" Evie slapped her hand on the metal plates of his arm. "Moving doesn't help, and you're shaking it all around."

That was enough to send Edu into a real laugh. He turned and scooped her up, lifting her easily into his arms. Edu knew how to control his strength such as he did not crush her against the metal of his armor.

She let out a yelp and a shrieking giggle as she now found herself up off her feet with her head, for once, even with his. Perhaps Dtu could wait a little longer. The wolf would certainly understand.

"Silly hunk of metal." She leaned her arms on his shoulders. "Now how'm I supposed to do that clasp from up here?"

"Let me help!"

That was a voice he had not heard in a very long time.

Edu's heart *soared*.

Evie let out a loud *"eep"* and squirmed in his grasp, vehemently insisting she be put down. Edu obeyed and placed her back on her feet. The redhead was nearly cowering, wide-eyed and looking behind him to the figure who must have appeared there.

Edu went to turn and face the sound of the voice but felt a pair of hands tugging on the undone buckle, so he waited. It was clasped within seconds, as the woman who had done the deed was far more skilled and dexterous than little Evie.

A pair of arms lazily draped themselves around his shoulders. It was an impossible task for anyone—that was, of course, unless they could fly. "Hello, my dearest stranger."

Edu turned within the delicate grasp of the woman and looked up at the beautifully painted mask of Ini. Her sapphire hair flowed around her as though caught in the current of a stream. He reached up and hugged her tightly to him, caring far less for her comfort than Evie's. Ini was hardly so fragile.

Ini laughed brightly, the sound like tinkling crystal glasses ringing in the air and hugged him back.

Edu felt a pang in his heart and realized suddenly, all at once, how lonely he had been. Tears welled in his eyes behind his mask.

How empty this world had been without the others there to fill it.

By the Ancients, how he had missed them *all.*

He and Ini had been close friends, and she had been the first to succumb to the hopelessness that had come with the press of the void. Edu shouldered the pain of her loss without a thought. It was not until this moment upon seeing her that he realized how keenly he had felt her absence.

"I have missed you too, my dear red dragon." Ini ran her hand along the forehead of his mask, stroking his face as much as she could. "How have you fared in these long years? Now that I think of it, how long has it been?"

"Twelve hundred years have passed since you went to your tomb." Edu answered her silently. Ini was a psychic and could read his mind. All the others guarded themselves from her intrusions, but Edu did not care. He had nothing to hide from anyone, a matter in which he took great pride.

"My goodness. No wonder my room is so dusty!" Ini giggled.

Edu shook his head and found himself grinning beneath his mask. *"It is beyond wonderful to see you."*

"And you, warrior." Ini tilted her head to the side and looked over his shoulder. She seemed to perk up suddenly. "Ah! And who is this little one?"

Evie let out another squeak and stammered, high-pitched and nervous. "I—I—should go!" Evie made a beeline toward the door.

"No, no, come here." Ini vanished out of Edu's arms and appeared in front of Evie, blocking her path. Wide-eyed and terrified, Evie pulled up short as Ini settled her feet down onto the solid ground to meet the girl eye-to-eye.

Edu merely watched, knowing Ini meant the girl no harm. The Queen of Fate was an endlessly curious thing and had little respect for the average distance a person wished to keep around themselves. Especially strangers.

Ini reached out her pale blue hands and placed her palms against Evie's face, cradling the girl's head in her hands. "How stunning... Oh, Edu, you have yourself quite the gem. Hello, Evie. I am Ini. It is such a joy to meet you."

"I—uh—" Evie squeaked. "I didn't tell—tell you—my name—"

"I know," Ini said through a breath and stepped into the girl closer. Edu tilted his head slightly, suddenly wondering what it would be like to watch the two women make love. And then to join in, himself. "I read minds, my darling. And on that topic—Edu, I see you have not changed." Ini laughed and seemed unoffended at his private pondering.

Edu shrugged. *Do you fault me?*

How wonderful it was to speak to someone—*anyone*—for himself. Edu adored Ylena. His empath was joined to his soul, now and forever. But the woman was always a barrier between him and his intentions. He had learned to speak without words as best as a man could, but still he often found himself frustrated.

"Of course not." Ini was now stroking Evelyn's fiery red hair, tangling the tight curls around her fingers as he so often found himself doing. Evie's eyes were drifting shut as Ini's power worked its way through the girl like warm wine. "I would wonder the same if I were you."

Ini the siren, the seducer, the destroyer. How many souls had she pulled to the grave with her song? The trap was inescapable for most, and Evie was no exception. Ini pulled the young girl into her arms, and Evie's head fell gently against her shoulder, lulled into her embrace.

Edu felt a twinge of sudden desire. *"Now you are just teasing me."*

Ini giggled and gently pulled away from Evie before disappearing. Evie shook her head, clearing the fog that had settled over her, and blinked in confusion. But Ini's goal was achieved —the young woman was no longer afraid. Evie rubbed her eyes and knew well enough to stay quiet, lest she bring more attention to herself.

Ini said from the air, invisible for the moment, "You know me, I cannot help it. Though this is not why I have come, though perhaps we will indulge ourselves later." Ini reappeared next to Edu, hovering off the ground once more. "I came to see you. I came to greet my old friend after so long and see how time has treated you."

"And how has it?" He wondered how she might see the passage of time in him. He could not see it himself, as he had lived every day of it.

"You feel weary. A tired guardian against the shadows, eager for a rest by the fire." Ini reached out and ran her fingers over the horns of his battle helm. "But other than that? You are whole. Unchanged. A rock barely weathered by time. I find the warlock far more affected than you."

"You have been to see him?" Edu was almost jealous that he had not been first.

"Vjo and I went to see the new darling dreamer. He is ever beside her, it seems. So, yes, I suppose so, but not on purpose." She folded the fingers of her hand under his chin. Her touch was like the whisper of the wind. "Isn't she quite the marvel? The Ancients have once more worked their great wisdom to bring us someone so... perfect."

Edu could not know if he would describe Lydia as perfect. After all, she turned down his own advances and somehow inexplicably chosen the warlock instead.

"You are jealous! I suppose you are so very rarely rejected, it must spurn you deeply to think that she found his embrace more appealing. Although, from what I have seen in her mind, Aon is a talented lover. Not merely the purely violent and selfish cretin we all assumed him to be."

"I do not wish to know such things."

"Though perhaps only with Lydia," Ini continued, unaffected by Edu's request for her to stop. Ini was accustomed to ignoring such requests from all comers. "He is different. Perhaps he finds pleasure in her that stretches past his love of other's suffering. I find him much changed in the time I have been gone. I am so very pleased. That is why I have come. Other than, of course, to see my dragon."

"How so?"

"Dtu does not trust me. But he trusts you. Work with him to gentle his nature toward Lydia. Coax the wolf to apologize to her. She is fearful of what we mean to her enough as it is. I will not have infighting so soon into our new world. I know of his pain over Qta, and for that, I weep for him still. But she is not at fault."

"But her lover is."

"Yes. I know. But he has paid for his crime. I feel from that man a contentment, a peace... a calm that I have never seen in him. Not once. Think of what a steady-hearted Aon may lend this world of ours? We must convince the wolf not to meddle, not to trouble the girl any longer. The glass is delicate. I wish for it not to break."

"You speak of meddling, Ini. That is all you ever do," Edu

rebuked. *"You are all too happy to play matchmaker between Lydia and the corpse."*

"I needn't play matchmaker. I merely wish to protect the bond before it is too weak to strengthen." Ini wrapped her arms back around Edu's neck. "Think on this, then—if Aon waged a war that destroyed our world in the search of love, what will he do if it is taken away?"

Edu felt a cold dread run down his spine. Edu did not wish to learn what form the warlock's wrath may take in such an instance. In that, she was correct. *"I have asked Dtu to be more forgiving of Lydia. As has Kamira, in far less kind a method. I will keep at my badgering of the boy."*

"He does owe her an apology. Attacking her, issuing such vile threats." Ini sighed thoughtfully. "I will do what I can as well. We will outnumber him. He can be convinced."

Edu nodded. Dtu was not a cruel man. He was emotional, prone to outbursts like an unpredictable animal. But he was not unkind. Dtu would adjust to Lydia's existence in their world. But it would take time. Time that may prove to be damaging, if they were not careful.

An idea sprung to him. *"I will wager him in our duel. If he can beat me, I will help him hurt Lydia. If Dtu loses, he must apologize to the girl and cease his aggressions."*

Ini giggled. She knew quite well that Edu would never lose a sparring match. For he had never once stood in battle against another and been felled. But the temptation of the prize would be too much for Dtu not to accept. "Devious, my dragon. You have spent too much time in the sole presence of the warlock. You are learning."

"Ugly words, elf." But he found himself smiling beneath his mask, all the same.

Ini tapped her fingers against the chin of his mask. "You asked me how time had changed you. I see it now. The man I knew when I retreated into my slumber was angry, broken, and sorrowful. Full of wrath and wrath alone. I see before me a man with... hope. Forgiveness, even. I find you not worn by time but tempered by it. Loneliness nearly shattered the warlock—but in you, it has built you stronger. Now, the silence is finally over, and we are whole."

Edu circled his arms around the woman and held her to him in a tight hug. Yes, the silence was over. The world had felt so empty, so desolate without the others with him. Edu was happy for the return of the chatter and noise of his fellows. Of a world finally restored.

Hope. It was a thing he had not considered for so very long. Their world had been dying. It had been withering away before his eyes, slipping through his fingers like sand. But Ini was never wrong. The Queen of Fate could see through him like a pane of glass. For now that she reflected upon what had been burning in his heart, kindled by the return of a dreamer, he could see it as well.

He only prayed it would last.

* * *

A few days had passed in peace and quiet. Lydia was still not letting herself believe it was real. Or that it'd last. But shit, if it wasn't *tempting*.

Slowly but surely, Aon was even coming to adjust to her home and the nest of pillows she used as a bed. The architecture of the Temple of Dreams seemed to have finally settled down, choosing something that was about eighty percent Boston, twenty percent Aztec temple. It fit.

That morning when she woke, she hadn't been able to find the warlock. He hadn't left her a note as he always did if he had business to attend to, so he must be around somewhere. Standing up, she yawned, brushed her hair, dressed, and went to go find him. It didn't take long. He was reclining on the massive stone steps of her home, his legs stretched out in front of him and his elbows propped up on the ledge behind him.

It took her a moment to realize why. The reflecting pool and the field in front of them was alight with what must have been millions of the little blinking insects, in a thousand different colors.

The lights from the insects glinted off the reflecting pool. It created the illusion that there were millions more. Mixing with the watery mirroring of the stars and moons overhead, it was stunning.

Lydia walked down the steps toward him, and he leaned forward at her approach. She sat behind him on the higher step and pulled him back to rest between her legs, leaning his back against her chest. Clasping her arms around his shoulders, she smiled down at him as he hooked his own arms over her thighs and reclined into her contentedly. He felt natural to her now—like this was where she was supposed to be.

She rested her chin atop his head and looked out at the fantastical light show in front of them. It felt like the first time she had seen a planetarium as a kid. "Wow."

"Ineloquent but effective." He ran the fingers of his metal clawed hand across the back of hers where it rested against his chest. The tips gave her goosebumps. "How did you sleep?"

"Good, and you?"

"I despise that bed of yours still. I wake with my leg in pins and needles half the time." He paused, and for a moment, she was worried what he was about to say. "I have never known peace like that which I have when I am with you."

Lydia laughed at his melodrama. "Jesus Christ, Romeo."

"I am not known for my subtlety. Though this newfound calm has come with an unfortunate side effect."

"Oh?"

"I am sitting here, *watching insects.* And finding I have

nothing else I desire to do more. What is wrong with me? What poison have you sunk into my veins?"

"It's called being happy, asshole," Q interjected as he swirled in the air overhead and then settled down on the stairs next to them. **"I know this is a novel concept in that busted-up head of yours."**

"Your commentary is not welcome." Aon didn't even turn his head to glance at the snake.

"But you're gonna get it, anyway. So, what're you going to do now that you don't need to be cutting people up? Stamp collecting? Baking? Knitting, maybe? Oh! I know. Gardening. You come with a built-in trowel with that stupid hand of yours."

The warlock sighed and went silent, not wanting to encourage the snake in his goading. Q snickered at his victory and fluffed up his feathers to settle in. He also seemed to enjoy watching the blinking bugs around them. If one drifted too close, he snapped his jaws at it playfully.

Lydia couldn't help but smile. She loved watching the two tease each other. It was mostly benign, after all. She turned her head down and kissed the top of Aon's head. "I still don't know what happens now. Between Rxa's paranoia and Dtu's, I'm still worried someone is going to start something." Lydia interlaced her fingers with his metal ones. The claws of his hand didn't worry her as much as they used to. He had astonishing control over them and had never once pricked her with the blades by accident. Plenty of times on purpose. But never once without intending to.

"I find myself in a similar state of mind," he observed. "You have not known freedom since the moment you arrived here. Every second of your days has been consumed by the chaos brought upon you by others. I, in turn, have never once not... had an agenda to pursue. This is a rare moment of quiet for both of us."

"Don't jinx it, shithead."

A roar of fire appeared at the base of the stairs. The giant swirl of flame curling up into the darkness. As it cleared, there stood Edu in full armor. Ylena at his side, and… Dtu. The enormous wolf was hunched beside him.

"See? You jinxed it."

Lydia and Aon both shot to their feet. In an instant, she was ready for a fight. But Edu shook his head and raised his hand as if to calm them both.

"Master Edu insists that we are not here for a brawl," Ylena said.

Dtu was growling like a spurned dog, hunched down low to the ground, his head lowered.

What the hell was happening?

Edu turned to Dtu and gestured him forward. The werewolf growled louder. Edu… smacked the werewolf upside the head. Just whacked him like a college drinking buddy and pointed him forward.

Dtu let out a long, rumbling sigh and obeyed. The werewolf king stepped forward until he was at the base of the stairs leading up to her home and cast a glowing, green pinprick of an eye up at her. "I am sorry for attacking you. I am sorry for what I said."

Aon burst out in a laugh. Rolling her eyes, it was her turn to hit a king. She smacked him in the arm, far less roughly than Edu had hit the shifter. The warlock fell quiet obediently and crossed his arms across his chest.

"Let me guess. You lost a bet." Lydia asked the werewolf, just as incredulous as Aon, even if she managed to be slightly more polite about it.

Dtu hesitated and let out another grumble. "Yes."

Lydia took a few steps down the stairs toward him. More to prove that she wasn't afraid of the sulking werewolf than anything else. "Then it doesn't count, dog."

"No, it is truth. I am sorry. I just wasn't going to say it. That is the bet I lost." Dtu sniffed the air, grumbled, and shook his head. The fur on his shoulders raised for a moment, and he seemed to fight with his urge to lash out at her. But he calmed himself and hunkered down further. "It is not your fault that Qta is dead. It is the warlock's crime. That is not your fee to pay, even if you and he are..." Dtu dug his claws into the ground and then growled low. "Lovers." He said the word with such disgust she was surprised he didn't spit when he said it. Maybe he couldn't.

"I get it. You don't have to like me. And you certainly don't have to forgive him." She finished walking toward the werewolf. Q was perched on her shoulder, still ready for trouble if it started. "I'd be livid if I were you. I can't even imagine what it's like. I won't pretend to say that I understand the pain you went through—are going through. You're five thousand years old." Letting out a sad laugh, she shook her head. "I'm twenty-eight. I'm just a kid. A stupid, insignificant blip on the radar compared to all of you. I can't even wrap my head around what you've all been through, what you've all put each other through."

She paused to gather her thoughts. "But, that said, I won't apologize for what I am or for what I feel. I know Aon can be an unmitigated asshole—" She paused as the werewolf huffed a laugh before continuing. "And I can't make what he's done right. I wish I could. I don't want to go into this with enemies, Dtu. I really don't want to have to worry about the goddamn family dog barking at me every time I come into the room."

"You speak plainly. I respect that." Dtu lifted himself up from where he had hunched down. "You fight your own battles. I will, then... recognize you as a queen. I will not hunt you or speak threats. Not until you give me a reason you have earned on your own."

"And I'll forgive you for attacking me and threatening to maim me. Deal?"

"Deal." Dtu turned away from her without another word and began to leave before glancing at Edu. "Was that satisfactory?" The big man in his armor was chuckling, and he nodded once at the wolf. "Good." And with that, Dtu disappeared and was gone.

Edu turned to go.

"Wait," she called after him.

Edu hesitated and looked to her with a curious tilt of his head.

Walking up to him, she stuck out her hand in front of her. "Thanks for that."

The warrior in red looked down at her hand for a moment, as if in disbelief. Just when Lydia was about to take her hand back in embarrassment, he clasped his hand to hers and shook it firmly. "Master Edu says you are very welcome, Queen of Dreams," Ylena said from his side, smiling.

He released her hand, took two steps back with his empath, and in a swirl of red fire disappeared.

"Unmitigated asshole?"

Lydia nearly jumped out of her skin at the sound of Aon's voice so close to her ear. "Damn it, Aon."

Arms circled around her, keeping her from turning around. "Is that what you believe?"

She would have been more threatened if the tone in his voice wasn't so playful. Dark, yes, but teasing. "Yup. You are."

"Hmf!" He gripped her tighter, digging his claws into her hip, almost breaking the skin. She gasped despite herself, unable to help the rush that brought. "I must work harder to earn this dubious reputation."

SEVENTEEN

Ini made good on her threat.

The House of Fate and its queen would not be stopped in its seemingly singular-minded goal—to throw a city-wide, Under-wide celebration.

A festival and a brand-new yearly holiday would be created to commemorate the retreat of the void, the return of the House of the Dreamers, and the reawakening of the sleeping kings and queens.

Under was whole again for the first time in fifteen hundred years. Ini insisted this was cause for an absolute bender of a party. It would stretch on for a week, Aon had warned Lydia. The main part of the festival was to be held in the capital city of Yej, out in the courtyard where the marketplace had been and at the foot of the Cathedral of the Ancients.

It was the same marketplace she had fled before Edu had killed her. But where she had been gifted the blinking false-insect necklace that she still wore. To say that she had mixed feelings about the courtyard of Yej was to put it lightly.

Tonight was the night that the festival would kick off. Everyone would be gathered in attendance at the gates of the

Cathedral of the Ancients. She had dressed up for the occasion. Everyone had. Aon looked damn good in his elegant tuxedo, the print an eccentric and gothic damask that was black-on-black silk print.

She had donned a dark turquoise coat printed with black feathers. Together with a short, silk turquoise dress over black leggings, and knee high dark turquoise boots, she hoped she looked the part. It felt like she was wearing a Halloween costume. She still felt ridiculous, but compared to all the other kings and queens, she looked dull. At least Q made her fit in a bit more.

Her nerves were on high alert as they gathered around in the sanctuary of the Cathedral of the Ancients, the main portion of the grand gothic cathedral. She had never seen it before, with its arching white stone walls and looming statues in the darkness. It was like everything else in Under—morbid but beautiful.

While she'd been in the cathedral before, she'd only been in the lower portions.

One statue drew her toward it. Seeing the swath of turquoise that hung under the altar before it, she knew why. This was "her" Ancient. The one from which she pulled her power. It was a gangly creature, with gaping black holes for eyes and a pointed, cruel grin. It was fascinating as it was horrifying.

She stood before it and couldn't help but feel like the statue was alive somehow. That the thing the carved stone was meant to represent was within it, staring back at her. Grinning its cruel, sadistic smile at her knowingly.

All the altars had candles on them, burning and lit. All the colors had souls in their house to tend to them. This one didn't. The candles upon it were unlit, dusty and old. This Ancient only had her for a "servant." Lydia smirked. *Poor son of a bitch. You got stuck with me.*

"You should light a candle." A hand fell on her shoulder. It was Rxa. "Out of respect, if nothing else."

She looked back at the statue of the eldritch, horrible monster that she was now tied to. "What does it care? That's the thing that always got me about religion. All powerful god, right?" She gestured up at it. "And it wants me to light a fucking candle? Why?"

His hand left her shoulder. "Perhaps it simply would appreciate the gesture of good will. Of gratitude for its gifts."

"Gifts. Right." Turning from the statue, she faced the faintly glowing angel. "Sorry. Maybe someday I'll be more thankful for all this." She gestured at the marks on her face. "But something tells me I'm here to save all of *you,* and that all they want with me is to make me suffer."

Rxa went silent for a long moment as he studied her. "You believe that you are not beloved of our Ancients."

She snorted. "Do I need to count off the shit that's happened to me since I've shown up here?"

"And you believe all of that was their doing?" His voice was quiet, his tone unreadable.

"They pull the strings. They give the prophecies. They put everyone in the right places." Grimacing, she looked toward the entrance of the church's sanctuary where a few others were gathered. She wanted to escape this awkward conversation.

Rxa had been desperate for her to come to the cathedral to talk to him about the Ancients for weeks. And she'd steadfastly ignored his request. Now, he seemed to be trying to shoehorn in the conversation, and now she just wanted to escape.

"Truth is, Rxa? I'm sick of being tugged around on puppet strings. From the moment that corpse showed up on my slab in the morgue, the Ancients have been dragging me along by the nose. I haven't had a choice—"

"You could have chosen death."

"I haven't had a *real* choice." She glared at him. "And I

haven't had a say in any of this. I'm real happy they wanted to save the world for all of you. But that doesn't mean I'm going to forgive them for it anytime soon."

The angel had gone impossibly still again. Even his shadow seemed locked in place, which was uncommon for him.

"I know you love them. And I know you want me to too. And I'm sorry I'm... all fucked up." She gestured down at herself. "I know I'm not what I'm supposed to be. I'll get there. But hey. We're immortal. We have plenty of time, right?"

For a second, she wondered if Rxa was having one of Aon's broken moments. But finally, after a few heartbeats too long, the angel answered. "That we do."

"I'm going to go see how Lyon is doing." *I'm going to go talk to the more approachable vampire. How the hell that's possible, I have no fucking clue.* Heading off down the aisle, she walked up to the taller, paler, somehow more normal vampire, and let out an exhale.

Lyon frowned down at her. He was standing a few paces away from the other regents and royals who were gathered behind the closed doors of the cathedral, waiting to make their exit into the courtyard to the waiting crowd. "Are you all right?"

She tried to shrug off the conversation, but it was difficult. It left a weird taste in her mouth. "Rxa."

Lyon subtly glanced over his shoulder to ensure the angel was nowhere near. "What did he do?"

"Nothing, I guess. He wanted me to light a candle for my Ancient. I refused."

"Ah." Lyon sighed and looked back toward the door. "Forgive him his zealousy. He... will have a hard time understanding the world from your perspective. He will have a difficult time being patient."

"I guess I should feel bad for that thing being stuck with me." She snickered quietly. "The Ancient."

"It will not be trapped with you alone for long. More will

fall to your House the next time Earth and Under align. Then you will be pestered by a regent of your own."

That turned her snicker into a full-blown laugh. She hadn't thought of that. She was going to wind up with people who... served her. "Oh, shit." The thought made her lose it in a fit of giggling. "That just makes it dumber! Can you imagine? A bunch of people shuffling around trying to do my bidding? That's going to go miserably, Lyon. I won't know what the hell to do with them!"

"Good. I am glad we will have a royal with some sense of humility about them." Lyon was genuinely smiling now. "Hold on to that as long as you can. It will fade in time."

"Time. I said that to Rxa, but I'll admit I can't quite grasp it."

"I struggled with the same. It was not for a hundred years after I lost my mortality that it truly sank in that I would no longer age nor die. That I would not see my wife and child in the afterlife."

"You... you had a family?" She looked up at the Priest, shocked. He vaguely resembled the statues around him, he was so pale. But instead of the sadistic glee of the marble figures around him, he wore sorrow.

"I did. They died when I was a mortal and before I fell to Under. They were victims of a war between the Romans and the Gallic empire. My son was four years old when he met the spear." He furrowed his brow just slightly. "I realize now that I cannot remember their names."

She slung her arms around him in a hug and squeezed him as tight as she could. There were no words for what echoed in his voice. It wasn't pain that made her want to hug him. It was the lack of anything at all.

Is that what time did? Is that what she had to look forward to?

The love of ancient gods and forgetting her humanity?

How many thousands of years would she go before she forgot Nick?

Lyon chuckled quietly as he hugged her back. "It was a long time ago, Lydia. But I thank you for your sympathy." When she looked up at him, he put his hand to her cheek and stroked it with his thumb. "You are a kind soul. I am glad that you have found your place here."

He didn't quite get why she was hugging him. But that was fine. "Later in this stupid party, I'd like to hear the story of your life, Lyon. I realized I really don't know anything about you."

"You know plenty. You know me, even if you do not know my history." He let her out of his embrace to look back up at the door before them. It seemed he couldn't keep her gaze.

"You really are shy, aren't you? I thought Kamira was kidding."

"I am." Lyon smirked, the barest twinge on his thin lips. "Painfully so."

"That's adorable. Everybody else here seems to want to jump all over each other's bones, and you're off blushing in the corner." *Speaking of horny idiots.* "By the way, where's Otoi? I haven't seen him in a while."

"I am now the Regent of Blood once more. With the return of Dtu and Rxa, I am restored to my previous position."

"Congratulations. I mean, if it's a good thing." She really didn't know if that was a role he wanted or not.

"I am glad to serve my people once more from a position of some authority."

"You still had authority. More than most, from what I could tell. Now, it's just back to being official. Hell, even Aon respects you. That has to count for something." She elbowed him in the side. "Besides, nobody is going to miss Otoi."

"His wife certainly did. I am sure she will be happy to have him at home more frequently."

Huh. Otoi was married? She wouldn't have guessed. *Every-*

one's always more complicated than they seem. "Lyon, I never did thank you."

"For what?" He seemed genuinely confused.

"For being nice to me when you didn't need to." She raised her hand to stop Lyon from interrupting her. "No. You were being compassionate with me, the whole way through. Thanks for being my friend. For being my *actual* friend, because you wanted to be."

He took a step back to bow, and his pale, ice-blue eyes were soft when he looked back up at her. "You are very welcome. It is my honor."

A bright-sounding giggle heralded Ini's approach before she appeared out of thin air next to them. "You are just quite the marvel!" she said, clearly beaming. "He smiles at you as much as he smiles at his wife. You melt the warlock and now the Priest. Hello, Lyon! My great white bat, how lovely to see you."

Q vanished from her shoulder the minute that Ini appeared. Lydia tried not to laugh at her snake's new fear of Ini and her "magic hands."

"I am pleased for your return, Queen Ini," Lyon responded but held a kind of dread in his voice as if he knew what was about to happen.

"I heard Dtu apologized to you," Ini said to Lydia with a playful glee to her.

"Did you have anything to do with that?"

"No! Nothing at all."

"Why don't I believe you?" Lydia narrowed an eye up at the floating elf.

"Because you are wise," Lyon said dryly.

"I did not speak to Dtu once on the subject. I merely encouraged Edu to do the deed for me." Ini put her hand to her chest in a delicate, ladylike gesture of polite offense. "It is very different."

"Right."

"It is!"

"Sure, it is." Lydia couldn't help it; she kind of liked Ini. Even if she did meddle. She was like every regency romance character's worst nightmare. Just full of drama and harmless intrigue.

"I enjoy you as well, Queen of Dreams. And I do not meddle," the floating woman responded to her thoughts. "And what is 'regency romance?' It sounds *fascinating*."

"Goddamn son of a bitch." She kept forgetting Ini was psychic.

Ini giggled at her silent tirade of obscenities. "You will adjust to it in time." She floated down to land next to her and drew herself in closer. She wrapped her arm around Lydia like a dear friend.

She could feel the draw of Ini's hypnotism but managed to keep it at bay. Probably by the benefit of her own power, more than anything else. "Look at them." Ini pointed to Rxa and Aon, who were now standing next to each other by the door. Black and white. Angel and demon. "Beautiful, aren't they? Our gentlemen peers are such gentle creatures in their hearts, don't you think?"

"Gentle?" Lydia tried not to snort in derision.

"See past the blood and violence that flows here like wine. Edu is a tender giant when it comes to matters of the heart. Dtu is loyal to the grave. Rxa is as sympathetic and kind as our dearest Priest here before us. And you cracked the last of them to keep himself veiled. Aon, the one with the most love in his heart to give of them all." Ini leaned her head against Lydia's shoulder. The Queen of Fate was shorter than her. Well, when she was standing on solid ground, anyway.

Lydia fought back the urge to push her away. She wasn't doing anything awful, only displaying an utter lack of understanding in personal space. At least her hands weren't anywhere they shouldn't be. Yet. "Just... don't go poking around in my head again, will you? I'm just a kid. I don't know how to stop you like the others can. It's not fair."

Ini sighed wistfully. "Oh, all right, if you insist. For my newest baby sister, I will try to respect your privacy. I have already seen some amazing juicy scenes, besides. I must say. Your ability to hold your breath for so long, even as a mortal, is *astonishing*. Where did you learn such a gift? Practice, I expect."

Lydia felt her face go warm, and she knew she had blushed a bright shade of red. Lyon looked embarrassed and stared down at his shoes. He'd probably be pink in the face as well, if vampires could even do that kind of thing.

"You are so bashful!" Ini teased and hugged her tighter. She smelled like flowers—not overly cloying but close. "How adorable. So easy to tease, like our Priest. But truly, I had no idea all this time that Aon was so talented. Or well endowed! My, oh my, what he can do with his claw. I didn't think it would be possible for a man to—"

"I should join the other regents outside. Excuse me." Lyon exploded into a cloud of white bats and flew up into the rafters and out an open window high above the pews.

Ini let out a peal of laughter that revealed that as having been her game all along. She was hugging Lydia tightly, giggling like a child, gleeful at her success. She had been needling the shy man until he "noped" out of the conversation in a spectacular fashion that only a vampire could do.

"You're awful," Lydia scolded Ini, even through her smile. "Did you just make him 'bat' out?"

"Oh, I truly am. And I am sorry, I cannot help it. He is so stunning when he is cornered and embarrassed."

"Try not to use my sex life as ammunition, though, would you?"

"Pooh, you're no fun." Ini let go of her to float up next to her. "I will amuse myself with your wonderful friend. Where is that lovely snake of yours?"

"Hiding from you and your magic hands."

Ini chuckled again, clearly amused. "You are just too much! But, come." She turned to face Rxa and Aon where they stood some twenty feet away. "The festival has already started, and we are all quite late."

As Lydia looked up, she realized that Aon and Rxa had both been watching the scene unfold. She mouthed "help me" to Aon, more for the humor in it than anything else. Sure enough, his shoulders shook in a silent laugh.

"My apologizes, Lady Ini," Rxa said. "I was too eager to learn from my old friend what I had missed through all the years."

"You were too eager to talk too much," the floating woman teased. Ini disappeared from Lydia's side and reappeared floating near Rxa. "Can we go now? There are lights, music, and there is much fun to be had! And the front landing just looked so silly with only the four of us gathered upon it."

Rxa bowed deep at the waist and gestured one arm out for Ini to lead them.

Lydia headed to Aon, eager for the comfort of his easy presence. Once she joined him, he began to lead her toward the door. "Not another 'important people have to stand here' kind of night?"

"Sadly, yes," Aon responded as she approached. "We are all expected to be seen together. It is a show of solidarity and peace. There will be a speech, I am certain. The task will fall to Rxa, as he is the voice of the people." He fell in step beside her, and she couldn't help but smile as he offered her his elbow like a gentleman.

She put her hand in the crook of his arm. "Shouldn't we not be seen together?" She could hear the crowd outside. As Ini had promised, it sounded like thousands of people were gathered. As many people as could fit in Yej had come to attend.

"Are you ashamed?" he chided her playfully.

"No, I just thought..."

"We are not wed. There is nothing but the opinions of others to greet us anymore. Our secret is well and truly 'out.' The rumors have already flown their coop and taken wing to every corner of this forsaken world." He sighed, clearly not enjoying the thought. "Ini saw to that."

"Maybe it'll do your reputation some good if people think you can actually care about something and aren't just hateful and violent all the time."

"That is precisely what I am afraid of. No, I will stand beside you, for I wish to show the world what is rightfully mine." He lifted his head haughtily. Lydia elbowed him hard in the ribs, and he made an exaggerated "oof!" as he played into the theatrics of her blow. She loved it when he was playful like this.

It made her smile up at him, and he turned his masked metal face down to her. "Rxa will make his speech, the crowd will cheer and while they are wasting away into bottles, you and I will retreat to our own dark corner. There, I will have my 'hateful and violent' way with you. Although, if he talks too long, my hand may wander, I warn you. And Rxa always talks too long."

Lydia's face went warm at his threat, and she glared up at him. "Don't you dare."

"You look too tempting to resist. So rarely do you wear something I might find so... easily accessible."

"I repeat—don't you *dare*."

"I do love a challenge." He chuckled.

The roar of the crowd grew louder as they stepped out of the front of the church and onto the landing. She saw Edu, Vjo, and Dtu already standing there, waiting. Vjo had chosen to be human for the evening, as she likely wouldn't have fit as a giant spider.

The others all turned to look at Rxa, Ini, Aon, and herself as they walked outside. Lydia's steps faltered, but Aon wouldn't have it. His other hand went atop hers, and he pulled her gently alongside him. So she had nothing else to do but just get dragged out there with him.

She focused instead on trying to get the pink out of her face as she must have been blushing heavily, standing out in front of the single largest crowd she had ever seen.

If she thought being on stage at the Festival of the Moons was bad... this was something else entirely.

But this was the first time the seven Houses of Under stood together in fifteen hundred years. She couldn't even comprehend that number. She could suffer through this.

Q, sensing his chance for praise, appeared and grew in size to stand behind her, some ten feet tall. His turquoise wings were illuminating the stone walls nearby with their constant glow. Her snake really did love to be adored.

Upon seeing them, all gathered around Rxa, the crowd cheered. The sound was nearly deafening. She tried not to retreat but couldn't help but try to take a step back. Aon's hand on hers tightened reassuringly.

Lydia wasn't afraid of the world anymore. She wasn't scared of what it had to offer. But still, she felt so lost all the time. Here she was, left in awe of the magnitude and size of Under and all the people and monsters who lived here.

The crowd was a multitude of colors, wings, scales, teeth, and tails. Of masks of every color, save hers. Down at the bottom of the stairs stood all the elders who had taken their places. One in red she didn't recognize—she realized she had never met Edu's second in command.

Under was together and whole. This was her home now. Her place was here, with them—with Aon.

Rxa stepped forward and spread his wings wide. The crowd silenced at the gesture. As he let his wings return to a relaxed state, he began to speak. His voice carried unnaturally out into the throng of people. Magic, she figured.

"Fellow Children of the Ancients... it brings me great joy to welcome you here tonight. For this evening, we celebrate a new holiday. A new occasion we will mark tonight, to praise our Ancients for the fate they have seen fit to paint before us!"

Aon shifted on his feet as if either already bored or bracing himself for a long speech. She nudged him again with her elbow, teasing him for being so difficult.

The crowd cheered Rxa's introduction. The angel continued after they quieted down. "Under has been saved. The void has retreated, and our world is once more whole. One person upon this stage deserves our thanks for seeing this done. One soul here is responsible for our mended world."

"Oh, don't," she murmured helplessly. "Please don't. No more speeches and stupid applause."

Aon chuckled beside her, moving his arm to wrap it around her to squeeze her against him briefly.

"Lydia. Queen of the House of Dreams. Our new savior, who rose from the pool once mortal, and rose again from the dead as you see her now."

Rxa turned to face her, gesturing an arm toward her.

The next words that left him felt like something from a fever dream.

"An aberration and a mutilation of our very nature."

Everything happened too quickly.

Chaos just happened—it was impossible to see it for what it was until it was over.

Until she could try and stitch things back together in the right order, everything was just a flurry of motion all at once.

Aon jolted next to her. His hand fell from her hip as he made a strange gurgling noise.

Q was shouting.

Something wrapped around her throat and yanked her backward and off her feet toward the cathedral. In a blink, Q vanished and was now yelling inside of her mind instead of out loud. Whatever was around her throat was tight and was dragging her across the ground as she kicked and thrashed. She might have been screaming; she didn't really know.

One sight fixed into her mind; a single thing struck her out of her panic and the chaos. Aon was impaled upon gold chains that stuck up from the ground, like razor-thin icicles jutting from the stones. He looked like a sick and morbid art sculpture, trapped in the crisscrossed gold. Rxa's magic. They had run through Aon like a hundred spears. He hadn't been expecting an attack. The crowd was screaming, running away, pushing back from the steps in panic and confusion.

By now, Lydia was already inside the body of the church. She was helpless as she watched Edu swing his sword at Rxa. A bright flash of blinding white light sent the King of Flames staggering backward. The doors slammed shut with a resounding *boom.*

White writing, esoteric and strange, appeared on the doors. They glowed with their own light, and she knew no one would be following her inside anytime soon.

The chain that was dragging her across the floor began to lift, yanking her up into the air and off the floor. It dropped her onto her knees painfully. She summoned her power and tried to will the chain off her, to do anything at all—but even though her symbols were flaring to life on her arms, nothing was happening.

Let me out, let me out, let me out! Q was shouting in her mind, almost drowning out her own thoughts.

Q was afraid. Panicking. Screaming.

She was in real danger.

The gold chain around her neck snapped around her arms, binding them to her sides. She was trapped. Rxa said his chains could hold the Ancients… what chance did she stand? And with them wrapped around her, Q was cut off and trapped inside her mind.

Rxa appeared in a shimmer, already in mid-stride as he materialized, moving toward her. "Ah. Yes. Now perhaps we can truly talk alone."

"Rxa! What the hell are you doing?" She tried to keep the panic out of her voice. But she knew it leaked through. "Get these things off me!"

The angel was standing in front of her now, his perfect porcelain face tilted curiously down at her. "I am sorry, I will not. I am protecting this world I love so much. This world you reject."

"I'm not—I don't reject this world!" She struggled desperately, but it was useless. The golden chains were coiled around her, binding her arms to her sides. They kept her lashed to the ground. The links came from small, gold, glowing circles on the floor, walls, or any other nearby object.

She was helpless.

With a flick of Rxa's hands, the chains hoisted her up to standing. "Forgive me for what I must do."

"I'll forgive you if you let me go. Why are you doing this?"

Rxa shushed her quietly and placed his warm fingertips against her lips. "Please... I understand your fear. There is little I desire more than for this situation to be different. I wish I did not have to do this."

Lydia yanked her head away from Rxa. "Don't you dare touch me."

"You needn't worry. That is not why I brought you here." He slid his hand to the back of her neck and stepped closer to her. There was nothing she could do to move away. "It is so rare to find any who are so guarded. So mistrustful of all others... any of those who live in the service of the Ancients. You are simply *wrong*."

"Is that what this is about?" Yet again, she was going to be blamed for something she couldn't help. Something the

Ancients had done to her. First Edu, now Rxa. History was repeating itself. "Please, Rxa, I can't help what I am!"

"You can. Come to the Pool of the Ancients with me. Kneel before them and beg to be made whole. Plead for their mercy. Pray to be made *right*. Give them your mind, your heart, your soul. The creature you carry about with you is amusing but an abomination."

"No." Lydia glared up at the angel.

"They are your masters. Kneel to them. Accept them."

"I'm not going to kneel to anyone. Not you, not them, not Aon. No one. I don't serve them. I'm nobody's slave, Rxa."

Rxa shook his head sadly and cupped her face in his hands. She struggled, but she couldn't get away from him. He kept shushing her quietly until she finally gave up and resumed quietly glaring a hole into that porcelain face of his.

"Reconsider. I beg you. For if you cannot be made right... if you do not accept them as your masters..." He trailed off. "Do not force my hand, Lydia. You seem like a kind, intelligent, strong soul. Do not make me destroy you."

Lydia went pale. Twice she had been wrong about the prophecy. She supposed that's all people ever did with prophecies—guess them wrong. She squeezed her eyes shut. It hadn't been about Dtu.

It was Rxa she shouldn't have trusted.

"Even if I did, it'd be a lie. Somehow, I think they'd know that." She couldn't even have the dignity to wipe away the tears that rolled down her cheeks.

Rxa did it for her, brushing them away tenderly. He tutted and turned her back to look up at him. "Yes. They would. Open your heart to them and all will be made well."

"I can't."

He sighed. "I know."

"When Aon wakes up, he is going to fucking *wreck* you."

Rxa lifted a hand to gently stroke her hair, brushing it back and tucking it behind her ear. She wanted to bite at him, but it would be pointless and childish. Whatever was going to happen, she could at least have some pride. "When he wakes, it will be too late for you, my poor unfortunate one."

"Too late for me?" Fear welled up in her throat. "What're you going to do... kill me?"

"No. I wish it were so simple. I wish it were so kind. I cannot doom our world to the void once more. What I will do to you is worse than death."

She knew then what he was going to do.

And she knew he was right.

EIGHTEEN

Lyon flew up the stairs, taking them three at a time. But when the doors to the cathedral slammed shut, he felt the surge of power that held them closed. Rxa had triggered a powerful shield that kept the cathedral under guard from any who might attack it. It had only once before been used, during the Great War. Edu and Dtu had tried to storm the building during a siege, and even against both, the gates had held in those days.

Now, Edu growled in his throat and shoulder-checked the door. It crackled with power and sent him reeling backward in the aftermath. It would prove unbreakable by that method.

The gold chains that held Aon suspended, impaled a hundred times over on the thin metal cable, had disappeared with Rxa. It left the warlock's lifeless body bleeding out on the steps. He would wake, and soon—but perhaps not fast enough.

Lyon was flabbergasted, shocked, and horrified at what had transpired. He stood there, uncertain and confused. His king's devotion to the Ancients came above all else. But to do this—to attack the girl? And for what? Did he not expect the girl's nature to be peculiar? She had been mortal but a few weeks ago. Now, she stood a queen! Rxa's zealous nature had come to bear in the past. But never like this. If Rxa saw Lydia as unnatural, who knew what the King of Blood may do?

A hand touched his arm, and he looked down at Kamira. Her eyes were wide and fearful, searching his for some sign that he may know what to do. He did not.

"Hm. So much for peace," Vjo commented darkly and looked up at the large door. "Lyon, can you pass through this gate? You are of its making." The Queen of Words, the rational scholar, was of course the first to gather her wits enough to react thoughtfully.

"Perhaps. But not here." Rxa's magic would be weaker against someone in his own house. And this place was Lyon's home. If anyone stood a chance on getting inside past Rxa's wards, it would be him.

Edu was not able to speak for himself. His empath was not present. But some things spoke louder than words. He pointed at Lyon and then jabbed his thumb toward the building. It was a clear and angry missive for Lyon to go and stop this madness.

Lyon bowed to the King of Flames silently. He moved to leave but was stopped once more by Kamira's touch. "Be careful, my love. I believe Rxa may have gone mad."

Kamira rarely expressed concern over his well-being. She knew he could handle himself, for all her teasing that she was the superior fighter. Lyon turned her to face him and kissed her. For she was correct—he did not know what to expect. Never had his king done anything like this before. He was walking into the unknown.

"I will do what I can." He placed a second kiss to her forehead. With one last glance at Edu, who nodded in silent appreciation for his willingness to go, Lyon exploded into bats and disappeared.

* * *

No. Please, no. Anywhere but here.

Not this place again.

Not this fucking lake.

Rxa had taken her and brought them both down to the platform that overlooked the Pool of the Ancients. That horrible, glowing red underground lake of blood held just as much terror for her now as it did then. All that had changed were the reasons behind it.

It had been horrifying the first time she had seen it, with its terrible waterfall and visages of skull-like masks for walls like the crypts beneath Paris. It seemed that every time she came down here, something horrible was either about to happen or had just happened.

The first time, she nearly drowned.

The second, she had crawled out after being murdered.

Now, she suspected what Rxa was going to do to her was going to be far, far worse than either of her previous adventures with it.

As she saw where he had taken her, she redoubled her struggling, jerking against the gold chains. Rxa merely sighed and gestured his hand, tightening the coils around her and making her gag in pain. It wasn't until he had nearly squeezed hard enough to crack her ribs that she finally gave up fighting and Rxa relented.

"I see why the warlock adores you so. You have quite the threshold for pain."

When she could breathe again, she decided to put her air to good use. "Go fuck a fire hydrant, flyboy."

It didn't even get a response from him. "For what it means to you, which I am certain is very little... I believe you when you say you are devoted to Aon. But when we spoke earlier of how you had no choice in anything here in Under... have you stopped to think whether or not you had a choice in that either?" He looked eerie—a glowing white and gold creature on a background of darkness, crimson and shadows. "Or whether or not you were led to love him, as well?"

"And here, I thought Aon loved the sound of his own voice." Lydia was on her knees near the center of the platform.

The angel reached down to lift her head to look at him, and she glared at him in return. Her anger didn't seem to bother him, and he kept talking as if she hadn't said anything. "You were his prisoner. A scared mortal girl trapped in a world of monsters and beasts that you did not understand. You could not contend against this place. You were helpless. Edu was cruel and unkind. Then in swoops our Dark King, and he treats you like an esteemed guest. His *princess*." Rxa shook his head. "He manipulated you. Played to your fears. Opened his arms to you and promised the rest of the world was worse than his own madness. He woke in you some latent desire and gave you shelter from your terror. Your love is a false one, born of desperation and granted solace."

"You don't know what you're talking about." Even if that had been how it started, it had evolved past that. She was committed either way. She loved Aon, and she knew that was the truth. "And you said this wasn't about him."

"Oh, it isn't. All manner of desires may be fed in Under, and I am not one to shame my brother's proclivities." Rxa crouched down to get closer to her and stroked her hair, straightening it and tucking it behind her ear where it had come loose in her struggles. "This is not about my eldest brother. This is not about the favorite of the Ancients. This is not even about the death of Qta or how Aon warped your mind and tricked you into loving him. This is simply about one thing, Lydia."

He stood slowly and looked down at her. His voice was full of pleading, of desperation. "You are not one of us. Pray to them to make you whole. Kneel in their blood and rise as the queen you must become. Please, I beg of you."

Staring him down, she knew what he was saying was suicide. No, not suicide. Worse than suicide. An eternity of *torture*. But the other option was an eternity of slavery.

She was done being on a leash.

"No."

"Everyone who has come out of that pool—every soul to ever set foot upon this world—has felt the influence of the Ancients upon their mind. They carry the marks on their faces because they are a part of our primordial gods. But you are *wrong*. You feel no bond with them. You fear them because you have been told to. You hate them because of how you feel they have wronged you. You went into their blood a corpse and came out a queen with no knowledge, no sense of veneration. This cannot stand."

"If you let me go right now, we can pretend none of this happened. I can talk Aon down from ripping your feathers out one by one and turning you into an art piece for the next thousand years." She was shaking. This was hopeless.

"I cannot. I am sorry. But you can free yourself. Pray to them, now. Kneel and surrender to them. Submit to your masters."

Lydia lowered her head and knew she was doomed. She couldn't do that. Just couldn't. Even if they were world-creating, all-powerful, ancient demi-whatever-they-were. But she still debated it for a long moment.

She should just give in.

Give them the rest of her and let it be over.

But it felt like a *lie*. It felt like surrender out of weakness, out of desperation to avoid the fate she knew Rxa had in store for her.

And she couldn't let herself do that. She lifted her head to look at the angel tiredly. "This world took everything from me, Rxa. My life, my home, my family... my friend. I won't give them my soul."

"It is already theirs!" Rxa pointed back at the bleeding waterfall. "You wear their marks. They already have you! You must only accept it!"

"I can't. I just... can't."

Rxa shook his head and turned to look up at the monuments in the lake. "Poor child. You are helpless in all this. A pawn in the games of the world around you. And now you shelter inside your soul, cowering against the storm that will bury you in its wrath. I would end your torment and send you to the grave, but that would doom us all. You are necessary, even if you are aberrant."

He turned to face her again, and if she wasn't mistaken, he might have been crying beneath his mask. His voice hitched, heartbroken, as he begged her. "I beg you. One last time. Enter the pool of your own will. Pray for their acceptance, their forgiveness for rejecting your servitude to them. *Please, Lydia.*"

Tears, far less hidden than his, rolled down her cheeks. She didn't answer. She was done fighting with him.

"Very well. I will send you to the one place where Aon cannot follow. I will place you in the one prison he dares not open."

She suspected. But it was very different to *know*. Dread and terror welled in her, fresh horror at the *knowledge* of what Rxa was about to do to her. Thrashing against the chains, she screamed as pure fear took over her body.

A white and porcelain mask framed with golden hair looked down at her. The image of an angel, cruel and beautiful in its perfection, emotionless and unempathetic. "If you will not enter the Pool of the Ancients of your own will, I will send you there myself. I will imprison you with the very gods you refuse."

* * *

Lyon had found his way in after a few moments of near disaster. The power that kept the Cathedral of the Ancients locked down was a vicious spell, but he was able to wriggle his way in through the chimneys once he had taken the form of bats. He was able to pass through the barrier at its weakest point, due to his own affinity with the source of its creation.

It was harrowing. One wrong move and he may never recover. But the stakes were too high—the cost of his failure too great to stop. Dismay was coursing through him as he moved from space to space, searching for Rxa and poor Lydia. When he could not find them anywhere in the chambers above ground, he realized with no small amount of panic where he must have taken her.

There was no single reason why the King of Blood would bring Lydia to the Pool of the Ancients that could end well. He raced there with all the preternatural speed he possessed and could only pray that he was not too late.

Pray to whom, he did not know.

* * *

"You're insane!" Lydia's fear was sending her voice to a higher pitch. Her usual mantra about panicking later was not going to work this time. There was not going to be a later.

Rxa was going to chain her up with the Ancients at the bottom of a lake of blood.

"Do not be concerned with what it may be like to drown without dying. I know that is what you fear. Think of it only as to sleep. To dream without end." Rxa was stroking her hair again with both his hands, trying to calm her like she was a child having a nightmare.

"Fuck you! Let me go, Rxa!"

"Calm yourself. Your mind will not last long under the torment, I assure you. You will go mad within hours, and you will no longer know pain. I am sure of it. Please, be calm—" He was honestly trying to *soothe* her.

"No, *no!*" The turquoise marks on her arms were flaring brightly, glowing and trying to break her loose. But the magic of Rxa's chains was too much for her.

Rxa sighed drearily, giving up on his attempt to calm her down. He gestured his hand as he stood. The chains cinched tighter around her, the gold bands biting into her skin. She cried out and doubled over as the metal cables dragged her closer to the ground.

Let me out! Let me out! Q was screaming in her head, and she felt his own fear rising, adding to her own.

"You're insane!" She couldn't keep fighting; she could barely move. But she could keep screaming at him.

"Perhaps I am." Rxa's voice was empty. Devoid of all feeling. "But this must be done."

"My king—please, stop!"

Rxa turned suddenly to look at a figure who appeared standing on the other end of the platform. A tall man in all white, a ghost against the background.

Lyon! Oh, she had never been happier to see anybody than she was right now to see Lyon. Hope blossomed in her heart. Lyon would talk some sense into Rxa. He had to!

She let out a sob of relief.

"Lyon. Leave here. This is not a deed for you to witness." Rxa's voice was dead and cold.

"What deed is that precisely?" Lyon stepped toward them carefully, wary of the angel and what he might do.

"She refuses to kneel and accept the Ancients as her masters. She cannot stand as a queen and mock them in her very refusal of their rightful rule. Her mind is spared of their influence. This cannot be." Rxa spread his wings just slightly as he talked, flexing them in his anger.

"These things must come in time, Master Rxa. She is

young, she is afraid... the power that has taken hold of her is too much for any to handle." Lyon took another careful step forward, his hands raised as if to calm a wild animal. "Take pity on her. Let her grow to accept their rule of her future in her own way."

"No, Lyon. For the warlock will fight to keep her this way. Preserved, as a capsule of a woman, separate from their influence for fear it may sour her against him. All who come from the lake fear him, even those that join his own House. He would have her like this to prevent such things. Either she kneels before them or she will *join them*." The angel's last words were a dangerous hiss.

"What?" Lyon exclaimed, his eyes wide. "You cannot... what you threaten—"

"Is what must be. Stand down, Lyon. Leave us. Leave this place."

"I cannot." Lyon took another tentative step forward. "I cannot walk away and let you do this. You are making a grave mistake, my king. Please, I beg you, reconsider. To send her to the depths... to doom her to that fate. Think on what you do."

"She mocks the Ancients by her very existence! I cannot let this stand. I will not stand down, nor will I release her. Either you must raise your hand to stop me or you must retreat." Rxa tilted his head back slightly on his neck as he challenged the vampire. "What shall it be, my elder and regent? Will you betray me, dear friend? Or will you obey the will of the Ancients you call master, and your king?"

"This is not their will, my king. This is yours," Lyon insisted. "I cannot let you do this. Lydia does not deserve this terrible fate. No one does."

"You are correct. She does not deserve this. She is innocent of all wrong in this tragedy. I respect her highly for being unable to lie to me. She cannot kneel to them. For that, she shall suffer regardless. Now, you must make your own choice, Lyon. Do you stand with me or against me?"

Lyon's pale blue eyes were filled with sorrow when they caught Lydia's gaze. She didn't know what to do during this whole exchange. She could only watch it unfold, stunned, feeling out-of-body and removed like it was happening to someone else. Like their conversation wasn't about her and deciding her fate.

"Go, Lyon—" She almost gagged in the pain.

It was easier than trying to wrap her head around the fact that she was going to be thrown into a lake of blood to go insane for eternity.

Lyon looked back to Rxa and sighed. He went to open his mouth to give his answer—but never had the chance.

Tragedy, like chaos, was another thing that happened too quickly. It came without warning.

Golden chains like spears, a dozen or more in a line, stabbed through Lyon's face from the back. They jutted up from the ground behind him and punched through his skull and out the front.

They ran in a perfect vertical line and through Lyon's marks that he bore on his face. Mutilating them, destroying them.

Killing him.

He was dead instantly... and permanently.

Someone was screaming, crying out his name.

It took her a moment to realize it was her.

Lyon was frozen, pale eyes wide, as blood oozed down the gold chains from the back of his head, painting the shimmering surface crimson with the liquid that dripped to the ground. As fast as the cables had impaled him, they retreated. They shot back into the small glowing circles that were their origins. A series of thin, dime-sized crimson circles on the man's face began to slowly ooze blood down his face and neck.

Lyon slumped to the ground on his knees, ice-blue eyes lifeless and glassy, staring at everything and nothing—caught in a moment of utter surprise.

Tears were running hotly down her cheeks. She didn't care for her dignity anymore. *Please, no. Please, not him!*

Twice she had to watch a friend be murdered before her eyes because of her.

Twice she had been dragged to this underground lake to suffer.

"We really are fragile creatures, Lydia," Rxa said to her emptily as he looked down at Lyon's lifeless body. "We make ourselves out to be impenetrable gods. But we are vainglorious and intemperate in our nature. We are but brittle things. You wonder why we wear our masks? You would not know, as you do not feel the connection to the Ancients as you should. They are not to hide our marks from prying eyes—they are to protect them. These marks upon our faces are our weakness. They are our strength. From them we draw our power. Without them, we are destroyed."

No. No, this couldn't be. Not Lyon. Not the kindly, doleful priest. Not him. His marks were destroyed; each of the gold chains had perfectly skewered one of the thin white symbols on his face. Blood was pooling around him, a stark contrast to his pale skin.

"Why?" It really wasn't a question for Rxa, she realized. It was for the Ancients who let this happen. *"Why!"*

But the angel answered, anyway. "Lyon was corrupted. By Aon or his own heart, I do not know. It does not matter which. But he was no longer a priest in service to our Ancients. He was no longer my loyal regent. He would fight me to save you from this fate."

"Because he was a good man! Not a maniac and a zealot!"

Rxa crouched down and picked up the tall man in his arms, carrying him like was nothing. Rxa moved to the edge of the platform and stepped into the glowing, bloody water. The red liquid soaking up into the white robes he wore wrapped around his waist. "He shall return to those who bore us. His power will live on in another who shall fall to us in time."

"Let me go, Rxa! Fight me. Beat me, and I'll kneel to your gods. I'll submit to them, if you stand toe-to-toe with me." Now, she'd moved onto the 'bargaining' stage of grief, she supposed. But she had nothing left. She'd try anything she could, even as she wept for Lyon. The Priest had only been trying to save her, and now he was dead.

"Clever, trying to play my ego against me. I fear I have none to use. I do not doubt you would escape, or you are merely buying time. That creature you wield is dangerous, and I do not wish to tangle with your beast. If you could fell Dtu, you may, in your grieved and desperate state, defeat me as well." With that, Rxa lowered Lyon into the water and let him go. The Priest sank beneath the surface of the lake and was gone.

She'd mourn him a lot more if she weren't about to join him.

Rxa climbed out of the water and walked up to her. He reached down and grasped her by the chains around her torso. It seemed he was going to do this by hand.

"You're going to pay for this, Rxa. You have no idea what Aon is going to do to you, once he wakes up."

"I shall suffer dearly for this, I am aware. Aon will pluck me, break me, and likely end my sanity as we all know he can." Rxa shook his head. "But he cannot kill me. He would not dare doom this world in such a way. The fee would be far greater than simply meeting the void once more. I take this cost upon myself for the good of our world. For the reverence of *our* Ancients." Rxa pulled her to the edge of the pond and stood her on the steps, her back to the waterfall. "Forgive me, Lydia. I truly am sorry. But if it is any consolation in your hatred, know that I will soon suffer as much as you. My madness will join yours. The warlock will see that I pay tenfold for your agony."

"Don't do this, Rxa. Please, don't do this." Now, she resorted to begging. Fear was consuming her, and she would do anything. "I'll kneel or do whatever you want—I'll try—I will—"

Rxa shook his head again. "You were correct when you said it would be a lie. I knew you could not surrender your strength. I hoped you might find it in you to accept them, but... now this is a pauper's plea, nothing else." He put his hand in the middle of her chest. "Goodbye, Lydia."

Rxa pushed. Sent her falling backward into the lake of blood. The liquid pooled up around her quickly. Wrapped up in the gold chain as she was, there was nothing she could do. Nothing but kick and writhe. But instantly she was beneath the surface.

The liquid punched its way into her body all at once, just like it had the first time. It forced itself into her body, into her lungs, driving all air out of her in one wicked hammer of the viscous substance. The violent jerk of it ended her struggles. She spasmed once, twice... and her body accepted it.

Surrounded by the red glow of the lake, Lydia drifted downward.

NINETEEN

Edu waited.

He sat on the edge of one of the columns on the front of the cathedral, near the corpse of Aon. He lay where he had been dropped by Rxa's sudden attack. The dead warlock was in a puddle of his own blood that haloed around him, crimson against the black fabric of his clothes.

Dtu, Ini, and Vjo had gone but stayed nearby. He could sense them in the city, gathering their people, calming the panic. Already the crowd had begun to wonder if another war was about to begin or curious as to what was to become of their new dreamer and her accursed luck. They had all hoped this may be the beginning of some manner of peace in this world. That although their new royal was not like the rest of them, she might be enough to patch this world back together.

Rxa had seen fit to end the tenuous quiet, one way or another. Whatever the vampiric angel had planned, Edu did not know. He was not creative enough to understand the depths of depravity to which the likes of Aon and the angel could sink.

The warlock and Rxa were so very separate yet so very aligned in their natures.

He merely knew, no matter what, this would not end well. It would end in war and an imprisoned King of Blood, at best. Or worse, a dead dreamer and the return of the void. Edu sighed. And so, he stayed and waited, sitting there on the column that supported the arch of the cathedral.

It had been a little under an hour since Aon had been taken down by Rxa's cowardly attack. He would wake shortly.

As if on cue, the index finger of Aon's metal prosthetic twitched. A split second later, and the man disappeared from the ground. He reappeared a few feet away in a roar of black fire, healed and with new clothing. Edu turned his head from the heat that stung his eyes.

Aon was already in mid-stride heading toward the door to the cathedral. His gauntleted fist was ablaze. Edu wondered if the sorcerer even knew he was there. Perhaps not. Perhaps rage had consumed him entirely. He would not be surprised.

Edu watched as Aon slammed his palm onto the wooden surface of the door. White energy crackled out from the blow like lightning, snapping and popping as Aon fought back against it. The spell that kept the church closed off was a powerful one. Edu was helpless to break it.

But not the warlock.

There was a reason they all feared him.

Aon's black flame roared over the surface of the door, overcoming the crackles of glowing power that held them, and every other surface of the church, barricaded against entry. Aon dug his claws into the wood surface of the door, digging deep trenches in the surface as he pitted his power against Rxa's. The angel's best work was no match for Aon's rage and dark magic.

With a roar of fury from the warlock, Rxa's spell broke with a shuddering *boom* and shattered under Aon's hand.

The force sent the church doors off their hinges, smashing in toward the sanctuary and crashing to the ground. Each portion of the door was well over thirty feet tall and several thick. Their impact upon the stone floor of the cathedral shook the whole of the structure.

Edu stood from where he sat, not having bothered to do so until now. It wasn't until then that Aon turned to look at him, his shoulders rigid in anger. "Do not try to stop me, Edu."

Edu shook his head. He was not here to stop the warlock. He hefted his sword onto his shoulder and began to walk inside.

"What are you doing?" The warlock's anger broke in his complete confusion.

He could not help but smirk behind his red mask. Edu turned to face the warlock and sighed through his nose. He had sent Ylena away—it was too dangerous for her. Edu could not stand to put her in harm's way. So he would have to do the best that he could. For once, Aon's latent intelligence might serve him well.

Edu pointed a finger at Aon, a thumb at himself, then gestured back into the church, as if it were the most obvious thing in the world.

"You cannot be serious. You wish to... help me?" Aon was dumbfounded. His shoulders lowered as shock and confusion clearly warred against his anger.

Edu nodded, then tilted his head thoughtfully and shook his head. He was not here to help Aon. Not precisely.

"You wish to help Lydia." Aon tilted his head back slightly. "Yes, that makes far more sense."

Edu nodded again.

Aon turned to face into the sanctuary of the church. He looked down at his metal hand and lifted the palm upward. He flexed his fingers slowly and then curled them in, one by one. When he talked, he did not have his ever-present tone of cynicism and derision. He sounded... oddly touched. Edu had never heard that tone on him before. "Thank you, Edu."

This truly must be the end times. What had the young

dreamer done to the warlock? That was reason enough to save her.

"I appreciate your gesture. But I must refuse. In what I will do this day, I do not wish you to sully yourself." Aon moved to walk away from him.

Edu reached out to put a hand on Aon's shoulder to stop him. He expected the warlock to brush it off, to snarl at him, to make some sort of comment. Or, perhaps, to sever his hand from his wrist.

But instead, by some miracle, Aon stopped his progress into his church. Edu removed his hand, not wishing to test fate.

Aon turned his head to look back at him. "Do you know, Edu, at the heart of it all? I think I have always been jealous of you."

Edu nearly pulled back a step. Not just at Aon's admission, but that the tone of his voice was like a man on his deathbed. Exposed and broken. He had never known the warlock to be as such. Not in five thousand years.

This... felt like a goodbye.

"The righteous king, the one they all adore." Aon looked back down at his prosthetic hand again, as if he were contemplating it for the first time. "How many men and women have loved you—truly loved you—in your day? I have always been so very jealous of that. I covet of your sense of morality. I envy a great many things, Edu. For that, understand what now has been taken away from me. And what all I am willing to destroy in return."

Edu knew first-hand what Aon was suffering. His own experience had been the warlock's doing, after all. Edu could mock the man in his pain, but he could not find the will to do so. Kicking a man who was down was not a fair fight.

Aon continued to speak as he dropped his hand back to his side. "If Rxa is a fool and I am too late—if he has done what I believe he may have—I do not wish you there for what I will do. Please."

Edu stepped to move closer to Aon. Fear tugged at him, and it was not an emotion he was overly familiar with. What Aon was suggesting Rxa had done—and what he was, in turn, saying he would do in response—would doom them all.

To something *far* worse than the void.

"Go be with your little bar wench." The moment was over. Aon's tone was once more cold. "You do not have much time."

* * *

Lydia was seriously sick of this shit.

She was still sinking.

The water around her glowed. She couldn't see anything through the crimson liquid. She couldn't breathe—and holy hell, it burned. It ached so badly she wished she could scream. For obvious reasons, that was impossible. But her mind had yet to shut down and hadn't let her slip into unconsciousness.

She wondered if she ever would go unconscious. Or if this was it. Just burning. And drowning. And suffering. There wasn't any point in struggling anymore. She just went limp as she sank deeper and deeper into the lake.

I wonder how far down it goes.

I guess I'm about to find out.

I really hate this fucking lake.

Everything hurt. Her body was screaming for air. Rxa was right—this would drive her crazy eventually. It'd only be a matter of time. Honestly, if this was going to be her new life? Living down here, chained to the bottom of a lake like an undead mafia victim? Crazy didn't sound so bad as an alternative.

Her body wanted to die. Her body begged for the silence of

unconsciousness at the very least. But it wouldn't come. She wasn't human anymore, and drowning wasn't an option.

I seriously, really, fucking hate this goddamn lake.

Maybe Aon could save her. When he found out what Rxa had done, he'd make the angel let her go. He'd find a way. He always did. Right?

I'm sorry, Aon, she pondered as she looked up into the glowing red nothingness of the lake. *I'm sorry I'm not stronger. I'm sorry I'm not more powerful. I'm sorry I can't stop this.*

Something shifted in the glowing liquid around her. A shadow. Lydia turned her head, unable to really do anything else but watch. Was madness coming for her already?

Great.

The shadow came closer. She watched in detached fascination as a claw or some sort of massive limb—like the leg of a giant spider or the finger of an enormous hand—closed around her waist. It was as thick as a tree. This thing was gigantic, whatever it was.

Now, she was no longer sinking into the water; she was being *dragged* downward. Whatever had grabbed her was a shadow that loomed around her. Drawing her into its body.

If she had air, she would have screamed.

The lake was no longer glowing. She was surrounded by darkness.

Darkness... and eyes.

Orange against the backdrop, like holes in the shadows back to the lake around them.

A voice filled her mind. Voices. It was like the sound of the wind howling yet forming words.

"Hello, child.
It is so very good to see you.
To see you as you really are.
As We really are.

And at such long last.
Do not fear. With Us, you are safe.
We promise."

* * *

Aon had sent Edu away. The massive warrior had not argued for long after he had hinted heavily at what he planned to do.

Or rather, at what Rxa may have done, and therefore what Aon would have to do in return. The warrior's compassion toward Lydia was appreciated and unexpected. To think that the young girl could bridge the seemingly insuperable gap between him and the King of Flames? She indeed was a creature of impossibilities.

She may be weak in comparison to him and the others— but the miracles she could work paled them all.

A shame it had to be revealed like this.

A shame it had to be in this moment.

Aon appeared standing upon the platform of the Pool of the Ancients, blinking himself there the moment Edu agreed to let Aon continue alone.

Rxa stood near the edge, looking up at the fountain of blood with the carved visages of their ancient gods. His hand was pressed over his heart, and his head was bowed in prayer. Hair like gold fell down his tanned back and mixed with his glowing, opalescent wings.

Rxa stood there alone.

Aon knew he was too late.

"She is gone." Rxa did not bother to greet Aon. The angel would have sensed his arrival the moment he broke down the door. "Her place is with the Ancients now."

Aon pulled in a slow breath and let it out. Lydia was alive, in that much he could take some relief. But what would follow... what would be required to free her?

*Do you believe I am not capable of such a deed, old friend?
Do I?*

There was blood on the stones. It caught his attention briefly. The color was too dark to be Lydia's. It had belonged to a vampire, perhaps. Whose was it? Who else had struggled here?

"What have you done?" Though there were no more travesties that Rxa could perform to add to his grief and rage, and he needed no more excuses, he was mildly curious all the same.

"Lyon betrayed me for your lover, and now his body is in the lake with our gods." Rxa turned to look at him finally, his wings unfurled.

Rxa had murdered Lyon. Aon's heart twisted in a pain that surprised him. Lyon had been a friend—one on a minimal list that recently had become one name shorter.

Hm. He had thought his anger could not compound further, and he was now proven wrong. His voice was a low, sharp hiss of rage. "I had nothing to do with her creation, Rxa. Free her. This will be the one and only time I ask."

"This is not about you. I have never hated you. I do not care if you love her and she you." Still, the angel would not face him. Still, he prayed to the abominations.

"Then explain yourself."

"She would not kneel to our gods, Aon."

"They are *not gods!*"

"Even you kneel to them. Even you recognize the power they hold over us. That we are nothing if not without them!" Finally, the angel turned. "She was devoid of a connection to them. They gifted her with power, with immortality, and she refused to give them what was rightfully theirs in return—her servitude."

Aon growled. "Lydia submits to no one."

"This was the problem. She was defacing our very faith. Mocking our very creators. Worse yet, that familiar of hers was a catastrophe. To have her power removed of her body? Her mind?" Rxa held his arms out to the world around him. "She was not a queen. She was a mutilation of all that we are."

"Regardless of your foolish dogma, you have taken from me something very precious. I will not let this stand."

"You cannot even deny it. Fah." Rxa waved a hand dismissively at him. "You are too late, regardless. I have murdered my own regent. I have sent your queen to the Tomb of the Ancients. I surrender myself to incarceration."

"*Incarceration?*" The laugh that left him would have made the fallen archdemons in their pits shiver. Slowly, he began to stroll toward Rxa, one step at a time. He enjoyed the way his wingtip shoes echoed ominously on the stone floor. They were the tick of a clock toward the angel's inevitable fate. "Do you think I will merely *imprison* you? Do you think I will remove your wings and curse them never to regrow, as I did to Edu's tongue?"

Fire burst around his clawed hand as he continued to speak. "Do you think that *torture* is what waits for you, now? No, Rxa. There will be no trial for your acts. There will be no tools of my trade waiting for you."

Rxa shifted, the first sign he may be nervous. "You would not dare," the angel whispered. "You know what it is you say. You know what will happen if you do this."

"To save her?" Aon was grinning behind his mask. Nothing else mattered. Nothing. "I will turn it all to *dust*."

* * *

There was sand between Lydia's fingers. As fine as dust.

She could breathe, and she gasped air into her lungs and felt the relief of the air that had been denied to her. It was hot like Arizona in the summer. She felt like she had just climbed into a car sitting in a parking lot at high noon. But she didn't care. There was *air*.

There was also no light. The world around Lydia was pitch black like a cave. She was lying on her back and could feel the sand around her. Lydia didn't bother standing up. It wasn't like she thought she could, anyway. Her body felt strange and disconnected.

"Hello?" She suspected this place wasn't real—that it was just somewhere inside her own head or someone else's head.

Voices laughed. Several at once, hissing and strange. It was a collective sound, and she shuddered.

"Are you the Ancients?" Her voice sounded small and far away.

"Yes.
And no.
We are no more the Ancients
than the wind is the sound of a storm.
We are everything.
We are all.
We are the very will of this world."

Cringing at the sound of the collective voices she heard before, she wished she had earplugs. But she also suspected it wouldn't help. They talked in sets of seven, like Greek fates taking turns. All at once, but one speaking louder than the other. Somehow audible and yet somehow inside her head, at the same time.

She didn't quite know what to say to their response. The way they talked sounded so epic and important. And here she was, some stupid girl, stuck on the bottom of a lake, talking to... Ancient primordial beings.

What in the hell was she supposed to say?

"Um... hi." She slapped a hand over her eyes. "Good going, you fucking idiot."

They only chuckled in response. The sand beneath Lydia

shifted, as though something was underneath her, burrowing deep beneath the surface.

"You are remarkable.
We are glad We chose you. Guided you here.
We must admit that We are proud.
Even We could not predict how well you have done.
At every pull of Our strings, you soared.
Oh, how our Only Son loves you. And you, he.
This will play out very well. Very well indeed."

Lydia furrowed her brow as she thought over what they had said. There was so much in those statements, so much unpack, that it took her a long minute to figure it out. "They" seemed happy to let her sit in silence as she thought.

Why did they call Aon their only son?

She knew that everything that had happened to her had been their fault. One way or another. They created this world, after all. But it was kind of nice to have them admit it.

These Ancient monsters had dragged her here. They made her like this. They hinted they weren't done with her. They hinted there was more to come. But she had to start with the first question she had wanted to know this entire time. The one thing she wanted to ask that nobody could answer for her but them. "Why me?"

"We saw in you what our Only Son desired.
We saw in you the spark that might grow to love.
As a mortal, you were free to let it blaze.
As one of them, you would have hated him like the others.
We saw in you the strength to endure
All that We would do to you.
All that We will do to you."

She didn't bother asking for them to send her home. She knew they would likely only laugh. At the best, they would simply tell her no. If they had gone through all this trouble to bring her here, it was for a damn good reason.

And... honestly? She didn't want to go home anymore. Her home was the Temple of Dreams. Her home was Aon's home. Her home was at Aon's side.

At least finally, she understood why they left her mortal. She couldn't have loved Aon if she was one of them from the start. Why they made everyone hate him, she didn't know. Now was probably not the time to ask. "You took me because I could love Aon? Then why work so hard to screw it up? Why let all of this happen to me?"

"He is Our Only Son.
He is Our Only Born.
He would love any who smiled upon him.
Your love must be true.
We do not yet believe.
We will have you prove it to Us.
We would have you prove your worth."

Only son? Only born? What the *fuck* were they talking about? They wanted her to prove her worth to them?

The reality of what they were saying sank in slowly, just as she had drifted to the bottom of the lake. Everything they had done to her had been a test to see if she was *worthy* of Aon. And it sounded like *they weren't done yet*.

Lydia tried to sit up, but something felt like it was pressing her back down, keeping her pinned into the sand. She gave up and obeyed, staying put without any other fussing. She felt so... very small.

What the hell was she thinking?

She couldn't stand up to creatures like this. She was an ant to them. She wished someone was there to help her make sense of any of it. Lyon would know what to do. What to say. *Oh god. Lyon.* "Please. I won't ask you to spare me. I won't ask you to take pity on me. I know you won't."

The sound of laughter echoed around her. But it wasn't cruel or mocking. It was the sound of a parent, pleased with a child's first steps.

Somehow it made her stomach twist even worse than if they had really been laughing at her. "But spare Lyon. He didn't deserve to die for me. He didn't deserve what happened."

> *"Our play has reached a crossroads.*
> *We will give you a gift.*
> *We love to watch you choose.*
> *You may decide how your future unfolds.*
> *Each option is equal in the joy it will bring Us.*
> *This is Our prize to you.*
> *In payment for your sweet suffering."*

Oh, great. That didn't sound foreboding or anything. When she didn't respond, they stayed silent. They wanted her to prompt them. "Okay? What?"

> *"Our Priest is dead.*
> *Our Dreamer is chained.*
> *We will spare one.*
> *But not both.*
> *One of you will rise.*
> *Will you save him?*
> *Or yourself?"*

She didn't even hesitate. "Bring him back. Let Lyon live."

The sound of laughter rang out again, pleased and gleeful. She put her hand to her head as images flashed before her.

Images of a desert world, blazing in a painfully bright sun. Of sand dunes and a city that stretched out over the pale abyss, pillars and monuments to horrible gods clawing at a blinding sky. Of a place of sand and fear.

A place where the Ancients were *free.*

The image of an angel, lying dead upon a platform, blood around him and staining his white wings. A man in black, looming over him. The sound of chains snapping like steel cable giving way under too much pressure.

Cold crept up her spine.

Oh God, no. She never considered what Aon might do. She never once considered the man might be angry enough—desperate enough—lonely enough to kill Rxa.

If he did that... the chains holding the Ancients...

The primordial gods had ruled this world, long before Aon and the others had imprisoned them in this lake. Aon and all the others had blotted the memories out of their minds.

The words that Aon had said to her in a moment of madness came back to her suddenly. "Into the darkness of my mind, my soul, I stare. Nothing shall gather within the shadows. In the twisting nettles, the briars, the thorns, I feel the pain that makes me whole. Balm not the biting sands that sting my flesh, for in that sorrow is my joy. To suffer is to live."

She hadn't even realized she had said them out loud until it was too late.

"You know Our prayer.
You know what Our Only Son will do.
You know We will be free.
Our Only Son
Kneels the world before the lash
For you.
All for love of you."

"No, please—don't let him. Don't let him do this! He can't possibly understand!"

There was only another laugh and no response.

"I change my mind, then!" More desperate pleading to no avail. She tried to sit up, but the same force that kept her pinned before had her still. She prayed that Lyon would forgive her. He'd have wished the same if he knew his death spared the whole world. "*Please*, let me change my mind—I didn't know—"

The sand lurched beneath her. It was like the ground itself was opening and giving way.

She knew she was too late.

> *"Heed Our words, Our Oracle, We said.*
> *A queen shall rest in her temple,*
> *Alone, weakened, afraid.*
> *A king shall rise and seek her doom.*
> *But know this;*
> *It shall be friendship...*
> *That proves to be her undoing."*

Cold rushed her as their words sank in. She shuddered as fear filled her. She knew what was about to come was pointless to fight. What was about to unfold was fated. Doomed. She had chosen the way they wanted her to.

The king who would rise to destroy her? They had meant Rxa.

The friend that would undo her? They hadn't meant Nick...

They had meant Lyon.

* * *

Edu felt the rumble of a fight taking place deep beneath the ground. He waited in the courtyard, standing with his elder Oanr. Kamira was there as well out of concern for Lyon, who had entered the building and had yet to resurface.

Twice already he had to physically restrain Kamira from going into the church herself. A pack of his people stood behind them, ready to deal with a war as it unfolded before them, armed for battle.

Aon would not kill Rxa. He could not. To do so would shatter the power that kept the Ancients in their prison. No one held such hatred for those primordial beings quite like the warlock.

Edu had long since wondered if his madness was born of the memories of what had transpired in those days when the sun burned in the sky.

Aon had instructed him to retreat to be with Evie. As if the choice were already made. Edu could only hold onto the fleeting hope that he had stopped Rxa before the deranged zealot could make good on his plans.

All of those gathered had to struggle to keep their balance as all the world itself seemed to shudder beneath them.

With a sense of creeping horror, Edu realized that was not the result of a blow. No impact in a fight could result in that.

The ground began to quake. As if something were moving deep below.

Aon, what have you done?

* * *

"You were my friend." Aon pulled his hand away from the burnt remains of the angel's face. He had torn the mask from him and looked down into the matching face of the angel—twisted in shock and fear. Now that he saw the features of Rxa, he remembered him from the old days.

From when the Ancients roamed the earth.

When the sun burned and the sand and dust bit his flesh.

The angel had always been so very beautiful. Now, his face was charred, his skull emptied. The marks were so easy to destroy for those of them who were so very old. For monsters such as Rxa and himself, the act was barely an effort. How many souls had he himself spent upon the stones, in all his five thousand years of life? he wondered. Too many to count.

Rxa had begged for freedom before death. He had pleaded for pity and mercy. He had wailed for Aon to come to his senses. That what he meant to do would destroy the world.

Aon had given him one last chance to release Lydia.

But his faith came above all else.

Even his own life. Even the fate of the world.

"May they consume your soul!" Rxa had shouted at him, just before Aon had done the deed.

Let it come.

This had to end.

Twice now, he had known the kiss of happiness upon him —the barest touch of what it meant to be whole. Twice now, he had felt it taken away. Once when Lydia was murdered and once more at the hands of the zealot who lay dead beneath him.

Aon would not allow himself to suffer any more of this. Under was not a world worth saving if she was not in it. If she was not there at his side, smiling. Those sharp blue eyes, unbreakable and looking at him with such tenderness. Her beauty, her resilience, her empathy, had all given him hope.

Only to be taken away.

This world meant only to hurt him. Five thousand years and all he had felt was pain. If that were his fate, then everyone else shall know the same.

Rxa was dead.

The chains were broken.

* * *

Someone was holding her.

Lydia blinked her eyes open and coughed, feeling something in her lungs. Whoever was near her turned her on her side and let her clear up whatever was there. Liquid. What had happened?

It took her a few moments to remember. The lake. Rxa. The Ancients.

She *really* hated that *fucking* lake.

When she could breathe again, she filled her aching lungs and let out a wavering breath. Where was she now? What was happening? Vague memories of a conversation came to her. Something strange, a voice that sounded like many people talking at once.

She must have been going crazy.

Someone held her close, tucked against their chest. The smell of old books and leather, a little like an old library. When she was finally able to open her eyes and blink enough times to focus, she wasn't surprised to see who was there. She knew the feeling of him against her. She could never forget it.

Aon.

He was holding her in his lap, his human hand stroking her damp hair back away from her face. Aon had removed his mask and was looking down at her, obsidian eyes creased in worry. She reached up to touch his face, and he leaned his head in to kiss her palm.

"Is this... real?" She sounded as wrung out as she felt.

"Yes, my dragonfly." His voice was strained, thin and pained. No, that wasn't worry on his face.

That was fear. *Terror.*

Lydia sat up as best she could and struggled to get up. Aon rose and gently lifted her, supporting her as she got up to her feet. They were in the grassy field outside of the Temple of Dreams.

She reached up to kiss him, and he met her embrace with fervor. With desperation. As though he thought he never would again. When she broke the kiss, she wrapped her arms around him and hugged him close. Her mind was still struggling to catch up. Desperately trying to remember everything that had happened.

"Forgive me, Lydia. Forgive me, I beg you. I could not—I just could not take any more." He sounded as though he were about to cry. He turned his face away from her, hiding his features behind his long black hair. "To free you, I..." Aon bowed his head and squeezed his eyes shut. Tears ran down his face, dampening her hands. "The chains are now broken."

It was then that she realized they had shadows on the ground. Not the oddly colored shadows cast by the strange and eerie moons. This was a shadow brought on by bright, amber light. She turned to find its source.

The sky was lit with brilliant and beautiful ruddy hues of copper, red, gold, and yellows. The clouds glowed and glinted as though a painter had put them there, dipping their brush into a mix of hues and spread them across the sky.

It was beautiful.

The sun was rising.

It was the end of the world.

The Ancients were free.

A LETTER FROM KATHRYN

Dear reader,

I want to say a huge thank you for choosing to read The Masks of Under series. This was my first series I ever officially published out into the world—and the tale of Lydia, Aon, and all the rest will forever be near and dear to my heart.

If you'd like to stay in the loop for all my future series and releases, just sign up at the following link. Your email address will never be shared and you can unsubscribe at any time.

www.secondskybooks.com/kathryn-ann-kingsley

There are several kinds of writers out there in the world—those who are happy to tell their story to a blank page, and those who thrive on hearing about how their readers engage with their tales.

I'm the latter.

I absolutely love hearing from my readers – you can get in touch through social media, my website, or even join my Discord (the link to join is on my website) to interact with both me and other fans.

Stay Spooky and Happy Nightmares,

Kathryn Ann Kingsley

KEEP IN TOUCH WITH KATHRYN

www.kathrynkingsley.com

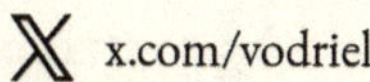
x.com/vodriel
instagram.com/kathrynannkingsley

PUBLISHING TEAM

Turning a manuscript into a book requires the efforts of many people. The publishing team at Bookouture would like to acknowledge everyone who contributed to this publication.

Commercial
Lauren Morrissette
Hannah Richmond
Imogen Allport

Cover design
BRoseDesignz

Data and analysis
Mark Alder
Mohamed Bussuri

Editorial
Jack Renninson
Melissa Tran

Proofreader
Catherine Lenderi

Marketing

Alex Crow
Melanie Price
Occy Carr
Cíara Rosney
Martyna Młynarska

Operations and distribution

Marina Valles
Stephanie Straub
Joe Morris

Production

Hannah Snetsinger
Mandy Kullar
Jen Shannon
Ria Clare

Publicity

Kim Nash
Noelle Holten
Jess Readett
Sarah Hardy

Rights and contracts

Peta Nightingale
Richard King
Saidah Graham